★ ★ ★ ★ ★ ★
★ ★ ★ ★ ★ ★
★ ★ ★ ★ ★ ★
★ ★ ★ ★ ★ ★
★ ★ ★ ★ ★ ★

TAKE BACK YOUR GOVERNMENT!

A PRACTICAL HANDBOOK FOR THE PRIVATE CITIZEN WHO WANTS DEMOCRACY TO WORK

BY ROBERT A. HEINLEIN

WITH AN INTRODUCTION BY
JERRY POURNELLE

TAKE BACK YOUR GOVERNMENT!

Copyright © 1992, by Mrs. Virginia Heinlein

A Baen Books Original

Baen Publishing Enterprises
P.O. Box 1403
Riverdale, NY 10471

ISBN: 0-671-72157-7

Cover Design by Carol Russo

First Printing, August 1992

Printed in the United States of America

Distributed by Simon & Schuster
1230 Avenue of the Americas
New York, NY 10020

An American Love Story . . .

This is a book for every American who wants to reclaim the political process. Are you mad as Hell and not going to take it any more? Have you tried to participate in the traditional political process only to discover that the traditional political parties have no place for you, won't listen, and don't much matter anyway? Have you turned to the Perot movement as a remedy? Do you want to see a fundamental change in the American political system?

If so, you need this book.

If you have never thought about politics, and hate the whole idea, you *really* need this book. As Pericles of Athens was fond of observing, because you take no interest in politics is no guarantee that politics will not take an interest in *you*.

If you look to H. Ross Perot to lead the nation to salvation, you particularly need this book.

———

. . . Everywhere there is an opportunity to, in the words of the old political rallying cry, Turn the Rascals Out. We *can* change the system. We very likely will.

With what, then, shall we replace the system of professional politicians? It's no good "reforming" the system only to abandon it to a new crew of professional politicians. That cure could easily be worse than the disease. We must Turn the Rascals Out, but we must rebuild our system of citizen-controlled government.

That, I submit, is the great value of this book. It's all in here. In this book, Robert Heinlein describes, lovingly and in great detail, the system of government which worked for this republic for nearly two hundred years. This isn't a blueprint, and it's not a treatise on political science. We will need those and they will come; but this is a love story.

— Jerry Pournelle
From the Introduction

Table of Contents

Why Touch the Dirty Business? The scope of this book: Mechanics and Techniques — the lessons of practical politics: people are decent — no dictators needed — what Americans *do* want — democracy is efficient but *not* self-operating — all government is representative — what good is one man's vote? — the amateur *versus* the Machine — the power of the little man — so you don't believe it? — the mess we are in — am I my brother's keeper? — the slopes of Vesuvius — democracy *versus* the Atom Bomb — the Smyth Report — what are your chances of staying alive? — let's get to work!

How to Start: "Put down your bucket where you are!" — the telephone book clue — how much will it cost me? — why not get paid for it? — the power of the amateur and what he gets out of it — how to shut up your brother-in-law — "Honest Money": a blind alley — the greatest game in the world — how it feels to be grown up

"It Ain't Necessarily So!" A few slips in the Great American Credo — a warning of disappointments to come — let's take our hair down — why consider a man's religion? — the sorry role of church groups — women, cut-rate corruptionists — how to spot an honest volunteer — the blind greed of the old folks — the honesty of crooked politicians — the virtues *you* need to compete with the

Machine — "A government should be run like a business"? — Compromise, an instrument of democracy — civil service and patronage — slim pickings in the public trough — the nonsense of "non-partisan" — the frailty of "reformers"

ground — 4th-of-July celebration — in praise of
bureaucrats — the Caliph and the precinct worker

● INTRODUCTION

Jerry Pournelle

This is a book for every American who wants to reclaim the political process. Are you mad as Hell and not going to take it any more? Have you tried to participate in the traditional political process only to discover that the traditional political parties have no place for you, won't listen, and don't much matter anyway? Have you turned to the Perot movement as a remedy? Do you want to see a fundamental change in the American political system?

If so, you need this book.

If you have never thought about politics, and hate the whole idea, you *really* need this book. As Pericles of Athens was fond of observing, because you take no interest in politics is no guarantee that politics will not take an interest in *you*.

If you look to H. Ross Perot to lead the nation to salvation, you particularly need this book.

I say this in full knowledge that much of the book — indeed its very heart — seems to be badly out of date. Ironically, being "out of date" is one of the book's major values. This book was written in a very different era of American politics; in a time when ordinary people could and did participate effectively in the political scene. This was a manual to show them how to do that. There were many such manuals. This one was unique in that Robert Heinlein both had practical experience

in politics and was one of the clearest (and most entertaining) writers of the era. Reading this book will be
good for you, but the good news is that it's fun.

Heinlein offers a number of timeless insights, but
many of his details are seriously out of date. That, however, is not a defect but a feature: because in describing
how to operate in a political world that vanished
during the "reforms" of the '60s and '70s, Heinlein
describes a working democracy: not as a dead world of
the past, but as the dynamic living world he knew and
lived in and loved.

It is a world we could reclaim. A world we must
reclaim. The United States went a long way down the
wrong road during the Cold War. It is time we return to
more familiar territory. This book can be vital to that
return.

Democracy, Robert Heinlein says, "is not an automatic condition resulting from laws and constitutions.
It is a living, dynamic process which must be worked at
by you yourself — or it ceases to be a democracy, even if
the shell and form remain." That was written in 1946,
at the close of World War II, before the Cold War;
before the federalization of much of American life.
When we look around at the disaster area that
American politics has become, it is all too clear that
Robert was correct. The shell and form of American
democracy remain, but much of what Robert understood about American democracy has vanished.

When Heinlein wrote, the typical professional
politician was what was then known as a political boss.
Most local, district, and county party leaders were
unpaid volunteers. Professional political managers
were distrusted. While some state legislators and congressmen were returned to office year after year, most
were not, and those who were, though powerful
through the seniority system, were often the butts of
political jokes — and were quite aware that they could

easily be turned out of office, either in a primary or a general election. It was a government by amateurs in a true sense, in that everyone had to live under the laws they passed. They worked hard, too. Heinlein could (and does) complain that members of Congress, and of the State Legislature, were underpaid and had too few perks of office; and offer the opinion that the main reason people went to their city council, or state capital, or Washington, and endured the hardships of public office, was patriotism.

It was all true in those days. Some politicians might have been motivated by greed, or a lust for power, but most thought of themselves as, and were seen by their constituents to be, public servants, sacrificing some of their productive years to the political process. Today things are different. However the professional politicians see themselves, poll after poll shows that the American people think they are a self-perpetuating elite motivated mostly by the desire to retain power.

Since Heinlein wrote this book, most states have changed from a part-time amateur legislature of citizens who approved laws they would have to live with and make a living under, to full-time paid professionals who spend most of their time in the state capital rather than in their home districts, exempt themselves from the laws and regulations they impose on others, and who, far from making a living under the laws they make, are paid by the state and sometimes prevented by conflict-of-interest laws from outside work. (A noted exception is, of course, lawyers, who have been allowed to retain their partnerships in law firms even if the firm does business with the government. They did that in Heinlein's day too.) Their idea of making a living is not yours.

It's doubly true of the Congress of the United States, which has multiplied its perks while invariably exempting itself from such laws as the Civil Rights Act; the Americans with Disabilities Act, the Wage/Hours Act, most of the reporting laws, and nearly all federal regulations. Far from a largely citizen body, the Congress has become a governing elite with high job security. Since this book was written, Congress went from an assembly of the people to an institution with 98 percent incumbency — a lower turnover than Britain's hereditary House of Lords. While private industry loses jobs, Congress multiplies its staff: there are over 30,000 "Hill Rats," as congressional staff are called in Washington. They serve 535 senators and representatives. Do you have nearly 50 people to mind details and run errands for you? Each of your legislators in Washington does, all paid with your taxes. Think about that before you contemplate running for office. Each congressman commands a political patronage machine that the old ward bosses would have envied.

Other things have changed. The budget has grown enormously. Government (federal, state, and local) now spends nearly half the money generated in this country. The national debt went from an irritation to an impending disaster. The civil service at all levels has grown well beyond anyone's ability to predict in 1946. Government, in a word, has become very big business indeed, while what we used to fear as "the big business interest" has faded into the background. I could multiply examples endlessly, but surely the point is made. Somewhere between 1946 and the present the American democracy as Heinlein knew it disappeared, to be replaced with our present system in which our local affairs are governed by Washington — a city that can't govern itself, but has no qualms about telling the rest of us how we should live.

The Opportunity

We have a new situation in this year of grace 1992 and of the independence of these United States the

216th. To say that the American people have come to distrust their government is a silly understatement. The polls show that they hate our present political system. They're mad as Hell and they aren't going to take it any more. There is a movement to take back control, and it may work. For the first time in our lifetimes there is an alternative. Millions of Americans, disgusted with politics as usual, have turned to a man who, as I write this, is still legally only an "undeclared candidate for President" — but who, as I write this, is the likely winner of the Presidency. In the state of New Jersey both houses of the legislature went from a majority by one party to a veto-proof majority of the other. As I write this we can predict that there will be at least 100 new faces among the 435 members of the House of Representatives; and it is entirely possible that there will be many more, perhaps even a majority of new faces.

There will be equally profound changes at the state and local level. Everywhere there is an opportunity to, in the words of the old political rallying cry, Turn the Rascals Out. We *can* change the system. We very likely will.

With what, then, shall we replace the system of professional politicians? It's no good "reforming" the system only to abandon it to a new crew of professional politicians. That cure could easily be worse than the disease. We must Turn the Rascals Out, but we must rebuild our system of citizen-controlled government.

That, I submit, is the great value of this book. It's all in here. In this book, Robert Heinlein describes, lovingly and in great detail, the system of government which worked for this republic for nearly two hundred years. This isn't a blueprint, and it's not a treatise on political science. We will need those and they will come; but this is a love story.

Jerry Pournelle
Hollywood, California
July 1992

Privileged Motions
Time and
Place to Adjourn

To Adjourn

To Recess

Questions
of Privilege *

Call for Orders
of the Day

Incidental Motions
Points of Order

Appeal *

Objection to Consideration
of Question 2/3

Reading of Papers

Withdrawal of a Motion

Suspension of Rules

Subsidiary Motions
Lay on the Table

The Previous Question 2/3

Limit or Extend Limits of Debate 2/3

To Postpone to a Certain Time #*

To Commit or Refer *

Primary Amendment *

Secondary Amendment *

Postpone Indefinately *

Main or Principle Motion *

---

* - Debatable
\# - When a "Special Order", 2/3 vote.
2/3 - Two-Thirds Vote, of members voting.

● Preface

(In which the defendant pleads guilty to the charge of being a politician but offers a statement in his defense.)

This is intended to be a practical manual of instruction for the American layman who has taken no regular part in politics, has no personal political ambitions, and no desire to make money out of politics, but who, nevertheless, would like to do something to make his chosen form of government work better. If you have a gnawing, uneasy feeling that you should be doing *something* to preserve our freedoms and to protect and improve our way of life but have been held back by lack of time, lack of money, or the helpless feeling that you individually could not do enough to make the effort worthwhile, then this book was written for you.

The individual, unpaid and inexperienced volunteer citizen in politics, who is short on both time and money, can take this country away from the machine politicians and run it to suit himself — if he knows how to go about it.

This book is a discussion of how to go about it, with no reference to particular political issues. I have my own set of political opinions and some of them are almost bitter in their intensity, but, still more strongly, I have an abiding faith in the good sense and decency of the American people. Many are urging you daily as to *what* you should do politically; I hope only to show some of the details of *how* you can do it — the mechanics of the art.

There are thousands of books for the citizen

interested in public affairs, books on city planning, economics, political history, civics, Washington gossip, foreign affairs, sociology, political science, and the like. There are many books by or about major figures in public life, such as James A. Farley's instructive and interesting autobiography, or that inspiring life of Mr. Justice Holmes, the *Yankee from Olympus*. I have even seen a clever, sardonic book about machine politicians called *How to Take a Bribe*. But I have never seen a book intended to show a private citizen, with limited time and money, how he can be a major force in politics.

This book is the result of my own mistakes and sad experiences and is written in the hope that you may thereby be saved some of them. If it accomplishes that purpose, I hope that you will be tolerant of its shortcomings. A decent respect for your opinions requires that I show my credentials for writing this book. A plumber has his license; a doctor hangs up his diploma; a politician can only cite his record — I have done the things I discuss.

I have been a precinct worker, punching doorbells for my ticket. I have organized political clubs, managed campaigns, run for office, been a county commit-teeman, a state committeeman, attended conventions including national conventions, been a county organizer, published political newspapers, made speeches, posted signs, raised campaign funds, licked stamps, dispensed patronage, run headquarters, cluttered up "smoke-filled rooms," and have had my telephone tapped.

I suppose that makes me a politician. I do know that it has proved to me that a single citizen, possessed of the right to speak and the right to vote, can make himself felt whenever he takes the trouble to exercise those twin rights.

— *Robert A. Heinlein*
April, 1946

● Chapter I

Why Touch the Dirty Business?

"He that toucheth pitch shall be defiled therewith — "
— Ecclesiastes XIII:1
*And the Pharisees asked Jesus: "Why do you eat and drink
with the publicans and sinners?"*
— Luke V:30

This book is on the *mechanics* and *techniques* of practical politics, and is based on the idea that democracy is worth the trouble and can be made to work by ordinary people.

If you can go along with me on that I don't care what party you belong to. I am registered in one of the two major parties, so chances are at least fifty-fifty that you can guess my affiliation, but any party bias I let creep into this book will be an oversight. The techniques of politicking are not the property of any party.

From politics I have come to believe the following:

(1) Most people are basically honest, kind, and decent.

(2) The American people are wise enough to run their own affairs. They do not need Fuehrers, Strong Men, Technocrats, Commissars, Silver Shirts, Theocrats, or any other sort of dictator.

(3) Americans have a compatible community of ambitions. Most of them don't want to be rich but do want enough economic security to permit them to raise families in decent comfort without fear of the future.

They want the least government necessary to this purpose and don't greatly mind what the other fellow does as long as it does not interfere with them living their own lives. As a people we are neither money mad nor prying; we are easy-going and anarchistic. We may want to keep up with the Joneses — but not with the Vanderbilts. We don't like cops.

(4) Democracy is not an automatic condition resulting from laws and constitutions. It is a living, dynamic process which must be worked at by you yourself — or it ceases to be democracy, even if the shell and form remain.

(5) One way or another, any government which remains in power is a representative government. If your city government is a crooked machine, then it is because you and your neighbors prefer it that way — prefer it to the effort of running your own affairs. Hitler's government was a popular government; the vast majority of Germans preferred the rule of gangsters to the effort of *thinking* and *doing* for themselves. They abdicated their franchise.

(6) Democracy is the most efficient form of government ever invented by the human race. On the record, it has worked better in peace and in war than fascism, communism, or any other form of dictatorship. As for the mythical yardstick of "benevolent" monarchy or dictatorship — there ain't no such animal!

(7) A single citizen, with no political connections and no money, can be extremely effective in politics.

I left the most important proposition to the last, on purpose. It is contrary to the beliefs of many but it happens to be true. You yourself can be a strong political force at less cost per evening spent in politics than spending that same evening at the movies and at less effort than it takes to be a scoutmaster, a good bridge player, or a radio hobbyist — about the effort it takes to be a Sunday School teacher, an active P.T.A. member, or stamp collector.

You may possibly think me unrealistic in some of the opinions expressed above. I may be self-deluded but I got those opinions from active politics through many campaigns. If your own experience in politics is really extensive you are certainly entitled to contradict me — but I don't think you will!

If active politics is fairly new to you — if, let us say, you have taken part in no more than one or two campaigns and have been left disheartened thereby — I ask that you suspend judgment for the time being.

I am puzzled by persons who take exception to the first proposition and seem to believe that crookedness is commoner than honesty. I can see how a citizen too long exposed to a corrupt machine might come to think the whole world is dishonest, but I am afraid that when I hear a man complain that everybody is crooked it makes me suspect that he himself is dishonest, especially if he complains that an honest man can't make a living in his line of business. I have met crooks, of course, but for every dishonest man I have met dozens, scores, of men so honest it hurt, both in and out of politics.

Any banker can confirm this. Ask your banker how many good checks come into the bank for every bad check. The figures will give you a warm glow of pleasure.

However, the occasional crook will band together with his kind and take your government away from you if you let him. It is very soothing to the conscience to tell yourself that, after all, *you* can't do anything to change the sorry state of things. It is much easier to sit in your living room, skim the headlines, and then make bitter remarks about those no-good crooks in the city hall, or the state capital, or Washington, and to complain about how they pay no attention to the welfare of the ordinary citizen (meaning yourself) than it is to put on your hat, go out in your neighborhood, and round up a few votes.

What do you expect for free? Chimes? If you wanted to round up a big order of yard goods, you wouldn't expect to accomplish it with your feet on your desk. This is just as important. Or have you forgotten that income tax form you made out? And your nephew who died at Okinawa because you let some senile congressman stay in office rather than bother with politics?[1]

Why should the average citizen bother with politics? Why touch the dirty business? Isn't politics loaded up with crooks you wouldn't want to eat with and crackpots you wouldn't want to have in your house? "Loaded" is hardly the word, but you will find plenty of each and they will almost drive you nuts. Besides that, and worse, your respectable friends — people who wouldn't be caught dead in a political club — will assume that you are in it for what you can get out of it. They will be very sure of it, for that is the only reason their peanut heads can imagine!

Then why bother? Why expose yourself to bad companions and snide remarks simply to make a single-handed attempt to clean the Augean stables, to bail the ocean, to clear the forest?

Because you are needed. Because the task is not hopeless.

Democracy is normally in perpetual crisis. It requires the same constant, alert attention to keep it from going to pot that an automobile does when driven through downtown traffic. If you do not yourself pay attention to the driving, year in and year out, the crooks, or scoundrels, or nincompoops will take over the wheel and drive it in a direction you don't fancy, or wreck it completely.

When you pick yourself up out of the wreckage, you and your wife and your kids, don't talk about what "They" did to you. *You* did it, compatriot, because you preferred to sit in the back seat and snooze. Because you thought your taxes bought you a bus ticket and a guaranteed safe arrival, when all your taxes bought you was a part ownership in a joint enterprise, on a share-the-cost and share-the-driving plan.

But the crisis is more than usually acute this year, the traffic is thicker, the curves more blind, the traffic signals less reliable, and there are a lot of places where the pavement is out which have not been marked on any map. More than ever your own welfare demands that you be alert and responsible.

Do you favor peacetime conscriptions? How did your congressman vote on it? Have you got any sons under twenty-one? Should the budget be balanced on a pay-as-you-go plan? If so, are you willing to vote to raise your own taxes? Or would you rather cut the budget for the army, the navy, and for veterans' benefits? Is there some other way to do it?

Should coal miners be forbidden to strike? Can you mine coal with bayonets? What would your rent be in a free market? Or are you still sleeping on a borrowed couch? When will a home be built for you and your kids? Can you afford it when it is built, if ever? Does your town have a building code which prevents the use of new materials and new construction methods? How do you feel about a loan to Great Britain? To France? To Russia? Are you willing to go on rationing to keep Germans from starving? How long should the occupation of Japan continue? Why? How did your congressman vote on FEPC? Do you know what FEPC is? How does it affect you?

The Filipinos become independent this year — should we let Philippine sugar in duty free? Do you live in the Colorado sugar beet country? Is a Senate filibuster a legitimate defense of states' rights, or a piece of tyranny? Should an oil man be in charge of military and naval oil reserves? Was Secretary Fall an oil operator? Does it make any difference?

Should we insist that Russia give us free access and uncensored news reports so that we will know what she is up to? Is it worth fighting about? How about the Big Five Veto power? Does it make for peace or war?

Should Russia get out of Iran?[2] Should Britain get out of Egypt? Should we get out of Korea? Are the three cases parallel? Or very different? Is a Manchurian communist the same thing as a Brooklyn communist? Why? Why not? Should a sharecropper be a Republican or a Democrat? Should a stockholder be a Democrat or a Republican? What is the American Way of Life? Does it mean the same thing on the Main Line as it does on Skid Row?

Are you sure about that last answer? Aren't we all in the same boat? Will an atomic bomb discriminate between bank account — or party labels?

Now we are getting down to cases. All the other problems were of the simple, easy sort that we have blundered our way through, not too badly, for the past hundred and seventy years.

We have a double-edged crisis this year, more acute on both its edges than any we have ever faced before, more acute, even, than Pearl Harbor, or the terrible War between the States.

The first crisis is political and economic. Our way of life is being challenged by a revolutionary upsurge in all corners of the globe. We can meet it with hysteria, persecution, and a new isolationism, or we can define our way of life in action and defend it by practical accomplishment. An American who is well housed, well fed, and holding a good job is poor pickings for an agitator. But let him miss seven meals —

The second crisis is amorphous but of even more deadly danger. We have entered the Atomic Era — but we are not yet used to the idea.

Have you read the Smyth Report?[3]

Do you know what the Smyth Report is? It is the War

Department's report on the atom bomb and is titled *Atomic Energy for Military Purposes* by H.D. Smyth. It is available in any bookstore and most newsstands at $1.25. It is dull reading but quite understandable and is easily the most important document to the human race since the Sermon on the Mount.

I won't try to tell you what it should mean to you. That's up to you. You are a free American citizen, for a while yet, at least. With good luck you should live another five or ten years. Whether or not you and your kids live longer than that depends on how you interpret the Smyth Report. But you must interpret it for yourself — no guardian angel will help you.

Get it and read it. Then get a copy of your own precinct list and start investigating this year's crop of candidates. If your interpretation of the Smyth Report and the world events behind it is correct, there is still a chance that the Star-Spangled Banner will continue to wave o'er the land of the free and the home of the brave.

Just a chance — that's all. But get busy, neighbor. There's work to be done.

• CHAPTER II

How to Start

"Put down your bucket where you are!" The late Booker T. Washington,[4] in his life-long attempts to advise his people on how to help themselves, had a favorite anecdote about a sailing ship, becalmed and out of fresh water off the coast of South America. After many days they sighted another ship, a steam ship, and signalled, "Bring us water. We are dying of thirst." The other ship sent back this message, "Put down your bucket where you are!"

They were in the broad mouth of the Amazon, afloat in millions of gallons of fresh water — and did not know it!

Here is how to start in politics:

Get your telephone book. Look up the party of your registration — or, if you are not registered in a party, the party which most nearly fits your views. I don't care what party it is, but let us suppose for illustration that it is the Republican Party. You will find a listing something like *Republican County Committee, Associated Republican Clubs, Republican Assembly*, or perhaps several such. Telephone one of them.

Say, "My name is Joseph Q. (or Josephine W.) Ivorytower. I am a registered voter at 903 Farflung Avenue. Can you put me in touch with my local club?"

The voice at the other end will say, "Just a minute. Do you know what ward you are in?"

You say no. (It's at least even money that you don't know, if you are a normal American!)

The voice mutters, "Fairview, Farwest, Farflung — "
The owner of the voice is checking a file or a map.
Then you hear, in an aside, "Say, Marjorie, gimme the
folder on the 13th ward."

"What do you want to know?" says Marjorie. She
knows them by heart; she typed them. She is a political
secretary and belongs to one of two extreme classes.
Either she is a patriot and absolutely incorruptible, or
she can be bought and sold like cattle. Either way she
knows who the field worker in the 13th ward is.

After a couple of minutes of this backing and filling
you are supplied with a name, an address, and a
telephone number of a local politician who is probably
the secretary of the local club. You may also be supplied
with the address and times and dates of meetings of the
local club, if it is strong enough to have permanent
headquarters. The local club may vary anywhere from
a club in permanent possession of a store frontage on a
busy street, with a full time secretary on the premises
and a complete ward, precinct, and block organization,
to a club which exists largely in the imagination of the
secretary and which meets only during campaigns in
the homes of the members.

Your next job is to telephone the secretary. This is
probably not necessary. If the local organization is any
good at all, the secretary of the local club will call *you*,
probably the same day. Marjorie will have called him
and said, "Get a pencil and paper, Jim. I've got a new
sucker for you." Or, if she is not cynical, she may call
you a new prospect.

She will have added you to a card file and set the
wheels in motion to have your registration checked
and to have you placed on several mailing lists.
Presently you will start receiving one or more political
newspapers — free, despite the subscription price
posted on the masthead — and, in due course, you will
receive campaign literature from candidates who have

the proper connections at headquarters. Your political education will have begun, even if you never bother to become active.

Note that it has not cost you anything so far. The costs need never exceed nickels, dimes, and quarters, even if you become very active. The costs can run as high as you wish, of course. The citizen who is willing to reach for his checkbook to back up his beliefs is always welcome in politics. But such action is not necessary and is not as rare as the citizen who is willing to punch doorbells and lick stamps. Some of the most valuable and respected politicians I have ever known had to be provided with lunch money to permit them to do a full day's volunteer work in any area more than a few blocks from their respective homes.

I know of one case, a retired minister with a microscopic pension just sufficient to buy groceries for himself and his bedridden wife, who became county chairman and leader-in-fact of the party in power in a metropolitan area of more than three million people. He was so poor that he could not afford to attend political breakfasts or dinner. He could never afford to contribute to party funds, nor, on the other hand, was he ever on the party payroll — he never made a thin dime out of politics.

What he did have to contribute was honesty, patriotism, and a willingness to strive for what he thought was right. It made him boss of a key county in a key state — when he was past seventy and broke.

I digress. This book will have many digressions; politics is like that, as informal as an old shoe, and the digressions may be the most important part. It is sometimes hard to tell what is important in the practical art of politics. Charles Evans Hughes failed to become president because his manager was on bad terms with a state leader and thereby failed to see to it that the candidate met the local leader on one particular occasion in one California city. The local campaign lost its steam because the local leader's nose was out of joint over the matter.

Mr. Hughes lost the state of California; with its electoral vote he would have become president.[5] A switch of less than nineteen hundred votes in the city in which the unfortunate incident occurred would have made Mr. Hughes the war-time president during World War I. The effect on world history is incalculable and enormous. It is entirely possible that we would have been in a League of Nations (not *the* League — that was Woodrow Wilson's League); it is possible that Hitler would never have come to power; it is possible that World War II would never have occurred and that your nephew who fell at Okinawa would be alive today.

We cannot calculate the consequences. But we do know that world history was enormously affected by a mere handful of votes, less than one percent of one percent — less than one *ten-thousandth* of the total vote cast.

An active political club[6] can expect to deliver to the polls on election day, through unpaid volunteers driving their own cars, as many votes as the number that swung the 1916 presidential election. It could be your club and an organization you helped to build.

Which is why you must now telephone the local club secretary. It may be your chance to prevent, by your own direct and individual action, World War III!

The club secretary, Jim Ballotbox, will not give you the brush off. Even if it is a tight machine organization, founded on graft and special privilege, an honest-to-goodness volunteer who is willing to work is more to be desired than fine gold, yeah, verily! If it is that sort of a club, presently you will be offered cash for your efforts, anywhere from five dollars per precinct per campaign on the west coast, through five dollars per day during the campaign in the middle west, to a sound and secure living month in and month out on the east coast.

(These figures do not refer to the Republican Party, as such, nor to the Democratic Party. They refer to the Machine, no matter what its label.)

Don't take the money. Remain a volunteer. You will be treated with startled response. Every time you turn down money you will automatically be boosted one rung in the party councils. And the progress is *very* fast.

But, no matter which sort of club it is, you will be welcomed with open arms. You have already caused a minor flurry at the downtown headquarters by volunteering during "peace time" — other than immediately before a campaign. It shocked them but they rose to the occasion and put you in touch with your local leader. They are used to volunteers during campaigns — and are aware that most of them are phonies who expect at least a postmaster's job in return for a promise to work one precinct plus a little handshaking at a few political meetings. If it should happen that you call up during a campaign, you will be treated a little more warily until you have established that you are in fact a volunteer and not a hopeful patronage hound, but you will be received pleasantly and given a chance to work. This applies to any political club anywhere at any time.

If Jim Ballotbox happens to be secretary of the other sort of club, the sort unconnected with a powerful, well-financed machine, he will be even happier to see you, although he may not be as schooled in the arts of graciousness as his full-time professional opposite number. *His* club will be in a chronic state of crisis financially, or even moribund; an enthusiastic new member is manna to him.

He will have plenty for you to do. You can be chairman next term if you want to be and share with him the worries about hall rent, postage, secretarial work, and how to get people out to meetings. At the very least he will place you in charge of one or more precincts (which will make you nervous as a bridegroom; it's too much responsibility too suddenly) and he will unburden his heart to you. You will learn.[7]

There remain two other possibilities which may result from your telephone call to the downtown headquarters. The first is that there may be no club in your district, in which case you will make your start directly at the downtown headquarters and will meet there the other active party members from your own area. You will join with them in organizing a local club before the next election. It is not hard to do; the process will be discussed in a later chapter.

The last remaining possibility is that your telephone book contains no listings for your political party. This will happen only in small towns or in the country. If you live in a small town or in the country, you already know at least one party leader in your own party — probably Judge Dewlap, who served one term in the state senate and has been throwing his weight around ever since.

Call him up. Tell him you want to work for the party. Perhaps you don't like the old windbag. No matter — he likes *you*. He likes all voters, especially ones who want to work for the party! He may suggest that you have lunch with him at the Elks' Club and talk over civic conditions. Or he may simply invite you to drop into his real estate office for a chat. But he won't brush you off. From now on you're his boy! — until he finds out he can't dictate to you. But by that time you are a politician in your own right and there is nothing he can do about it.

(That knife in your back has Judge Dewlap's finger prints on it.)

We have covered all the possibilities; you are now in politics. As a result of one telephone call you have started. Stay with the club or local organization for several months at least. Attend all the meetings. Help out with the routine work. Don't be afraid to lick stamps, serve on committees, check precinct lists, or distribute political literature. Count on devoting a couple of evenings a month to it for six months or a year. Your expenses during this training period need not exceed a dollar a month.

At the end of that time you are a politician.

I mean it. You will have become acquainted with your local officeholders and political leaders, you will have discovered where several of the bodies are buried, you will have taken part in one local or national campaign and received your first blooding in meeting the public. You will find that you are now reading the newspapers with insight as to the true story behind the published story. You will have grown up about ten years in your knowledge of what makes the world go 'round.

You will either have experienced the warm glow of solid accomplishment that comes from realizing that you performed a necessary part in a successful campaign for a man or an issue, or you will have taken part in the private post-mortem in which you and your colleagues analyze why you lost and what to do about it next time. (The answer is usually to start your precinct organization earlier, with special reference to getting your sure votes registered and to make sure they are dragged to the polls.)

You will feel that you can win next time and probably you will. Politics for the volunteer fireman is not one long succession of lost causes — far from it!

But the point at which you will realize that you are in fact a politician with a definite effect on public life is the time when your friends and neighbors start asking your advice about how to mark their ballots. And they will. Perhaps not about presidential nor gubernatorial candidates, but they will ask *and take* your advice about lesser candidates and about the propositions on the ballot.

You may discover in the course of the first few months that you are in the wrong club, or even in the wrong party. This does not matter in the least insofar as your political education is concerned. In fact it is somewhat of an advantage to make a mistake in your first affiliation; you will learn things thereby which you could never possibly learn so well or so rapidly if you had found your own true lodge brothers on your first attempt. *It does not matter by what door you enter politics.* If you have belonged to the party wrong *for you*, by habit or tradition, a few months of active politics will disclose the fact to you. You can then reregister and cross over, bringing with you experience and solid conviction you could hardly have acquired any other way.[8]

If the trouble lies in your having fallen first into the hands of a gang of unprincipled machine politicians, the mistake is still a valuable one, for you will discover presently that there is a reform element in your party, unaffiliated with the Machine. You can join them, taking with you a knowledge of the practical art of vote-getting which reformers frequently never acquire.

You will be invaluable to your new associates. Most of the techniques of vote-getting are neither dishonest nor honest in themselves, but the machines normally know vastly more about such techniques than do the reform organizations. The honest organizations can afford to copy at least 90% of the machine techniques. It is curiously and wonderfully true that a volunteer, reform organization can use the machine techniques much more effectively than the Machine does, with fewer workers and less money. It is like the difference between the ardor of unselfish love and the simulated passion of prostitution; the unorganized voting public can feel the difference.

Recapitulation — How to start: Take a telephone book. Look up your political party. Telephone, locate your local club. Join it, attend all the meetings, and do volunteer work for several months. At the end of that time, let your conscience be your guide. You will know enough to know where you belong and what you should do.

I might as well admit right now that the above paragraph is really all this book can tell you. The matter discussed in the later chapters are things which you will learn for yourself in any case, *provided you do everything called for in the paragraph above.*

If you have skimmed through this book to this point without, as yet, laying the purchase price on the counter, you can save the price of the book without loss to yourself simply by remembering that one paragraph — and doing it!

On the other hand you might buy the book anyhow and lend it to your loud-mouthed brother-in-law. Aren't you pretty sick of the way he is forever flapping his jaw about the way the country is run? But when has he ever done anything about it except to go down and kill your vote on election day by voting the wrong way? Give him this book, then tell him to put up or shut up!

You can point out to him that he owes it to his three kids to take a responsible part in politics, instead of just beating his gums. If he won't get off his fat backside and get busy in politics but still refuses to stop being a Big Wind, you are then justified in indulging in the pleasure of being rude to him. After all, you have wanted to be for years, haven't you? This is your opportunity; you've got nothing to lose politically since he votes wrong anyhow, when he remembers to vote, and it will come as a relief to be rude for once, now that you are a politician and usually polite to all comers.

Tell him that he is so damned ignorant that he doesn't have any real opinions about politics and so lax in his civic duties that he wouldn't be entitled to opinions if he had any. Tell him to shut up and to quit holding up the bridge game.

The faint sound of cheering you will hear from the

distance will be me. I don't like the jerk either, nor any of his tribe.

You may not believe that getting into politics is actually as simple as I have described it. Here is my own case: I returned to my own state after an extended absence. My profession had kept me travelling and it happened to be the first time I had ever been at home during a campaign. I walked into the local street headquarters of my party and said to a woman at a desk, "I have a telephone, an automobile, and a typewriter. What can I do?"

I was referred to another headquarters a couple of miles away — I was so ignorant that I did not know the district boundaries and had gotten into the wrong headquarters.

That very same day, to my utter amazement and confusion, I found myself in charge of seven precincts.

Six weeks later I was a director of the local club.

Six months later I was publishing, in my spare time, a political newspaper of two million circulation.

During the next campaign I was a county committeeman, a state committeeman, and a district chairman. Shortly after that campaign I was appointed county organizer for my party. And so on. It does not end. The scope and importance of the political work assigned to a volunteer fireman is limited only by his strength and his willingness to accept responsibility.

Nor is the work futile. The volunteer organization with which I presently became affiliated recalled a mayor, kicked out a district attorney, replaced the governor with one of our own choice, and completely changed the political complexion of one of the largest states — all within four years. I did not do it alone — naturally not, nothing is ever done alone in politics — but it was done by a comparatively small group of unpaid volunteers almost all of whom were as ignorant of politics at the start as I was.[9]

Or let me tell you about Susie. Susie is a wonderful girl. She and her husband volunteered about the same time I did. Susie had a small baby; she packed him into a market basket, stuck him into the back of the family car and went out and did field work.

In the following four years Susie replaced a national committeeman with a candidate of her own choice, elected a congressman, and managed the major portion of the campaign which gave us a new governor. She topped her career finally by being the indispensable key person in nominating a presidential candidate of one of the two major parties. I'll tell more about that later; it's quite a story.

All this time Susie was having babies about every third year. She never accepted a cent for herself, but it became customary, after the house filled up, for the party to see to it that Susie had a maid during a campaign. The rest of the time she kept house, did the cooking, and reared her kids unassisted.

During the war she added riveting on bombers during the night shift to her other activities.

We can't all be Susies. But remember this — all that Susie had to offer was honesty, willingness, and an abiding faith in democracy. She had no money and has none now . . . and she had *no* political connections nor experience when she started.

I could fill a whole book with case histories of people like Susie. Most of them are people of very limited income who are quite busy all day earning that income. One of the commonest excuses from the person who knows that he should take part in civic business is: "I would like to but I am just so tarnation busy making a living for my wife and kids that I can't spare the time, the money, nor the energy."

The middle class in Germany felt the same way; it brought them Hitler, the liquidation of their class, and the destruction of their country. The next time you feel like emulating them, remember Susie and her four kids. Or Gus. Gus drove a truck from four a.m. to noon each day; he had a wife and two kids. By sleeping in the afternoons and catching a nap after midnight he managed to devote many of his evenings to politics. In less than three years he was state chairman of the young people's club of his party and one of the top policy makers in the state organization.

What did he get out of it? Nothing, but the satisfaction of knowing that he had made his state a better place for his kids to live.

The Guses and the Susies in this country are the people who have preserved and are preserving our democracy — not the big city bosses, not the Washington officeholders, and most emphatically not your loud-mouthed and lazy brother-in-law.[10]

I have said that the rest of the book will tell only things that you will learn anyhow, through experience. They will be recounted in hopes of saving you much time, much bitter experience, and in the expectation that my own experiences may make you more effective more quickly than you otherwise might be. I also hope to brace you against the disappointment and sometimes disheartening disillusionments that are bound to come to anyone participating in this deadly serious game.

One warning I want to include right now, since you may not finish reading this book.

You are entering politics with the definite intention of treating it as a patriotic public service. You intend to pay your own way; you seek neither patronage nor cash. Almost at once you will be offered pay. You will turn it down. Again and again it will be offered and patronage as well.

There will come a day when you are offered pay to campaign for an issue or a man in whom you already believe and most heartily and to whom you are already committed. The offer will come from a man who is sincerely your friend and whom you know to be honest and patriotic. He will argue that the organization expects to pay for the work you are already doing and that you might as well be paid. He honestly prefers for you to be on the payroll; it makes the whole affair more orderly.

Everything he says is perfectly true; it is honest pay, from a clean source, for honest work in which you believe. It happens that just that moment a little extra money would come in mighty handy. What should you do?

Don't take it!

If you take it, it is almost certain to mark the end of your climb toward the top in the policy-making councils of your party. You are likely to remain a two-bit, or at best a four-bit, ward heeler the rest of your life. A volunteer fireman need not *have* money to be influential in public affairs, but he must not accept money, even when it is clean money, honestly earned. If you take it you are a hired man and hired men carry very little weight anywhere.[11]

There is a corny old story about a sugar daddy and a stylish and beautiful young society matron. The s.d. offered her five thousand dollars to spend a week at Atlantic City with him. After due consideration she accepted. He then offered her fifty dollars instead. In great indignation she said, "Sir, what kind of a woman do you think I am?"

"We settled that," he told her. "Now we're haggling over the price."

Don't make the mistake she did. There is however some sense in haggling over the conditions. If you reach the point where your party wants you to accept a state or national party post, for full-time work in a position of authority, or your government asks the same thing of you, under circumstances where it is evident that you must surrender your usual means of livelihood, go ahead and take it, if you honestly believe that your services are needed and that you can do the best job that could be done by any of the available candidates. It is well understood in political circles that public office or major party office is almost always badly underpaid for the talent and experience the jobs need. The salaries, therefore, are regarded simply as retainers to permit the holder to eat while serving the public.

But don't be a paid ward heeler!

On the other hand, it is not wise to hold the petty hired man in the party in contempt. You will have to work with many of them no matter what party you are in. The biggest reform movements in this country include areas where the Machine is dominant; the most perfectly oiled political machines include areas where all the work is volunteer and unpaid. You will find the paid precinct or headquarters worker as honest and as conscientious as employees usually are; almost invariably he or she will be sincerely loyal to the party employing him. They usually do more work than their wages justify. Remember this, and be careful what you say to them or about them. Most of them are as honest as you are and just as anxious for your man to win.

But don't become one of them if you expect to have any major effect on the future of this country.

Well, then, if you are never to accept pay, except under remote circumstances in which the job even with pay is likely to be a financial sacrifice, what can you expect to get out of it?

The rewards are intangible but very pleasing to an adult mind. The drawbacks are easier to see. You must expect to be regarded with amusement and even suspicion by some of your acquaintances. Most of the station-wagon crowd you used to run around with will be certain that you are in it for what you can get out of it, for that is the only reason their unmatured minds can imagine. They are the free riders in the body politic; despite the fact they do nothing to make our form of government work, they serenely believe that the wheels go around by their gracious consent and think that gives them the privilege of caustic and ignorant criticism of the laborers in the vineyard.

Moreover, you won't be seeing so much of them from now on. You will find that you are beginning to select your social contacts, your dinner guests and your golf partners from among your political acquaintances. You will do this because you find more intelligence, more brilliant conversation, and more worthwhile solid human values among your political acquaintances than you found among the free riders. You won't plan it that way, but it will work itself out.

You will play less bridge. Bridge is a good game, but it is dull and tasteless when compared with politics.

Your brother-in-law will shun your company. That's clear gain!

There will come to you the warm satisfaction of being in on the know every time you pick up your newspaper. News stories that once were dull will be filled with zest for you, because you will know what they mean.

From the stand point of sheer recreation you will have discovered the greatest sport in the world. Horse racing, gambling, football, the fights, all of these things are childish and trite compared with this greatest sport! Politics is a game where you always play for keeps, where the game is continuous, always fresh and full of surprises. It will take all of your intelligence and wit and all that you have ever learned or can learn to play it well. The stakes are the highest conceivable, the lives and the futures of every living creature on this planet. How well you play it can make the difference between freedom or a firing squad, civilization or atomic

conflagration. For this is the day of decision, the hour
of the knife, and none but yourself can choose for you
the correct path in the maze.

Over and above the joy of playing for high stakes is
the greatest and most adult joy of all, the continuous
and sustaining knowledge that you have broken with
childish ways and come at last into your full heritage as
a free citizen, integrated into the life of the land of your
birth or your choice, and carrying your share of adult
responsibility for the future thereof!

● CHAPTER III

"It Ain't Necessarily So!"

This chapter will be devoted to smearing a few cherished illusions.

I do not suppose that you are suffering from all of the misapprehensions listed herein; however, if you are typically American and have not had extensive political experience, it is likely that you are subject to one or more of them. Before we go ahead with detailed discussion of the practical art of politics it is well to correct the record with respect to many items in the Great American Credo — items which happen to be wrong and which have to do with politics. It will save your time and mine in later discussion.

With the possible exceptions of love and religion probably more guff is talked and believed about politics than about any other subject. I am going to discuss some of that guff and try to puncture it. Most of the items I have chosen because I myself have had to change my opinions through bitter experience in politics.

My present opinions are subject to human error. However, they are based on the scientific method of observation of facts; they are not armchair speculation. If you don't believe me, go take a look — several looks! — for yourself. But I suggest that you will save yourself a lot of the mistakes I made if you assume that what I say is true until through your own experience you reach a different opinion.

Warning! Every generalization I make about groups

of people is subject to exceptions. You must meet each citizen with an open mind. For example, there is no natural law which prevents club women from being intelligent and quite a few of them are.

Now let's let our hair down and speak plainly. We are going to discuss a lot of sacred cows and then kick them in the slats. We are going to mention a lot of unmentionable subjects, using everything but Anglo-Saxon monosyllables. We are going to discuss Catholics and Communists and Jews and Negroes, women in politics, reformers, school teachers, the nobility of the Irish, civil service *vs.* patronage, and whether Father was right. I will try to tell the truth as I have seen it. I hope I won't splash any mud in your direction but I may.

"One should never consider a man's religion in connection with politics." This is a fine credo, based on the American ideal of freedom of religion. It happens to be cockeyed and results from mushy thinking. One should always consider a candidate's religious beliefs; it is one of the most important things about him. Whether a man is a Catholic, a Protestant, a Communist, a Mormon, or a Jew has a very strong bearing on how he will perform his duties in certain jobs. (Communism is, of course, classed with the religions—more about that later.)[12] The important thing to remember is to consider a man's religion objectively, in relation to what you expect of him, and not in an attitude of blind prejudice.

There is nothing discriminatory nor un-American in scrutinizing a man's religious beliefs in connection with politics. A man's religion is a matter of free choice, even though most people remain in the faiths to which they were born. A Catholic can become a Jew; a Communist can become a Quaker.[13] A man's religious beliefs offer a strong clue to his attitudes, values, and prejudices and you are entitled to consider them when he is in public life.

For example — let us suppose that you live in a mythical community where the school board can, at its discretion, assign public funds to the support of private schools which are open to the public — parochial schools, of course. Let us suppose that you believe that public funds should be used only for state-controlled schools. Two tickets of candidates are before you, one Catholic, one non-Catholic, all equally well qualified, good men and true.

Should you vote for the ticket which will support your own opinion, or should you ignore what you know about the candidates and vote for the one with the pretty blue eyes?

Or let us suppose — same election; same town — that you are a non-Catholic who believes that tax money should support popular education but that the government should not be allowed to determine the nature of that education, except, perhaps, for the three R's. It is your belief that the individual parents should control the training received by their children; you fear state domination. Whom should you vote for?

Or suppose you are a Catholic but believe that public funds for support of Catholic schools would be the first step toward state control of those schools. Which way do you vote?

The problem can become still more complicated. Congress is considering subsidizing scientific research; many of the best colleges and universities in this country are controlled or dominated by members of a particular faith. Would you refuse a research subsidy to Notre Dame but allow it to some state-owned college in Tennessee, the state where biology is subject to the vote of the state legislature?[14] Or how about the great University of Southern California? It was a Methodist college once; there has been a divorce of sorts but the influence is still there. Can USC be trusted with a subsidy in mechanical engineering, or does nothing less than outright atheism meet your standards for freedom of thought?

In passing it might be added that private schools with church leanings were an indispensable factor in the scientific research that won World War II.

What bearing does all this have on the problem of tax funds for parochial schools? It obviously has some bearing and you yourself will have to consider the factors when you decide whether to campaign for the ticket made up of Catholics or the one made up of non-Catholics.

In my home state recently there were introduced in the legislature a group of bills concerning birth control and a group of bills concerning liquor licensing, local option, and prohibition. The governor received hundreds of letters about these two groups. Analysis showed that practically all of the letters about the birth control measures came from Catholic groups, whereas the letters about liquor measures came almost exclusively from Protestant church groups.

Is it not obvious, then, that you have a legitimate interest in the religious persuasion of your state legislator, your state senator, and your state governor?

Suppose you are a Christian Scientist; how do you feel about socialized medicine? Suppose instead that you are strong for socialized medicine; is it of interest to you that a candidate for the legislature is a Christian Scientist? Or should you ignore it?

Is a Jewish congressman more likely or less likely to vote to open the United States to any and all displaced persons in Europe? Who is the more likely to put a rider concerning Palestine on a bill to end money to Britain — a non-Zionist Jew or an Irish Catholic from Boston?

The ramifications of the political effect of a man's religious beliefs are endless. I do not intend to suggest answers to any of these questions; I simply mean to make it clear that to shut your eyes to this factor is to handicap yourself grossly in the analysis of men and issues. To vote always for a person of your own religious persuasion, or, at the other extreme, always to ignore a candidate's religious beliefs, is equally stupid and unrealistic. The first attitude is narrow and un-American; the second is custard-headed.

Call 'em as you see 'em!

Now let us discuss church groups.

(Before shouts of dirty red, fascist, papist, Jew, atheist, or whatever, start coming in, let me put this on record: Like all my great grandparents, I am native born, an American mixture, principally Irish, with a dash of English and French and a pinch of German. My name is Bavarian Catholic in origin; I was brought up in the Methodist faith. I believe in democracy, personal liberty, and religious freedom.)

American church groups as a whole are frequent sources of corruption and confusion in politics. This is a regrettable but observable fact which runs counter to the strong credo that if only the church people would get together and assert their strength we could run all those dirty crooks out of town. In fact, the church members of any community, voting as a bloc, could swing any election, institute any reforms they wished, and make them stick.

It does not work out that way.

I do not question that we are more moral, more charitable and more civilized as a result of church instruction and the labors of priests, ministers, rabbis, and countless devout laymen. Nor do I question the political good intent of church groups. The evil consequences result from good intentions applied in too limited a field.

Only rarely do churches become interested in the way in which paving contracts are awarded, how the oral examinations for civil service are conducted, or the fashion in which real estate values are assessed for tax purposes. Towing fees for stolen cars, the allocation of gasoline tax monies between city, county, and state, or the awarding of public utility franchises are likely to be too "political" for discussion from the pulpit.

Instead church groups are likely to demand laws which prohibit practices contrary to various religious codes of morals. A crooked political machine is happy to oblige each church as such laws do not hamper the machine; they help it — first, by providing new fields of graft and corruption, second, by insuring the votes of the madams, bookies, etc., engaged in these fields, and third, by obtaining support from the very church groups which demanded the legislation.

If you believe that laws forbidding gambling, sale of liquor, sale of contraceptives, requiring definite closing hours, enforcing the Sabbath, or any such, are necessary to the welfare of your community, that is your right and I do not ask you to surrender your beliefs or give up your efforts to put over such laws. But remember that such laws are, at most, a preliminary step in doing away with the evils they indict. Moral evils can never be solved by anything as easy as passing laws alone. If you aid in passing such laws without bothering to follow through by digging in to the involved questions of sociology, economics, and psychology which underlie the *causes* of the evils you are gunning for, you will not only fail to correct the evils you sought to prohibit but will create a dozen new evils as well.[15]

If your conscience requires that you support legislation of the type referred to above, then you must realize that your overall problem of keeping honest officials in office to enforce the laws is made much more difficult and that you must work several times as hard and be much more alert if you are to have an honest government.

As an amateur, unpaid, volunteer politician interested in certain reforms, don't expect any real help

from the churches even in accomplishing the moral
objectives of the churches, or you will be due for a
terrible disappointment.

Women in Politics[16]

We were told, when Votes-for-Women was new, that
women would bring higher moral standards and
would eliminate the graft and corruption which the
nasty old men had tolerated.

Women have had an effect — they caused the instal-
lation of a powder room in the Senate's sacred halls;
they changed the atmosphere of conventions from that
of a prize fight to something more like a college
reunion, and they broadened the refreshments at
political doings from a simple diet of beer and pigs
knuckles to a point where the menu now includes ice
cream and cake, little fancy sandwiches, coffee, and
wine cooler. The change in refreshments is a distinct
improvement; I don't like pigs knuckles.

They have also brought political corruption to a new
low.

Whoops! Easy, girls — please! Quiet down. There are
exceptions to all rules — you may be the exception to this
one. That is for you to determine. Judge yourself.

A great many women are willing to go to hell in a
wheel barrow. Their husbands may be politically just as
dishonest but the gentle sex are usually willing to sell
out at a lower price. They go in for cut-rate corruption.
If you file for office, or become the manager of a candidate, you will quickly be besieged by telephone calls
from women who want to help in your campaign.
They sound like enthusiastic volunteers; you will find
very quickly that they are political streetwalkers who
will support any candidate and any issue, without
compunction, for a very low price.

Brush them off, but politely — a practical politician
should never go out of his way to make anyone sore;

your purpose is to win elections, not arguments. Let the opposition hire them. They are hardly worth the low price they charge, even to him. Later on in the campaign you will find that he hired one of them a little sooner than you had expected; she worked as an unpaid volunteer all through the campaign in your office and turned in nightly reports to the opposition.

Don't let it throw you. As a politician you must learn to expect such little disappointments. And don't let it shake your faith in human nature. If you take the trouble to count up you will find that you know many more people who are certainly honest than the number who are just as certainly crooked. The crooks just seem more numerous because they get in your hair more.

I am inclined to believe, although I am not sure, that the average difference in political honesty between men as a group and women as a group in this country is actually considerable and not just a matter of a lower pay scale for corruption on the part of women. As a result of punching thousands of doorbells and talking with many, many men and women I am of the opinion that women usually know less about political issues than men and consequently are less inclined to realize that political issues are of moral consequence. This probably results in part from the fact that most women, in their daily occupations, are not thrown out into the world to the same extent as their men folk and consequently never really find out what makes the wheels go around.[17]

Furthermore, the husband is inclined to encourage the little woman to remain in ignorance; it gives him a chance to show off at home how much he knows without betraying just how little it is — since it is still more than she knows.

In any case, I have heard hundreds of times, in campaigning from door to door, this remark: "Oh, I leave everything of that sort up to my husband!" And she does, too — she doesn't know a filibuster from first base and she thinks an alderman is something to hang clothes on.

So, when somebody tips her off that she can pick up a few dollars in a campaign year by a little light work in her neighborhood, she is ripe for it, gullible, willing to work for low wages, and so naive she doesn't know that it's loaded. It won't even worry her to work for the candidate George is voting against, because she does not think it matters. She can work in a dozen campaigns and never find out anything about men nor issues; she just knows that State Senator Slotmachine is *such* a nice man and here is some literature about him and would you like to have a car sent around to take you to the polls?

Slotmachine is a nice man, too — he's an old hand in this business; his public personality is a work of art. You would enjoy having dinner with him.

After a while, if she is bright enough to mark a sample ballot, she does notice a few things, but it does not wise her up to what she is doing; it simply makes her utterly cynical about politics. She becomes convinced that the shoddy business she has been associated with is the only brand of politics in existence. Nothing will change her junior-size mind on the subject and she is forever lost to your side.

So don't hire her and don't bother to try to convert her. The women volunteers who work for you, free, can get ten votes to the one she can round up for Slotmachine.

All through it she remains a good wife and mother and a respected member of the P.T.A. You can't tell her from an authentic volunteer by sight nor, very quickly, by conversation. There is however one simple touchstone which works in nine cases out of ten. The sincere volunteers will look you up in person and offer their services; the political prostitutes will telephone, offer their services over the phone, and then ask you to come to see them. (I think they believe it improves their bargaining position.)

The rule is not infallible, but it will help you to be on your guard. It won't help you much when you encounter this particular bird of prey by chance, on ringing a doorbell, and it won't help you at all when the opposition hires her and then sends her to see you; nevertheless it will save you a lot of grief. After a while you will acquire a sense of smell concerning this sisterhood. In the meantime don't trust too far any volunteer previously unknown to you, who has great enthusiasm for unpaid work but does not seem to grasp the issues in the campaign. Don't put such a person to work in the headquarters; let her (or him) distribute literature — and then make a spot check on its distribution.

Still another breed of cat is the club woman politician. She organizes women's political clubs. She may not be dishonest; she is usually ambitious and stupid and she is almost never of any use in winning an election, although she may help you lose one and her enmity is to be dreaded. Look, ladies — don't be a woman politician, or a women's politician! Be a politician who happens to be female.[18] You are the equals of men — remember? It isn't necessary to go off and form little groups of your own; stay in the main event and start swinging.

After the above nasty cracks about women in politics I am very happy to be able to say that a sincere and enlightened female volunteer is the best political worker you will find. She is a pearl beyond price, but, thank Heaven, not too hard to find. She will average from twice to many times as useful as the general run of sincere male volunteers. She is not nearly as choosy as the men are about what kind of work she will do. She'll punch doorbells, and sweep the office, and type letters, and distribute newspapers, and watch the count, and drive a car on election day.

She doesn't expect anything out of it but the satisfaction of serving. Somebody told her once that a good citizen finds it a privilege to work for the betterment of her country. She believed it and she still believes.

Bless her heart — she is the backbone and sinew of *every* honest political organization in the country.

"*Mother knows best, dear!*" or "Remember, Father is usually right." It is standard practice for the elder generation to harry the younger generation with saws about "older and wiser heads." The youngsters resent it, until they get old enough to pull it on the next crop.

There is just enough truth in it to keep the practice going. Wisdom mellowed by years is beautiful to see. In public life the occasional George Norris, Henry Stimson, or Justice Holmes are as breath-takingly inspiring as the Lincoln Memorial. However, in most cases, what passes for the wisdom of age is merely the sophistication of experience, knowledge of precedents, and familiarity with details.

In politics our senior citizens habitually assume that their years entitle them to respectful attention from their juniors on the assumption that they have mellowed, grown broader, and increased in patriotism and social responsibility through the years.

It ain't necessarily so! Although there are shining exceptions, the average run of our elder citizens are notably avaricious, self-centered, unpatriotic, and devoid of any notion of social responsibility, as compared with their sons and daughters.[19]

Before I am accused of personal bias let me state that I am no longer a youngster myself. I've reached the shady side of the street, short of wind, and fat in the middle. To my regret, young women now call me "sir" and stand when they speak to me.

And I do not speak primarily of political office holders. I do not refer to the congressional practice whereby senility is an asset rather than a liability in reaching key committee posts, nor am I repeating the arguments about "The Nine Old Men." As a matter of fact old men in politics seem to keep young better than their non-political contemporaries. (Try shadowing a seventy-year-old congressman during a campaign; he'll wear you to a frazzle.)

In any case, the problem of superannuated officeholders is a political issue outside the scope of this book. I am speaking of the ordinary run of elder citizen, your neighbors, your parents, your grandparents. They may be kind to children and dogs and sweet to look upon in church and at family dinner, but politically speaking the average lot of them are the sorriest bunch of old vultures you will find.[20]

Remember that when you start punching door-bells.[21]

I am sorry to say these things. I like Great Aunt Mary's apple pies, her neat grey hair, and her wrinkled smile as well as you do. I had the opinion forced on me.

For example — several years ago I was covering a district which lay, half and half, on the right side and the wrong side of the tracks. I interviewed young and old, rich and poor, men and women. I expected and found certain trend differences in view point on the two sides of the tracks. But I was surprised to find an amazing and almost unanimous similarity in viewpoint on the part of the elderly rich and the elderly poor.

Mellowed and altruistic interest in the welfare and future of the whole community? Far from it! The elderly poor wanted $200 every month, or some other pension which would pay them more income than they had ever earned while working, and they didn't give a hoot what it did to the country! The elderly rich wanted the highest possible return from mortgages, rents, dividends, or other investment income, and they didn't give a hoot what it did to the country!

Naturally they tended to vote for different men and

different issues — except when a candidate managed to kid both groups. But the motivation was identical and utterly shameless — blind and narrow selfishness, short range in nature and quite unconcerned with the welfare and future of their children and their country.

Nor were they driven to it by hunger. One can forgive the selfishness of hunger, but even on the wrong side of the tracks they were neither hungry nor cold, as it happened to be in a state with, possibly, the most favorable and generous welfare conditions in the country. No, it was the greed of old age.

There appears to come a change in most people somewhere around the age of fifty when they cease to think of the rest of the human race except in terms of what others may be induced to do for them. A divorce from the human race is not a good thing for a man's inner being; it reduces his spiritual life to its lowest common denominator — the animal level. It is absolutely imperative that a man care for something more than for himself for him to remain human. Most tragically, many people, when they have reached the age when their own children are no real responsibility and are thereby not forced to think in terms of the welfare and future of their children, find nothing to replace such interest. The more nearly truly human of us substitute, for a preoccupation with the needs of our own children, after they are grown, a wider interest in all children everywhere, and the future of the nation and the race.

An elder citizen who has come safely through this difficult transition is a joy to know and is likely to make your best political worker. He will labor until the day he dies for the public welfare as he sees it, without the slightest expectation of personal reward. He usually has enough free time to be very effective, his views are respected, and the physical labor of politics is within the limits, in most cases, of even the elderly and infirm.[22]

I remember in particular one old lady who was the mainstay in a dozen campaigns. She lived along on a pittance and was nearly seventy when I met her. Her first name was Laura. (I never dared call her by her first name.) Not only did she work her own precinct and campaign among her friends, she was usually headquarters manager and handled the field workers and the public with cheerful tact.

Laura wanted to know only whether it was a private fight or could she get in it, too? She was never indifferent to any public issue; she would study, decide what was right by her values, and start pitching. I recall with pleasure watching her shake her finger under the nose of the chairman of a school board while scolding them all. "You gentlemen should be ashamed of yourselves! To have the temerity to sit there and tell *me*, a citizen and taxpayer of this state, that you do not intend to carry out your sworn duty!"

The fight was none of hers; it involved discrimination against a group in which she had no remote interest. But Laura won the fight; the school board backed down.

(Incidentally, keep your eye on school boards; they tend to disregard the constitutional rights of the public even worse than do judges.)

Churches, women, and elderly people have come in for quite a lambasting in this chapter; it is gratifying to emphasize that from these very groups you will get your most effective and altruistic volunteer workers. Embattled grandparents, militant housewives, and crusading clergymen will be your best shock troops. The rank and file of your organization will be young people, usually less than thirty-five years old — a man under thirty-five who cannot be induced to take any action for the welfare of his community and nation is morally dead and blind to his own personal interests; it is usually easy to interest young people in volunteer political activity. They have not yet acquired the case-hardened selfishness of their elders; they are enthusiastic, energetic, and they believe in the future.

But of the four groups, the young, the old, women past girlhood, and the clergy, young people are the only ones to be approached with no particular caution. The others are guilty until proven innocent from a standpoint of usefulness in volunteer political work.

Clergymen, although usually worse than useless, make wonderful altruistic politicians when they happen to possess both love of humanity and hard-headed realism. Too often the ones that are bright aren't good and the ones that are good aren't bright. Catholic priests are usually both and you can work with them to limit the issues in which you both see eye to eye. If you happen to be Catholic yourself the problem is simple.

The same may be said of rabbis, to a lesser extent.

"Politicians are usually crooks." This statement is false; it is likely that no other canard has done more harm to the United States of America.

The statement is false even when it is limited to machine politicians and bosses. Political bosses are not more crooked than the average run of non-political laymen; they are less crooked.

I know my statement runs contrary to popular prejudice. I am aware that graft, bribery, nepotism, special privilege, and outright official connivance in crime and racketeering have stained and continue to stain our public life. I still stand by the statement.

Consider how a political boss operates. His purpose is to stay in power not this term, but next term, and the term after that. To do that he has to have a majority of satisfied customers — the public — you! Despite all stuffing of ballot boxes, despite thuggery and intimidation at the polls, there is rarely (I am tempted to say "never") a time when aroused citizenry cannot throw him out of power and sometimes into jail as well. He cannot operate with the impunity of a Hitler. On the average he has to please *you*.

The successful political boss has to stay fairly honest. Just how honest that is depends on how honest the electorate is. His success depends on delivering to the public what the public *really* wants; not what you the public *say* you want when you are busy complaining, in private conversation, about those crooks in the city hall.

Have you ever had a traffic ticket fixed? Have you ever slipped an underpaid building inspector ten or twenty bucks not to report some violation of the building code? Have you ever patronized a prostitute? Have you ever taken a drink of bootleg liquor? Have you ever patronized a black, or even a light grey, market?

If you have done any of these things your own moral state is no higher than that of the Machine under which they exist. The man who believes in capital punishment cannot afford to turn up his nose at the hangman, nor can the man who offers a ten dollar bribe to a petty official afford to be righteously indignant when he finds that the scoundrels have stolen the city treasury. Nor can you expect a judge to fix a parking ticket for you on Monday but refuse to spring a known criminal on Tuesday. The difference is one of size, not of kind. Being a private citizen, your contact with graft and corruption is likely to be retail, but the man you deal with is a professional — necessarily! For him it is wholesale.

Your own record of civic virtue may be absolutely spotless; I have known many, many people who *never* violate public morals in any way. Nevertheless, even if you are such a person, you are aware that your friends and neighbors do such things as those listed above. Sometimes they give the excuse that the system forces such derelictions on them. This excuse is rarely if ever valid, but how often is it accompanied by an all-out effort to correct the conditions complained of? I have yet to find such a case.[23]

Very well — political dishonesty is a condition shared by the boss and the body politic. I have stated that the boss is *more* honest than the average of the lay public. I will attempt to prove it.

I am speaking here of the boss who *stays in power*, year after year, not of the man who suddenly climbs to power, overreaches himself, and gets promptly thrown out. The boss who stays in power is a businessman. Like all businessmen he deals daily in numerous transactions which are intended, over the long pull, to cause a profit to accrue to him. These transactions strongly resemble those of other businessmen, i.e., they are intended to benefit, one way or another, both parties to the transaction, and they must be, if not legal, at least not of such a nature as to cause the formation of vigilante societies by angry citizens. Most of them are mild in nature and stack up favorably when compared with the daily labors of the second hand automobile business, the cosmetics trade, the public relations profession, the undertaking business, the real estate business, and the "opportunity" schools.

But the business of the machine boss differs in an important respect from that of these respectable, legitimate occupations. His business is transacted orally, usually for future delivery on his part. And his word is better than the bond of most people!

Consider how it *must* be. (Later on you will find that I am right, through your own experience, but now let us tackle it by analysis.) This man deals in wind, in oral statements. Political commitments are not written down. These contracts are settled with such remarks as, "Okay, Joe, I'll see the commissioner next week and take care of it," or "All right, then, we'll support your man," or "That street will be repaved in six weeks." That's all.[24]

His word has *got* to be good — or he goes out of business.

It *is* good. Under circumstances where a written contract is necessary, and sometimes a law suit, to force a layman to carry out his solemn promises, a business politician will meet his commitments without a murmur, even though the situation may have changed so that it costs him immediate loss or embarrassment. His personal reliability is his stock in trade; he must not jeopardize it.

I can hear a snort of derision; everybody knows that broken political promises are common as flies around a garbage dump. Whose promises, citizen? The promises of a "reform" ticket? The promises of some office-happy candidate? Or the flat commitment of a *successful* boss of an entrenched machine? If you know personally of a broken promise of the last-named sort, I would appreciate it if you would write to me, care of the publisher, giving me the details.[25]

The commitments of a successful boss are made with a careful eye to what his experience has taught him the majority of the people really want. The Pendergast Machine, now moribund, of Kansas City, Missouri, was a perfect example of a machine which gave the people what they cared most about and stayed in power for more than a quarter of a century thereby. People want good pavements and aren't too interested in the cost; Kansas City had excellent streets all through the reign of the Machine. Parents want good schools; the Old Man saw to it that high-minded citizens sat on the school board and forbade the members of the organization to monkey with the school system.

People also want personal service from their government. The Old Man was in his office daily and the door was open. Any bindlestiff or solid citizen could walk in his office, make his complaint, and get a decision. The decision was backed up with action, and most of the decisions and actions would have met with your warm approval. The cop who had shoved around the bindlestiff was ordered to cut it out; the solid citizen got the chuck holes in front of his house repaired.

In addition, Widow Murphy got free coal and free food to help her and her kids through the cruel midwestern winter.

It is alleged that there was a Machine ruling which forbade shooting south of Twelfth Street. True or not, the respectable citizens worried very little about killings around the water front. Later on, when the Boss grew older and the Machine lost its careful attention to detail, it was certainly true that the sound of gunfire was not too uncommon in the "respectable" neighborhoods; the gangsters had moved south and set themselves up in fine apartments on Armour Boulevard, Linwood, the Paseo, and the Plaza.[26]

This was the beginning of the end; the Machine had overreached itself and permitted things which the citizens really disliked. Shortly thereafter the Old Man was so old and sick that he was unable to attend personally to one campaign. The "Boys" decided to make him a present, a really fine majority. Ghost votes were common in Kansas City, but this one reached a new high — or low. The Machine majorities were so enormous; the tallied opposition so microscopic, that it was easy for a federal grand jury to dig up proof of fraud from the persons who were willing to swear that they had voted against the Machine.

Does all of the above mean that I approve of political bosses and political machines? Decidedly not! The people of Kansas City paid a terrific price, both in money and intangibles, for their complacency, all through the reign of the Machine. Toward the last, as the Boss grew old and the invisible government became less well disciplined, the price became outrageous and intolerable. Bombings, shootings, and other crimes of violence became commonplace.

But the greatest loss was in their own attitude toward civic virtue. They had become — the "respectable" citizens — cynical about the possibility of honest and efficient government. They had lost faith in themselves. There were many times in the early decades of this century when a concerted effort could have cleaned up their city; they were too indifferent and too cynical to attempt it whole-heartedly. When the change came, it resulted from decay of the Machine and from organized efforts outside the city, not from the inhabitants thereof.

Something very like the disease of Kansas City caused the downfall of France.[27]

If bosses were the utter villains the "respectable" citizens think they are, political reform would be easy. In addition to being no crookeder than the average of the public and notably more meticulous in their personal honesty in one respect, successful bosses and successful machine politicians have many other virtues.

No matter how twisted are their attitudes toward public money and private graft, successful machine bosses have these positive virtues: They are friendly. They are helpful. They are tolerant. They are good tempered. They are conciliatory. They are personally reliable. They give patient attention to the personal problems of people who ask them for help, without being stiff-necked about it.

In short they like people and they show it, in practical, warm-hearted ways. If you expect to compete with them successfully you've got to emulate them in their virtue while shunning their vices. You can be as pure in heart and motive as Sir Galahad but it won't make your strength as the strength of ten unless you get down off your horse.

Roark Bradford has John Henry tell how to get along with a hog. "First you got to be a friend to the hog. Then he friend you back." John Henry knew his political onions.

Take a tip from the Salvation Army. Sal remains pure in heart by never failing to extend a hand to anyone who asks for help.

Possibly you don't like Jews. Perhaps you think the Negro should be kept "in his place." A foreign accent may annoy you. You may consider the poor to be loafers and bums. Or, vice versa, you may consider all the wealthy to be crooks. Perhaps Catholics come in for your special scorn. Whatever it is, if you hold any of these attitudes, you had better search your soul and change them, or you will never be a success in politics.

I don't mind in the least injecting discussion of racism and minorities into this book. There is no partisan bias here; both major parties are forthright in their *official* attitudes condemning these things, despite the mouthings of individuals or groups, despite filibusters by members of one party and the silent, guilty consent thereto by the other.

The bosses understand democracy better than many who turn up their noses at political machines. That is why you find the minorities supporting the Machines with such regularity.

You must meet the competition or you might as well go back to your ivory tower and wait for the dictatorship. It may suit you better, for dictators stand for no nonsense from people of the wrong race, or the wrong religion, or the wrong place of birth. Of course he is equally likely to liquidate you — stand you up against a ditch and shoot you. Or take your business away from you and give it to a party member.

I am sorry to raise these issues but this book is intended to be truthful rather than diplomatic. If you expect to beat the machine politicians in the practical arts of democracy, you have got to be at least as democratic as they are. It is not necessary that you *like* any particular man nor group; it is necessary that you be friendly in manner and that you honestly treat all comers with fairness, tolerance, and decency. If you do have any strong prejudices against particular minorities you had better learn to guard most carefully against showing them, both in public and in private.

"A government should be run like a business." This is a common saying and it is rather silly. Look, citizen, a machine boss is a man who runs a government like a business. Is that what you want? A business is an organization run from the top down for the personal profit of the persons who run it. Businesses provide the public with something they want in return for money. Isn't that what a political machine does?

Our Constitution is quite explicit about the purposes for which we formed this government. They are: " — to form a more perfect Union, establish justice, insure domestic tranquility, provide for the common defense, promote the general welfare, and secure the blessings of liberty — " That's all. Nothing about making a profit, nothing about being "businesslike."

The methods of business are appropriate to the purpose of business; they are quite incompatible with the purposes of the Constitution. I do not mean to imply that a businessman cannot serve well in public office; I do mean that he had better not try to run things with the high hand with which he bossed his own business or the public will throw him out on his ear once they get wise to him.

It is quite true that some areas of government administration could stand more "businesslike" handling, but most attempts to tidy up government service to the public results in screams of anguish from any who are annoyed by the changes, without any compensating applause from those who are helped.

Take for example the new income tax form. It has been functionalized and made explicit, with all the turns clearly marked, to the point where a moron with a hangover can make out his own income tax return unless he is in the habit of keeping his business records in the bottom of his laundry bag. (Or unless he keeps two sets of books, one for tax purposes and one for his eyes alone!)

The thing that makes the new income tax form a marvel of bureaucratic genius is that the tax bill it defines with such graphic simplicity is a hodge-podge of second thoughts, blind guesses and compromises, resulting from the agonized efforts of officeholders of both parties to be reasonably fair to all hands while paying for the most expensive war in history.

Have you heard any applause for the result? Like fun! The mere mention of March 15 by a comedian produces sour laughter.[28] The effort of figuring out the form is regularly portrayed as being more difficult than understanding Dr. Einstein's relativity.

Forget that notion about running a government like a business. A government should not be run for profit and a democratic government can't be run by a boss. And as for "businesslike" — are you sure you want it yourself? Do you want your home confiscated if you fall behind on a tax payment with the same speed with which a mortgage holder will foreclose if you fail to pay up, or a landlord will kick you out if you fail to pay rent — or do you prefer the present practice in which the government will stall around for years before putting your place up for auction?

By the way, why do people kick so much at having to stand in line in the post office, or the recorder's office, but are docile as little lambs when queued up in a bank? Is it because they expect service rather than a businesslike attitude from the government they own? Could be, maybe?[29]

"Politicians are always compromising." This statement is quite true but the implication that the process is dishonest is so much balderdash. Compromise is the core of the democratic process. Without it there is no democracy and can be no freedom. Compromise is the process by which we meet the other fellow halfway and agree on a joint course of action not quite pleasing to either party. Every happily married couple is quite used to the system; if it is good at home, is it bad on Capitol Hill? The man who won't compromise is not a lily-white idealist; he is merely a conceited ass and undemocratic to boot.

We will discuss this further under techniques, particularly under "caucuses" and "primaries."

Civil Service *versus* Patronage. This subject is not nearly so much a matter of all black and all white as most people seem to think. Let us concede that civil service is a good idea in most public jobs below the policy-making level — if the regulations have been drawn with the intent of producing an honest, spoil-free service and if those regulations are honestly administered. Otherwise — and this applies to many cities, counties, and states — it is merely a dodge to entrench the henchmen of a machine in public jobs, beyond the reach of the electorate to "turn the rascals out!"[30]

The wrangle is generally managed through the device of an oral examination for applicants which counts as much, or nearly as much, as the written examination. If your local civil service makes use of an oral examination you are justified in assuming that it is crooked, a racket.

Nor is patronage, or the "spoils system," the benefit to practical politicians it is supposed to be. If a politician once gets started on the road of paying off political obligations with patronage, he quickly finds that there is never enough patronage to go around. Some of our senators meet this situation by becoming insatiable patronage hounds — one of them recently proposed a bill which would have made holding a job as a senior aeronautical engineer at Wright Field a matter of political faith! Others meet it by dropping the matter

entirely, refusing to touch patronage, or by delegating
it to the official local organization of their party.

Many officeholders have told me in private that the
system of refusing to have anything to do with
patronage is the only one which is free from headaches
and unnecessary loss of votes.

The reason is very simple. For every patronage job
there are at least a dozen candidates with good claims
— in their own minds, at least — for appointment on
the score of political services rendered. That means
one man whose loyalty, such as it is, may have been
purchased by the appointment — and eleven who are
almost certainly antagonized.

After a few terms of this a congressman finds himself
surrounded by a sea of disappointed postmaster candidates, each anxious to elect his opponent.

Still, if you are going to be in politics, you will have to
face up to the problem of patronage. If you steadfastly
refuse to accept it yourself, someday you will find that
the job of dispensing it has been laid in your lap. What
to do will be discussed under "techniques."

The federal civil service is almost entirely free from
the dishonesty which is so prevalent in state and local
civil service. It need not concern you too much as it is,
by and large, well run and moderately efficient. It is not
free from politics; federal civil servants maintain quite a
lobby in Washington, but it is almost entirely free from
partisan politics. Their efforts run mostly to pressure to
obtain larger appropriations, higher salaries, and big-
ger organizations.[31]

Senator Byrd seems to feel that this is one of the most
important problems facing the Republic. I don't happen
to think so. You will have to decide for yourself.[32]

The worst thing wrong with the federal civil service
is the fact that the salaries and working conditions are

not sufficiently high to attract enough competent men in the more responsible administrative positions — a section head in agronomy, let us say, or a division supervisor in aerodynamics research, or a chief physicist for the Bureau of Standards.

This problem is not limited to federal civil service but extends all through government. We pay a congressman $10,000 a year for a job that costs him $15,000 a year to hold under present conditions, *exclusive of his campaign expenses*, and then wonder why things get fouled up in Washington.[33]

One of the commonest misconceptions has to do with "eating out of the public trough." By popular superstition, every officeholder, appointive or elective, is suspected of living by a process midway between cannibalism and vampirism, and classed with robbing the dead.

Truthfully, comrades, eating out of the public trough is mighty slim pickings. As we just mentioned, it is slow bankruptcy to become a congressman. The situation with state legislators is much worse. A hundred dollars a month is high pay for a legislator or state senator; most states pay less than that. None of them pay a living wage, yet carrying out the duties of the office properly in these complicated days is a full-time job at nearer sixty hours a week than forty.[34]

How do they live?

One of two ways: (a) honestly, through private income or private work done at the expense of public business — and the legislator's own health; it's too big a burden — or (b) by graft, either polite or shameless.

If the legislator is a lawyer, as too many of them are, polite graft is simple.[35] Get your own lawyer to explain the process. Shucks! We might as well be frank. In most states (all states, as far as I know) a legislator who is also a lawyer may practice his profession on the side. He may receive legal fees, size not limited by professional code, for legal services, nature undefined. These fees may be legitimate fees, honestly earned; they may be "clean" graft — fees that fall in his lap because of his prominence as a public official but with no definite strings attached (there is a lot of that and it tends to make a man a tame dog without buying his vote outright); or it may be outright bribery, done in such a manner that it can never be prosecuted.[36]

If you should happen to get interested in cleaning up this particular evil in your home state — it's there! — the method is simple: Pay your legislators about $10,000 a year, which is what they should be worth for what you expect of them; forbid them to earn money through outside business; and institute some type of required publicity of their financial conditions on entering and leaving office, each term.[37]

Simple to state, that is — you will find it hard to formulate in law and very hard to put over, not because of the opposition of the legislators but because of the blind and angry opposition of a great part of the population who hate to see a public official paid a living wage and hate still worse for him to be paid a salary commensurate with the responsibility of the office.[38]

Most strangely and wonderfully, in spite of the nominal salary and impossible working conditions, in spite of the fact that they are usually treated disgracefully by their constituents (who seem to feel that an elected legislator is something between a paroled convict and a chattel slave), a very large percentage of our legislators are earnest, honest, hardworking public servants doing their level best for their state and their constituents.

Why do they do it? Why would any man expose himself to such a fate? In England the profession of government is the highest and most respected occupation a gentleman can enter; in this country a man who dares to offer himself for the public service might as well kiss his reputation goodbye.

Then why do the honest men in public office (and their numbers are enormous compared with the crooks) ever chuck their hats in the ring? Or, once having had their fingers burned, why do they run for re-election? Is it a power complex? Are they publicity-mad exhibitionists? Is it some sort of a vice?

All of the above may enter into some cases to some degree, but I have a different theory as to the main reason. My theory is based on intimate knowledge of many legislators; it may be wrong but here it is, for what it's worth.

I think it's patriotism.[39]

There is a strong conceit held by a large part of the population that it is somehow a little *déclassé* to be an active partisan, that all really nice people are non-partisan. You will hear, "I vote for the man, not the party," said in a smug tone of voice, as if expecting for that pious sentiment at least one more star in the heavenly crown. Among middle-aged and elderly women this attitude is almost universal.

With rare exceptions, I vote for the party, not the man. *Be partisan!*

Be party regular. Vote the ticket in the fall of the party whose primary you voted in earlier in the year. Do all you can to enforce party discipline, not only among political workers, but, after election, on the part of your party office holders. Make 'em stick to the party's platform.[40]

Like all generalizations, this rule is subject to some exceptions, but the exceptions are *very* few, and you should spend several sleepless nights before deciding that a special circumstance merits an exception.

I can give you the thumb rule I use. I won't vote for a man whom I know to be an outright crook, or treasonable to our form of government, or, in my opinion, having some other moral defect so gross to make him a public menace in public office.

But I will vote for a dunderhead against a smart man of the party I am opposing.

After all, all I am asking of the poor devil is that he represent me; the dunderhead, if subject to party discipline, can do so; the smart man from the other party is already pledged to vote contrary to my wishes in the respects in which the two parties differ.

The belief that it is somehow more "idealistic" to ignore party lines arises from a failure to understand the nature of the democratic process. Democratic government is the art of reconciling the desire of every man to do just as he damn well pleases with the necessity of setting up rules and agreeing on programs for the general welfare of all and the protection of each individual.[41]

When there are 140,000,000 individuals concerned the procedure has to be more formalized and more complicated than it is when a single family decides what movie to attend. The process is necessarily as follows; no other system has ever been invented:

Individuals who are somewhat like-minded get together, discuss candidates and issues, iron out their differences, compromise, and agree on a program and a slate for the party primary. The primary they take part in is, of course, that of the party which, in their opinions, most nearly fits their needs. As a result of the primary they hope to make it still closer to what they want.

Other groups have been doing the same thing. After the party primary the groups, successful and unsuccessful, get together in larger groups and make further compromises. Many, perhaps most, of the concessions are made by the successful groups to the unsuccessful ones, for the successful groups are acutely aware that they cannot win in the final election single-handed.

Somehow, a party platform is hammered out. It is a conglomeration of compromises, representing an average of the hopes and beliefs and needs of many people. No one is satisfied, but half a loaf, etc. — they pledge support.

A campaign organization is worked out. The campaign manager is not infrequently the strongest unsuccessful rival of the head of the ticket; all through the organization you will find disappointed candidates and their supporters pitching in to try and elect the man they opposed a few weeks before. Hypocrisy? Hell, no! It's brotherhood and civilized cooperation.

After the election the compromising process starts all over again, for the successful candidates of each party are now public officials. From unlimited considerations, out of strongly opposed needs, and violent differences in viewpoint they must arrange programs, pass laws, produce an administration.

From this endless and involved series of compromises comes the government of these United States, and of our states and counties and cities.

There is no other way — for a government of free men.

But the point is this: You can't take part in this process without being partisan. What is a political party? It is a large group of people who have agreed to compromise their differences to accomplish a program reasonably satisfactory to all but which none could accomplish alone.

The definition applies to all political organizations. In this country we call that group just below the level of government itself the political party. The groups which make up the national parties are little parties, no matter what they are called — clubs, groups, blocs, wings, leagues. I want to point out that a "non-partisan league" is a political party. So is an "independent women voters' league," or a "civic affairs committee." Mr. Lincoln made it clear a long time ago that calling a tail a leg did not make it a leg.

However, these parties without party labels are usually less responsible and more subject to dishonest manipulation than the parties which openly avow their party nature.

But why be partisan? Why not vote independently, after an earnest scrutiny of the candidates and issues, for the welfare of the people as a whole? It sounds good and it would be very nice if it would work. It would also be nice if *pi* were exactly 3.000 instead of a bothersome 3.14159 plus.

There are two reasons, one moral and one practical. The practical reason is this: You simply cannot be effective in politics unless you join in the process of compromise and conciliation whereby free men merge little groups into big groups until they accomplish a government. If you are not partisan you are on your own, everybody is out of step but Johnny, and the chances that you can have any effect on how this country is run are 140,000,000 to one against you.

If you write to your congressman about some issue that matters to you he will recognize you for what you are, a free rider, a political zombie, and he will give your opinion the casual attention it deserves.[42] But if he knows you to be an acting worker in the South Side (Democratic) (Republican) Club, he will write you a careful explanation of his own views in the matter and ask you to elaborate yours.

It does not matter whether or not your congressman is of the same political party as the club you belong to, just as long as he knows that you take regular part in the basic democratic process of partisan politics.

Now for the moral reason: Whenever you take part in the group processes of democracy there is an unwritten but morally binding contract between yourself and the other members of the group that you will abide by the will of the majority. If you know ahead of time that the will of the majority is likely to be something that you can't stomach, then you are in the wrong pew and should go find a group more to your liking.

But you have no right to take part in their proceedings, accepting from them a voice and a vote, unless you intend to abide by the outcome of the vote.

The issue can be quite crucial. You will one day find yourself engaged in the process and will see coming out of it a result which you had not anticipated but which you cannot support with a clear conscience. There is then only one answer—get out. Resign. Retire.

But don't go over to the opposition! You've had your chance; through your own bad judgment you've muffed it. Wait it out and choose your associates more carefully next time. Change clubs, change groups, change parties if necessary, and try again. But do not expect to run with the fox and hunt with the hounds, all in the same campaign.

Being partisan does not mean that you must stay in one party all your life. It is proper to change parties, or to help to form a third party, if you find that the party of your former affiliation no longer represents your views.[43] It is also proper to join a straddle-party, a group which announces its intentions of selecting and supporting candidates on the basis of some issue or program which they regard as paramount, irrespective of party labels. Such a venture although highly speculative is legitimate, but it automatically bars you from any moral right to take part in the regular party processes, including the primary.

It is *not* legitimate to vote in the Republican primary in the summer, turn around and vote for the Democratic ticket in the fall.

When you accepted a voice in the selection of a particular party's candidates you contracted with the other members of that party to abide by the outcome. Some state's recognize this principle; others are so lax that it is possible in such a state for a man to be registered in one party, run for office in a second party, then support the ticket of a third party. The moral issue is the same anywhere.

The principle is formalized in a caucus. The caucus is a device used to bind a group to unanimous action and is used both for programs and for the selection of candidates. It works like this: A group of people with something in common get together for the purpose of a political action. Some member moves to caucus. This is a motion on procedure; no issue or candidate is as yet before the group. If the motion carries the group as a whole is bound to act unanimously to carry out the will of the majority.

Pretty rough on the minority? Wait a moment — anyone who at this point decides that he is not willing to bind himself *gets up and walks out*. He has been deprived of none of his rights as a free citizen, but he has decided of his own free will not to work with this group.

The doors are closed and the remainder arrive at a majority decision which is binding on them all as the unanimous wishes of the caucus.

Simple, isn't it? You never have to join a caucus, but if you do you promise to live up to the contract. Yet I have met people so politically naive that they refused to bind themselves but demanded that they be allowed to remain and vote and debate. Others will break the caucus after the doors are opened. One "reformer" type is particularly prone to this sort of political dishonesty; he can always find reason why "the greatest good of all the peepul" demands that he go back on his word.[44] It marks him as dishonest, he is not invited to caucus the next time, and he never gets an opportunity to serve the people he claims to love so well.

I have tried to make it clear that it takes a nice sense of honor, personal self discipline, and meticulous respect for the obligations of contract to be partisan and party regular. It takes ideals and integrity, despite the common opinion to the contrary. The political free-lance, who proclaims that he wears no man's collar and boasts of his independence, should not be admired, for he is merely irresponsible. He is the cuckoo of politics, who claims the privilege of laying eggs in a nest he refused to help to build.

You may still have misgivings. You may still feel, quite honestly, that you want to be free to pick up your ballot in November with unlimited choices to split the ticket any way you like for the men you believe to be the most able. Well, no one will stop you. But an adult is never free in that sense. He is bound by his conscience, his sense of responsibility, and his commitments to other people. If you have taken an adult part in the preliminary democratic processes which led up to that ballot in your hand, then you already have obligations and are morally bound to carry them out.

Let us mention one more practical consequence of the evil of being "non-partisan." When you elect a man to office you expect him to make an honest effort to carry out his platform pledges. Very well — don't give a Democratic governor a Republican legislature and then expect him to rear back and pass a miracle. Remember the second half of Hoover's administration. The Executive and the Congress were headed in different directions and the processes of orderly government came to a stop. Mr. Hoover never had a chance. Neither did the Congress.[45]

• CHAPTER IV

The Practical Art of Politics

Field and Club Organization [46]

We could call this chapter the *Art of Kissing Babies*, or *How to Win Friends and Influence Voters*.

I will try to make this as objective as a book on automobile repairing and as non-partisan as a rain storm. I hope to keep moral issues out of it but will not consciously recommend any practice which is not honest and fair.

Politics is not a science but an art, an incomplete and unorganized art as untidy as the bottom of a closet. One can start anywhere and go anywhere. This chapter cannot be complete; I will content myself with sticking up a few sign posts in the maze and posting a few boggy places.

Your object as a politician is to win elections, not arguments. If you will always remember that, you can't go far wrong.

The second thing to remember is that elections are won with votes; those votes are out in the precincts, not down in the politico-financial district, not in political clubs, not at political rallies.

The third thing to remember is that a vote for your side never becomes a reality unless you see to it that the holder thereof gets down to the polls and casts it. This should be printed in red ink and set off with flashing lights.

The fourth thing to remember is not to waste time arguing with a hard case. In the years I have spent in politics I cannot honestly say that I recall ever having persuaded anyone to change his mind about how he was going to vote on an issue or for a candidate if he had already made up his mind when I approached him. Yet I know that I have influenced and sometimes changed the outcome of elections through my own efforts.

How? By organized effort in applying the first three points-to-be-remembered while observing the injunction contained in the fourth. The first campaign I was in I thought that campaigning consisted of going around and trying to persuade people by sweet reason to vote for my side. I used up a lot of shoe leather, met a lot of interesting people, and learned a good deal. I don't suppose I did my candidate very much harm — oh, I may have lost him a dozen votes or so — but I certainly did him no good.

Long before you punch the doorbell: the person on the other side has usually made up his mind as what party and what head of the ticket to support. He has reached this decision through a process of rearranging his prejudices which he laughingly calls "making up his mind" — unless he is a very exceptional citizen. He now holds his opinion as an emotional conviction; if you try to attack it you probably succeed only in making him angry. This is a good way to insure that he will take the trouble to go to the polls, for the satisfaction of voting against you.

Some very successful campaigns have been run by the expedient of providing the opposition with the wrong sort of a "volunteer" precinct organization, who lose votes for the man they pretend to support by being belligerent nuisances. It is a dishonest practice but an amazing illustration of the old saw that the way to lead a pig is to pull its tail.

*   *   *

How to Punch a Doorbell: You are clean, you are neat, you have a smile on your face and a friendly attitude in your heart. Someplace about your person you have some campaign literature. You are facing a closed door; behind it, according to the precinct list, lives Mr. and Mrs. Seldom, both members of your party.

You punch the doorbell. After what seems an interminable time the door opens; you see Mrs. Seldom. Her face is flushed, a baby is squalling in the background, and your eyes and nose detect clear evidence of cooking in progress.

You look pained, you look embarrassed — it isn't hard to do; you *are*. And you get out of there fast!

You say, "Oh, I'm sorry, Mrs. Seldom — I sure picked a bad time to butt in, didn't I? Excuse me, please!" You start backing away.

If she's human she will at least say, "What do you want?"

Don't take this as a cue to hang around. No woman wants to be held up when the potatoes are about to burn. Say, "I'm Fred Glutz, representing the East Squamous Demican Club. We're making a survey and we wanted to get your opinions on the coming election. But I certainly did not mean to butt in and make a nuisance of myself. Here — may I leave this with you and get out?" You place appropriate literature in her hand. Keep on backing away.

There is a fair chance that she will apologize for being tied up and suggest that you come back some evening when her husband is at home.

If so, close the deal fast. Suggest that evening. If she demurs, suggest the following evening. If she still demurs, ask if you can telephone for an appointment. Then follow up without fail.

If she doesn't suggest some sort of follow up, leave at once and pray that you haven't annoyed her.

Let's try the next house. The precinct list gives it as the residence of the Squiffle family. You ring, the door opens. A small dog sails out and begins to circulate around your feet. You squat down and begin scratching his ear, then grin up at his mistress. "What's his name?" you ask.

"We call him Snuffy. Here, Snuffy, get back inside and quit bothering the man!"

"He's no bother. Had one myself that looked like him, but he got run over last year. Streetcar." (Make it true. There must be *something* you can say at this point that a dog owner would recognize as sincere shop talk.)

This goes on until *she* brings up the matter of why you are there. You tell her — same words as next door. It develops that her name is not Squiffle, but Bedrock. "I think there used to be some people here by that name, but they moved. I don't know where."

You've struck pay dirt, pal. Careful, now! Find out what party they are in. Use a direct question if she does not volunteer the information. If it is the wrong party, end the interview quickly. Leave some literature if she will take it, but don't argue and get out fast. Thank her for her time, reach down and pat Snuffy, and get out.

If it is the right party, tell her the Club is glad they moved into the neighborhood. Ask her whether or not she has registered at this new address. The chances are she has not. Offer to have a deputy registrar call to register them. Follow up on this.

Invite them to the club meeting, then see to it that an invitation comes by mail.

Ask her if she would like to have some one come to watch the kids while she goes to vote. Ask her if she would like to have an automobile sent to take her to the polls. Even if she says this isn't necessary, follow it up on election day. If she has not voted as yet a couple of hours before the polls close, send a car for her anyway.

Continue the interview as long as she is interested.

Discuss issues if she wants to and listen respectfully to what she has to say. Don't argue with her views. Let the points of difference pass and bear down on the respects in which you agree with her. As soon as she shows signs of restlessness, after two minutes or thirty minutes, get out promptly.

Record everything you have learned on a 3 x 5 file card, noting the action to be taken, before you ring the next doorbell.

You have almost certainly obtained one, and probably two or three, brand-new votes for the whole ticket. If it is a primary campaign your chances of swelling the total for your favorite candidates are even better.

With good luck you may have added a member to your local club, a member who may later do some precinct work herself. That remains to be seen. Gold is where you find it. Her husband may turn out to be one of those commendable individuals who will reach down in his pocket for a five spot to help pay for printing or hall rent, even if he won't do precinct work. He may own a filling station, or be a barber, or be in any of the many trades or professions which lend themselves to political contact work.

All this remains to be determined. Probably all you've gotten is a pair of new votes, but that is not to be sneered at. The Great Wall of China was built of individual bricks. In any case all that you have learned is recorded on the file card — including the dog Snuffy's name. When you send her the invitation by mail, to attend a club meeting, write on the printed form or typed letter, in long hand: "Does Snuffy still speak to strangers?"

Here is another doorbell. Behind it (it says here on the precinct list) should be Mrs. Grassroots, her son and daughter-in-law.

And so they are. They own their own home and

haven't moved. They are on your side already; the record shows that they habitually vote even in the primaries. Your job is too easy; you might as well not have bothered.

Don't be too sure. Out of three votes, even with conscientious citizens, at least one will probably fail to show up for the primaries unless you follow up and, possibly, provide transportation. Furthermore you have a chance to win new club members and find new precinct workers. *New* club members, *new* precinct workers, are behind those closed doors. You must ring the doorbells.

We have covered all the important types, though you will encounter infinite variety in the types. You will encounter crackpots, and lonely people who will talk to you endlessly, and serious people who welcome a chance to exchange views. You will find some who will sit you down and ply you with cake and coffee and others who are obviously suspicious of you. Once in a long, long time you will encounter outright rudeness and it will leave you shaken, sick at heart, and reluctant ever to risk another rebuff.

Don't let it drive you home. Smoke a cigarette. Walk up to the corner drug store, buy a malted milk, and look at some comic strips. Then go back and tackle the next doorbell. The chances are that the person behind it will be as friendly as a puppy. Most Americans are.

You will find out a lot about your fellow citizens and what you find out will usually increase your faith in democracy and make you proud to be an American and a member of the human race. It will warm you up inside and give you new confidence about the future.

Why is a political club? I have already stated that elections are won in the precincts, not in clubs. Political clubs are hard to keep alive and require constant attention; why should you bother?

The political club is the organization of the doorbell pushers. It is the means by which you get them together and keep them together. It provides the necessary minimum of loose organization necessary to any cooperative enterprise.

But it does more than that. It is your principal means of keeping up morale among the volunteers. Field work in politics can be a lonely business; after a day or even an evening of punching doorbells you may feel that nobody cares but yourself, to hell with it, let the country go to the dogs, why should you knock yourself out — it isn't appreciated.

Then you need the company of other politicos, citizen. You need shop talk from others who have been through the same mill. You need to listen to how they are tackling things down in the twelfth ward and what the chances appear to be. You need to hear the ever hopeful comments of the old timers and the optimistic predictions of the campaign managers.

You'll listen to gossip about what the governor told Joe Shortterm in a secret conference last Wednesday and just what Joe thinks of the governor. You'll hear that Dr. Toplofty has decided to run for Congress in the third district and you will agree that that stuffed shirt doesn't stand a chance unless he quits spending all his time speaking in front of organizations made up of other stuffed shirts just like himself.

You'll stay up a little later than you should and drink a little more coffee than you should and you'll buy two tickets to the Fourth of July dance. Next day you will feel like punching some more doorbells. It doesn't look quite so hopeless. After all, your district has a more favorable registration than the twelfth ward and Jack Sidewalk seemed to be fairly confident that the party could carry the twelfth.

You'll go to the dance. You may not dance more than three or four dances, but it seems you had a swell time.

You picked up a couple of ideas from the chairman of the Westside Club and heard two wonderful pieces of scandal about, respectively, the street commission and Senator Shortchange.

In addition to building morale and acting as a clearing house for political information the club performs the serious function of acting as a school and a seminar in government. The candidates speak before the club and are there subjected to questioning and searching examination impossible at the public rallies. No candidate nor office holder, up to and including the level of governor, can afford to refuse a summons to appear before a club. If circumstances interfere, he will be apologetic about it and try to arrange another date.

This fact gives you a chance to know intimately the men who run our government. In a country as large as ours this is a most valuable opportunity and one of which most people appear to be unaware. If you avail yourself of it, the mysterious and remote processes of your government will become as familiar and personal as the ministrations of your family physician.

The club is also the work shop of democracy. It conducts much the same business and under much the same rules as does our Congress — with this difference: The club conducts such business frequently in advance of the Congress. Many a bill has been submitted, and passed, in the sacred halls of Congress because some private citizen, a tailor, or a grocery man, or a school teacher, first submitted that bill as a resolution before some small and amateurish political club.

The political club is in fact part of our government, although an unofficial part. New ideas are tried out in it, debated, referred to committee, modified, and made ready for the public arena, just as plays are sent to Atlantic City for a try out.

How to Form a Political Club: Just one person is necessary to a successful political club. He (or she) is usually the secretary, though he may be the chairman, the treasurer, a member of the membership committee, chairman of the program committee, or not even an officeholder. Whatever the title this person is the *de facto* executive secretary through willingness and energy.

He sees to it that invitations and notices are mailed out. He is a day-in-and-day-out one-man membership drive. He sees to it that the hall rent and postage costs are collected from the membership. He arranges for speakers and plans for social events. He borrows chairs, promotes refreshments, dickers for halls, inserts notices in newspapers, and welcomes newcomers.

In a large club he may be twins, triplets, or even quintuplets. But no club is without him. He has the qualities of a Sunday School superintendent, a Scoutmaster, or an amateur orchestra leader. You have met him, or her, in lodge meetings, in the Rotary Club, in the Parent-Teachers' Association, or in the ladies' aid. All human organizations are dependent on such persons; it takes just one to make a political club.

When to Form a Club: Don't try to form a club unless you yourself are prepared to be this spark plug. I can recall at least two clubs, well and carefully planned by persons who had the temperamental qualifications, which never got further than a couple of meetings because the persons who planned them were tied up with other work and had assumed that they could start the ball rolling and then let the rank and file carry on.

It ain't so . . . except by rare accident.

Don't start a club unless you are prepared to stay with it and nurse it along during its lifetime. You may plan to keep it alive during one campaign and then let it die if it can't walk alone. Such a club can be very useful. Or you may plan it as a permanent community organization in which case the job never ends. However, in the latter case, you will probably come across one or more foster parents who can be depended on to carry on the good work even if you move out of town.

It is a lot more trouble to found and run a club than it is simply to be an active member and a precinct worker. However, if you live in an area where one ought to be founded and are willing to put out the amount of effort it takes to run a scout troop, then go right ahead. It takes no special talent as long as you are willing and know the techniques.

It is not even necessary to be the sort of person who makes friends easily and is known as "popular." I have seen clubs, successful clubs, run by persons who were neither intelligent nor pleasing in manner, but who had the single virtue of industry. However, the ability to make friends is so useful in running a club, and is, in fact, so useful everywhere in politics, that we will digress again and discuss it before taking up the techniques of forming and running a club.

Remember what John Henry said about the hog? "You got to friend him first. Then he friend you back." It's as easy as that.

The secret of popularity is to let people know that you like them.

Find something to like about a person and *say so*. There is always something about a person you can approve of — if the devil showed up you could at least compliment him on his industry.

I am not suggesting that you be insincere; I do suggest that you avoid being reticent. If you like something, say so.

You are standing beside Mr. Brown at a club dance. Mrs. Brown is on the floor. You say, "My, but Mrs. Brown dances beautifully, doesn't she? Nobody would think she was the mother of three kids."

It will please him without making him jealous; it's a tribute to his good taste. Ask him if he's got any new pictures of the kids. He has, he hauls out his wallet.

If you can't find something pleasant to say about

pictures of kids I can't help you. But you can. At the very least you can note that one of them looks like his old man. There is always some sincere small remark you can make which is pleasant for him to hear. You don't have to lay it on with a shovel. Don't gush. Just be on the alert to say the nice things that occur to you and keep your mouth shut when a nasty crack seems opportune.

You can even compliment women on their hats. All right, all right, I know that is painfully close to outright dishonesty if you look at it from the stand point of scientific truth, but we are not now in a physics laboratory — we meet on a social occasion; the rules are more flexible.

When you compliment a woman on her new hat, you are not necessarily making an esthetic endorsement; you are taking notice of the fact that she has made an effort to make herself attractive, for her husband, for you, and for others. It matters not that the thing on her head looks like a battered bird cage. You are praising in her a commendable social effort.

So, when you see a woman in a hat you don't recall having seen before, remark on it. Say, "I like your new hat," or, if you can't carry that off with a straight face, say "I see you have another new hat!" in an enthusiastic tone of voice. The word "another" implies that she is the sort of stylish female who has a new hat every week; the tone of voice implies that it is always a pleasant event for her friends, nevertheless.

If she says, "Why, this old thing is two years old!" you need only answer,

"It looks like a new hat to me. It reminds me of one I saw in *Life* magazine last week." And it does, too. After all, there is a limit to the hideous shapes which can be devised using only three dimensions.

If she persists, "You saw me in this hat last week," then you can answer, "I don't remember seeing it. I must have been looking at your face," thereby winning trick, game, and rubber.

(If you are sure of your ground, very sure, you can say "legs" or "ankles," instead of "face." But *keep your hands off the women*. Don't mix your love life with your political work. Many politicians have — and it frequently lands them in retirement. Emulate the troubadour who sang the praises of his fair lady but never laid a finger on her.)

When a man deals with a man it is not necessary to compliment him on his clothes, but if you feel like it, go right ahead. They like it, too. But the easiest approach is to ask him about his business, then listen attentively. *You surely will learn something* — and you will impress him as a man of intelligence, well worth knowing.

I will not venture to tell women how to flatter men. The woman who does not know how to flatter a man and make him believe it is already embalmed.

There are many opportunities for legitimate praise in the course of a club's activities. Be liberal with such remarks as, "That was a fine suggestion. Will someone put it in the form of a motion?" or, "Good speech you made tonight, Charlie. You certainly told them," and, "Mrs. MacIntosh contributed the cake you see over by the coffee cups. Homemade."

Possibly the most important thing you can do to make yourself liked, aside from the elementary necessity of speaking to people and telling them you are glad to see them, is to get their names right. A name may be an arbitrary symbol, but it does not feel that way to its owner.

I've heard many people say that they could never be in politics because they can't remember names. But you *can* — look, compadres, you know about 50,000 English words, or more, all of them arbitrary symbols; you have memorized hundreds of mathematical relationships in order to get through eighth grade; you know street names and land marks without limit — is it impossible for you to associate a name with a human face?

It *is* possible and here is how it is done — here is how I do it and I have a memory like a pocket with a hole in it; I forget my own wedding anniversary.

When you are introduced, look the man in the eye and repeat his name and ask, "Is that the way you pronounce it, Mr. Lovell?"

He will either correct you, or agree. Then spell it and let him correct you. Respell it and pronounce it. (All this time you are looking at his face and listening to his voice.)

If possible, add, "I knew some people named Lovell in Grinell, Iowa. Cousins of yours, maybe?"

His remark will be something like, "Could be. There are Lovells all through the middle west. We're a big tribe."

You have pronounced his name four times and you have heard him pronounce it four times. You have spelled it. All through this the busy little workmen who throw the switches in your brain are, with no real effort to yourself, soldering tight connections on a new memory circuit. The next time you see that face you will hear that voice, in your mind, saying "Lovell," and another one of your silent servants will be spelling the name for you.

By this means I can learn to pronounce, spell, and *remember* in connection with a face even Turkish, Japanese, or Polish names — and I have no talent for languages.

In the next few minutes, try to find an opportunity to say something, anything to Mr. Lovell, and tack his name on the remark — such as "Have any trouble finding a place to park, Mr. Lovell?" This puts a coat of varnish on your new memory track.

He will have forgotten *your* name and it will embarrass him slightly. He will then get the man aside who introduced you and whisper, "Who is that guy you just introduced me to? The one with the red nose?"

The answer will be, "Him? Oh, that's Jack Doorbell. He's the king pin around here. Nice guy." It will all be perfectly true and Mr. Lovell will remember *your* name and face. You're in, pal!

All of this takes surprisingly little time and no effort, and it is a sure way to solid political influence. A man does not mind you mispronouncing or misspelling his name when you are meeting him, when it is evident that you are trying to get it correctly. Your minor effort is flattering; it shows that you want him to be an individual to you, not a blank face in a crowd. But thereafter you *must* have his name right, if you are not to offend him. The spelling is quite as important as the pronunciation, as you will want to write it on club invitations and political mail advertising. It annoys a man named MacGregor to have it spelled "McGregor" . . . the same goes for Stinkfish.

If you emulate these few illustrations in spirit if not in detail you will be well liked, even with B.O., halitosis, and tattle-tale grey. Your infirmities will be forgiven you. Let me repeat the rule: Feel friendly in your heart and watch for opportunities to let people know that you like them, admire them, or approve of them.

One cold and dismal morning a young man waited outside the gates of a great walled city. He was a country lad, come to seek his fortune, but at the last moment he was overcome by cold feet, homesickness, stage fright. He inquired of the gate keeper, "What sort of people live in the City?"

The gate keeper considered. "What sort of people were there in your own village?" he asked.

The boy's eyes shone. He answered in a choked voice, "They were the most wonderful, the kindest, the finest people in the whole world!"

"Go on in, son," the gate keeper told him. "You'll find the people inside much the same."

It is an old story and I have forgotten who told it first,

but it contains the whole key to success in politics. There is a possible sequel, though history is silent: With the gate keeper as his manager that boy could have been elected mayor of that city in three seasons.

Now back to our club. Invite everybody you know who is of your registration to the organization meeting. Hold it in a *small* hall if you can afford it, otherwise in a house, preferably not your own.

You will be lucky if eight people show up. Don't let that discourage you. A smaller meeting planned the American Revolution. You can probably get the central party organization to send some affable individual, full of enthusiasm and political anecdotes, to help you fill out the evening, not with a formal speech but with intimate talk, while you are all gathered in a circle.

Call the meeting to order yourself as chairman *pro tem*, and appoint some conscientious person, preferably female, as secretary *pro tem*. Elect a chairman. Have yourself elected executive secretary (or executive vice-chairman). If suitable, have the secretary *pro tem* elected permanent recording secretary. Have the club select a name and have a committee appointed to draft a constitution, with yourself as a member.

I speak as if all these matters were entirely a matter of your own volition; they are. You have programmed the matter ahead of time, deciding who should serve in what capacities and you have arranged for friends of yours to propose the various nominations and motions. There will probably be no opposition at this first meeting since you will have invited no one known to you to be a trouble maker. If you don't program ahead of time the club is likely to be stillborn. Your tactics should not be a steam-roller; it is very likely that there will be no opposition to your program.

If you are surprised by unexpected initiative on the

part of someone, don't let it worry you and don't try to freeze it out. It is likely that you have struck gold again by finding a person who will help make it a live, active organization. See to it that this person lands on some of the committees.

With respect to the selection of a chairman it is best to select some friendly, gregarious, extrovert who has served as a Rotary Club president, a lodge master, a veterans' organization commander, or as a Sunday School superintendent, but be sure it is someone you have seen preside in the past and whom you know to be capable of conducting a meeting, of keeping it alive, and who combines an adequate knowledge of parliamentary law with a sense of fairness. You will be able to discern these traits in a person only by seeing him, or her, in action. Don't try to form a club until you have one lined up.

You may decide to take the gavel yourself. In any case, in the course of your political life you will many times preside, at least at committee meetings. Presiding seems to frighten many people, but it is easier than driving a car. You can pick up a copy of Roberts' *Rules of Order* for two-bits at any second-hand book store. Read it, study it, but do not think that it is necessary to learn it by heart — it isn't.

Here is all you really need to know: Roberts' *Rules* are not law; every body of people is free to make its own rules of procedure. However the *Rules* are well nigh universal because they are practical. They are founded on the idea that each member shall have a fair chance to speak his piece and to have his ideas voted on by the other members. If you keep that in mind you won't go far wrong, even if parliamentary rules are a mystery to you.

There is one expedient which will get the man with the gavel out of a jam at any time: Somebody gets up and complains that you have made a mistake ("Point of order, Mr. Chairman!") and demands that you make some change, reopen nominations, refuse a late nomination, stop the debate, reopen the debate, change the order of business — it matters not. Let him have the floor; you must listen to him; a point of order takes precedence over everything else.

You have to listen to him but you don't have to do what he wants you to. *You* are the chairman! Review the situation quickly in your mind. If you can let him have his own way without gumming the works, do so. If not, come out with a ruling against him, quickly, and give him a chance to appeal. Do it like this, all in one breath, without punctuation:

"The Chair rules against you and the nominations are closed you have a right to appeal from the ruling of the Chair to the House do you wish to appeal?"

If he decides to take an appeal turn at once to the assembled group and say, "The ruling of the Chair has been appealed. The motion is not debatable and has priority. The chair has ruled that nominations are closed (or whatever the ruling was). All those in favor of sustaining the Chair make it known by saying 'Aye.' " (Short pause) "Opposed — 'No.' "

If you have tried to be fair you are almost certain to be sustained by an overwhelming shout, but be sure to take the negative vote, if any, as well. Then turn to the objector and say, "I am sorry, Mr. Smith, but the house has overruled you." Bang your gavel. "Next order of business!"

If he does not subside (he may even shout "Steamroller!"), you may use whatever means are necessary to bring him to order, even to the expedient of appointing several of the huskier male members as deputy sergeants-at-arms to assist the elected sergeant-at-arms in ejecting him from the hall. This is quite unlikely but I have had to do it, at least once. You will have the full support of the house, your own influence will gain, and the disorderly person will be discredited.

It is more likely, however, that a rap of your gavel and a reminder that he has been overruled by the house will shut him up. It is still more likely that he will hold no resentment, since you gave him his day in court.

If you are overruled, take it with a smile. Say, "You have been sustained, Mr. Smith. The floor is yours. Suppose you come up in front where we can hear you better." Let him swagger up and let him talk as long as he likes, while you relax. It's even money he'll dig his political grave with his tongue.

Either way you have increased your reputation for utter fair dealing, whether you know much parliamentary law or not.

There is another situation which comes up less often but is even more ticklish. Someone rises to a point of personal privilege. This means probably that he thinks his honor or integrity has been impugned; it is loaded with dynamite. It may result in a dog fight on the floor which will destroy your club.

You may have been warned that the matter was likely to come up, but, if you are caught flat-footed, allow the person to talk just long enough to establish what is eating him. If it will cause a fight among members of your own party, cut him off short. Announce, "By the customs of this body, all such matters must be investigated by the grievance committee and an attempt made to work out an amicable solution before they may be aired on the floor."

You may be setting a new precedent. The by-laws may not provide a grievance procedure. Go right ahead. Appoint a grievance committee, if one does not exist, at once, of the "old heads" and "steady horses," refer the matter to them and direct them to report back at the next meeting. Rule further discussion out of order.

As a matter of fact, *you* are out of order unless a grievance procedure is already on the books, and you

may be forced to ask the house to sustain your ruling.
Since your purpose is quite evidently conciliatory and
in the interests of the body as a whole you are likely to
be sustained. In any case — don't let Samson tear down
the temple just to salve his ego!

Very frequently someone will want to bring up a
matter out of the regular order of business. Rule firmly,
but kindly, that the matter must be brought up under
new business. If you know ahead of time it is a matter
which is no proper business of a political club, you may
be able to avoid it entirely by the simple expedient of
calling on the speaker of the evening before you transact business — this can be done as a courtesy to the
speaker to permit him to leave the meeting before
adjournment. By the time new business comes around
your audience is likely to be too tired to give much time
to letting one person ride a pet hobby. A motion to
adjourn will almost certainly intervene, once the
proper business of the meeting is out of the way — and
a motion to adjourn is always in order!

To be fair, remind the body as you submit the motion
to adjourn that Mr. Doakes wanted to bring up the
matter of pantaloons for Patagonians (or perhaps it
was memorializing the board of aldermen to change
the name of Swamp Street to Rosebud Avenue —
Doakes owns vacant lots on Swamp Street). But do not
let the matter be debated while a motion to adjourn is
before the house. A successful motion to adjourn at this
point, after such a reminder, is all the hearing he is
entitled to. Free speech includes the right not to listen,
if not interested.

I seem to have wandered into the subject of how to
dominate a club by legitimate means, which was meant to
be a separate subject. The two subjects are intermixed.
Domination of a club is a legitimate, necessary practice.
Democracy requires leaders quite as much as does
fascism, if anything is to be accomplished. But you can

dominate by methods which give everyone all of his democratic rights at all times. You will rule because you have the support and the approval of the club members. It is much easier to rule through popular support, gained in recognition of your fairness and common sense, than it is to be a little tin dictator. Remember always to warn the man you overrule of his right to appeal and you will remain a popular leader.

Someone will protest that you are refusing to recognize him. Point to him; say, "You're next, after this speaker," then turn to the person you have already recognized and say, "Go ahead, Mrs. Blodgett. You have the floor." But don't give in.

If the person complaining has already spoken once on the subject before the house, tell him that he will be recognized just as soon as everyone wishing to speak first has had a chance. This will happen frequently; the loud-mouths complain the worst.

Don't let anyone speak three times without permission of the house. Rule against them — unless your common sense says that here is a time to be lenient.

The cry of "question" from the floor for the purpose of stopping debate may be ignored; it is not in the rules. If somebody gains the floor and moves the previous question and the motion is seconded, you must vote at once, without debate, on *that* motion. The motion is to close debate on the previous question (the motion which has been under debate). State it as such, for many people do not understand this and may lose their right to speak if you do not make it clear. Say,

"The previous question has been moved and seconded. This is a motion to stop the discussion on the motion before the house, which is a motion to send a delegation to the intercity convention (or whatever the main question is, or the amendment to it which is under debate). If this motion carries, the debate will stop and we will then proceed immediately to vote on the main question, the question of sending a delegation." Then call for a vote.

This may seem unnecessarily wordy. I assure you it is not. If you do not explain this type of motion clearly and completely each time it comes up, you will gradually accumulate a group of people who don't like you and don't like the club simply because they do not understand what you are doing and feel that they have been tricked out of their equal rights. Use the whole elaborate explanation every time — it takes fifteen seconds only and it will keep your club from being dominated by the smart alecks.

And speaking of smart alecks — you will run into the Communist cell someday. How to cope with Communists will be treated in detail in the chapter "Some Footnotes on Democracy." In this connection let it suffice that you will have to depend on the body of the club to support you in your rulings. Don't argue with Communists. Cut them off short and rule them out of order (usually for not following the order of business). If you let them argue they will make a monkey out of you, for every Communist Party member has been carefully trained in parliamentary law and is skilled in parliamentary dodges — but he has only contempt for the democratic procedures; he uses them only to twist them to his purpose.

Get the body's support behind you, shut him up, and ignore his cries of "Free speech!" or "Fascist!" *Your* club hired the hall; let the Communist Party hire their own hall — and drag in their own audience.

I believe in the right to free speech for everyone, including Communists and fascists. I think that our constitutional guarantee in this case is wise and that the Founding Fathers knew what they were doing. But my own right to say what I think does not give me the right to barge into a Catholic church while the priest is saying mass, interrupt him, and make a speech for atheism. If I should happen to want to make such a speech (I don't) I should hire a hall of my own, or find a soap box. I have no right to interrupt others in the orderly pursuit of their business to spout my own views.

We have come a long way from our first organization meeting of a new political club to the rude manners of our pinko citizens, but all has been pertinent to the conduct of a club and was intended to show why it may be necessary to take the gavel yourself unless you can find an experienced and tactful presiding officer. You need no experience yourself if you follow these hints; later on you may be able to train someone to preside. It is not to your advantage to preside yourself if you can find another able person.

Two more hints and we will drop parliamentary procedure: Most motions come before the house improperly worded. If it is a matter you think should cool off, you can point out to the member that he has not formulated his proposal in such a fashion that it can be debated and voted on and then recommend to him that he consult the resolutions committee in order to whip it into shape. He may take your suggestion, or he may put it into motion anyhow. In the latter case this is a cue for your unofficial floor leader to move to refer to committee. If the matter is unclear, involved, or the facts are not all available (these are usually the reasons why you want the matter postponed), the body of the club will be happy to postpone the action.

On the other hand a member may make a suggestion from the floor which seems to you wise, but you can't handle it since it is not a motion. You may then put words in his mouth by rephrasing it as a motion, in the form that seems best to you, and ask him if that is what he meant. He will gratefully agree, or perhaps suggest some change. You can then open it to debate as a motion.

A chairman can usually get a meeting adjourned or

keep it from being adjourned, without violating any of the rights of any of the members, if he handles it carefully. A mere suggestion from the chair that the hour is late will produce the motion to adjourn, having priority and undebatable; a motion to adjourn almost always carries. On the other hand a spontaneous motion to adjourn usually comes from someone who is annoyed at the way things are going; this annoyance will usually lead him to shout his desires without waiting to be recognized — like this:

"Mr. Chairman, I move we adjourn!"

You can recognize him if it suits your purpose — after all, the house has to vote on it; it's not a "railroad." But if you think the business at hand must be finished, there is always someone standing behind him, out of his sight, who wants the floor. Tell him that he will be recognized in turn and recognize the other party.

Perhaps someday someone will invent an electronic device with all of Roberts' *Rules of Order* built into it which will be an automatic and infallible chairman — if so, politics will lose a lot of its zest. Until that day presiding will remain an art in which a sensible chairman may have a great deal to do with the outcome of any body's deliberations while retaining the respect of all — simply by remembering that the *final* arbiter is the assemblage itself. A word of caution — in the two cases in which I have recommended the maneuver of referring to committee, the intention must not be to bury or sidetrack. You have only thereby created an opportunity to have a word in private with the interested parties in order to clarify a confused issue or in order to smooth over a row. You can probably settle out of court — but if you can't, then you *must* permit a full and open hearing at the next meeting, come what may. That's democracy.

If you can't find a chairman for your club who can conduct meetings along the lines described above, then you must accept the gavel, but continue to search for such a person. You can do more from the floor where your latitude is greater. But let us suppose that you have managed to select a fair group of provisional officers at your first meeting. Your remaining business is to plan for your first public meeting.

You must group the novel but for monstro...
such a person, to retail it more from the...
your fortune to term... But by fo supp...
have mumbled to see... carry compen...
on know your snap in term. Your man and...
is of camera your first public met...

● CHAPTER V

The Practical Art of Politics (continued)

Club Meetings and Speech Making

Pick a date for the first public meeting of your baby club at least two or three weeks later than the organization meeting. This will give you time to insert notices in the local papers, send out postcard invitations, arrange for extensive telephone follow-up, and, if you can afford it, print and distribute handbills. You can do none of these things until you arrange for a hall; you'll need the time.

Make the hall small. Not only is it cheaper, but, more important, it is much, much better to have standing room only in a small hall than to rattle around in too large a hall. I know of nothing more dispiriting than to face a meeting in which more than half the seats are empty. Twenty people can have a rip-snorter of a meeting in a small room and build up to a fine campaign; a hundred people can be overcome by contagious melancholia in a hall which would seat five hundred.

Plan to get there early in order to fold up and hide most of the folding chairs, then don't get them out until you see that you need them. People always slip into the rearmost vacant seats at a political meeting (I don't know why — but I do it myself). This habit makes a half-filled hall still more gloomy. So if you must accept a hall with lots of floor space, go easy on the chairs and fill up some of the rear with refreshment tables, or card tables covered with literature, signs, or registration forms.

About chairs — the local undertaker usually owns several dozen folding chairs of the more comfortable and unnoisy variety and he can usually be persuaded to lend them, rent-free for good will, even if he is of a different political party, if you will pick them up after business hours and return them the same night or earlier than any scheduled funeral the next day. A couple of dozen make one automobile load.

The loan of chairs may solve your hall-rent problem for your first meeting as it will permit the use of space not ordinarily used as a hall, such as a retail store owned by one of the members (set up chairs between the counters).

In many states the use of school buildings is permitted for public meetings. I have used them fairly successfully but do not ordinarily recommend it. You are likely to have to choose between an auditorium much too large, or a classroom in which adults feel silly in the little seats and can't sit chummily together. Smoking is usually prohibited and you are likely to have to agree to get out by 10 p.m. Furthermore, regulations frequently prevent taking up collections and collections are necessary to a political club which is not to be a burden on a few. But many a fine meeting with worthwhile results has been held in a school building. It is your problem, with local factors.

A lodge hall is a best bet, with a small American Legion hall a close second. You will find if you poke around that there are many little halls concealed above store buildings and in back of restaurants which are available for surprisingly small fees — $3 to $10 per evening, heat and light thrown in, and even less on a permanent arrangement. Before you take a $10 hall remember that the hall rent should not run more than ten to fifteen cents per person per evening. How large will your crowd be and will they be good for more than two-bits a head in the collection?

Your problem depends on the average economic status of the constituency in which the club is formed — as will be almost all of your practical problems of mechanics, as opposed to techniques.

Publicity for the first public meeting. Don't depend on the persons at the organization meeting to supply the audience at the first public meeting. They will be full of enthusiasm and promises and some dunderhead will point out triumphantly that if each one of you brings ten friends to the next meeting the crowd will be one hundred (or two hundred, or a hundred and fifty). You will be justified in shooting him on the spot for this piece of asininity, but don't do it.

Agree heartily that that is just what we are looking for — and bear in mind that getting out a crowd is still up to you. Some of those present will in fact bring friends; Joe Pollyanna won't show up at all.

How to get a crowd — how indeed! This is a cause of grey hairs to all amateur politicians. The most important point you have already covered — don't let the hall seem empty. The next most important point is to see that you have an attraction. Get the central organization, through its secretary rather than through its speaker's bureau — the things that hide in speakers' bureaus should crawl back into the woodwork! — to provide a really good rip-snorter of a speaker, preferably with a name which is a public drawing card. Be firm about this. Point out that they want a club in that area, don't they? Threaten to throw up the sponge. Kick your heels and scream. But get a good speaker even if he has to fly down from the state capital.

Provide some entertainment. Tap dancers, even bad ones, go over well. There is probably a children's "talent" school in your town or neighborhood; the coach will display her proteges free of charge, but don't let her schedule more than fifteen minutes and make it all dancing. Be firm in refusing recitations, little plays, and singing. Never use singers — unless it's Paul Robeson, Bing Crosby, or Frank Sinatra.

A man or woman who plays popular piano well by ear and can lead singing in old-time favorites is worth his weight in marked ballots. There is one somewhere, of your party, within ten blocks of your house.

Okay, you've got your program. Now to haul them in off the sidewalk. If there is an editor-publisher-owner of a small town or local community paper of your party in your area, he should be at the organization meeting and you will see to it that he is appointed chairman of the publicity committee — not "publicity man"; you keep that open for the man who is going to do the work, when you find him; the editor won't. But he will give you a free half-column ad and he will write up a little story himself. He will probably donate some throw-away hand bills as well. Get volunteers to distribute them, or see what you can do with three boys and some small change.

More involved methods of publicity are covered in the ninth chapter; the same principles apply here. The daily papers will print (but just barely) your notices; announcements tacked to telephone posts are illegal some places but entirely practical in most cases; and bumper signs (see ninth chapter) are good. But direct mail coverage followed by telephone calls on the day of the meeting are your best bet. This will take a little money — not much but, if you can't afford it yourself, you must raise it at the organization meeting. (The hall rent can wait; it will be covered by the collection at the first public meeting.)

Passing the hat in a private home, if that is where your organization meeting is held, is probably in bad taste. I suggest that you approach two or three persons privately, selecting them for their ability to cough up, and nick each one for a share. A dollar buys a hundred postal cards, it need not be much.

Your editor victim may print the postal cards. Otherwise, borrow a mimeograph or pay for it.

The ladies present will address them for you and will make the telephone calls on the day of the meeting. This will give you a chance to locate your girl Friday, too — the woman who is as devoted to the cause as you are and is willing to do quantities of routine clerical work and telephoning, provided you tell her what to do. When you find her, you will wonder how the party struggled along without her.

You will have to supply the addresses. You have some; the others present have some; you can get quite a list, not very well weeded, from the central organization. Any lists available to any present, such as lists of customers, members of clubs, and church lists, are useful provided they are trimmed down to your party by checking for registration. Don't use a non-political list without this trimming for direct mail advertising. It is wasteful and unnecessarily annoys American citizens who happen to differ with you politically.

As a last resort you can always use local precinct lists, but it is rather expensive and not too productive to work at this stage from precinct lists which have not been trimmed to live prospects.

The first organization meeting is over as soon as you have picked the provisional officers, discussed plans for the first open meeting, and got all available commitments for help in preparing for the meeting. Adjourn at once, serve refreshments, and encourage the man from headquarters to reminisce and everyone to gossip.

Refreshments should be coffee and cake, or something else simple. Make a rule from scratch that refreshments must be simple and that the treasury pays the bill, else the ladies will start competing, upping the ante, and the whole thing will get out of hand. Refreshments are a social lubricant in politics, not a meal.

Don't start the coffee until you see how many are to be served. Put out half a dozen tea bags and a pot of hot water for those who can't drink coffee at night. Doughnuts are the simplest food, but they are perishable; if you are in doubt as to numbers, get some boxes of soda crackers, a couple of those small packages of cream cheese and a quarter-pound of yellow cheese. Cheese, crackers, coffee, and tea bags will keep. Plan to take a loss on doughnuts. (Naturally the cost — and the loss — on this first small meeting is not much, but the rule will save quite a bit of money later. The economical use of money is one of the prime secrets in volunteer, self-supporting political activity.)

You may wonder at my repeated emphasis on the economical use of money in politics. You yourself may not have to pinch — you may be a millionaire. But bear in mind that the average income is less than a thousand dollars per person a year, and is considerably less than that for the great majority of people. Elections are won by majorities, not dollars. Some expenditure of money is necessary to any political work. In a popular, volunteer political movement, the costs must be paid by the small donations of the volunteers themselves. The cost of living being what it is, it is hard for the average run of volunteers to make even small donations, so cultivate the habit of mind of getting the very maximum possible in political results out of every dime spent.

Therefore, even if you are rich — save those unused tea bags!

You can never beat a political machine through the lavish expenditure of money. You would be meeting them on their own grounds and they will beat you — they would match and double, or triple, every dollar you spend. Your weapon is the enthusiasm and sincerity of the free citizen.

It is a shining fact that most votes in America can't be bought. There is an unpurchasable majority of votes in any community. You and other volunteers can round them up to beat the socks off any machine, no matter how rich, while taking care of unavoidable expense by passing the hat — provided you are a little more careful with the collection money than you are with your own.

The night of the first public meeting of your baby club can be almost as distressing as a first night performance for an actor. You get there early; the hall is empty and seems cold. People straggle in, stand around and look at you; there aren't enough of them to permit you to start at the hour set. (This is a minor vice of most political meetings; it can be beaten and is worth beating. It requires just the determination to bang the gavel and start anyway — you and the janitor and the cat. It will surprise and please everyone.)

Let's bust up that empty-hall feeling first. Bring along your own radio or radio-record-player, plug it in, and get some loud music into the joint. If some of the young people start to dance, so much the better. This is a private, non-profit club; you don't need a license for dancing. (If somebody wants to make something of it, it's a fine chance to get some free newspaper publicity on a personal freedom issue.)

Later on you should be able to get some radio shop to supply a used radio-recorder-player for nothing more than a display, on the machine, of an advertisement. It is then worthwhile to buy a microphone to hook in through the speaker — and you are all set for the biggest hall in town. But the principal use of the gadget is to warm up the crowd — and to turn the conclusion of each meeting into an informal party and dance. This is especially useful in hanging on to the young people, who will be the bulk of your precinct workers.

The people are straggling in. Everyone who comes through the door must be greeted. You will do a lot of it but you will need help — provide for it ahead of time. You will want a careful record of every person present, name, address, and anything else at all that you find out about them, and that information must be recorded for each person on a 3" x 5" file card. Cards mimeographed or printed into a form are convenient but not necessary. The blank ones available at 10 cents a hundred in dime stores are all right.

Don't wait until the audience is seated and then expect to get this information by passing out cards, because many of them will leave the cards blank. If you button-hole them at the door and ask them to fill out cards right then you will do better, since you have provided card tables, chairs, and pencils for the purpose, but the best way is to fill them out yourself — or have one of your alter egos do it — while asking them the necessary questions and keeping up a running fire of conversation. Don't say "Name? Address? Any other adults in family? Telephone? Occupation?" Such an approach acts like a cold shower. Say, "Glad to know you, Mr. Brewster. Half a minute and let me get that down in writing. My wife says I can't be trusted to buy a pound of butter unless she writes it down. I wouldn't want you to miss getting an invitation to the Spring Dance through my poor memory. That's 'James A. Brewster,' isn't it? Mrs. Brewster come with you tonight? So? My wife's doing the same thing — we've got two kids, both in grammar school, and they have to be in bed by nine. How old are your youngsters? Maybe some day we can arrange a sort of game room or nursery for the kids and get a lot of folks out who are otherwise chained down. Do you think it would help if we moved up the meeting time half an hour? Is that address right? That's your home address, isn't it? Business address you say? Oh, of course — that's the same block the Safeway Market is in. It's not the same

address, is it? Oh — I think that's the same block of offices
Dr. Boyer is in. Hey — Fred! Doc! Want you to meet a
neighbor of yours — Dr. Boyer, Mr. James Brewster. You
know each other already — fine. Doc, see that Mr.
Brewster meets some of the folks, will you?"

Sounds corny? It is corny — but it works, and it's not
hard to do. You have recorded:

Brewster, James A.
    June 8, 1946 — mtg.
    1232 Oak St., r. tel Br 4395
    1010 Tenth Ave., b. tel Cl 8482
    Insurance business, Bedlow Bldg.
        married, 3 chil. 13 junior, 11 Alice, 2 (?)
    Masonic pin in lapel, and VFW. Heavy set, bald,
        well dressed, manner of a professional man.
    Assign to Doc Boyer? Follow up.
    Mr. S. Check registration.

Put the card in your pocket and make another, later,
for the club files, minus the personal comments. That
card, the file of your own it goes into, is your most valuable physical asset in politics. We will refer to it again and
again, but first one example now of how you will use it:

Let your wife answer the telephone at home. Get her
in the habit of getting the name and repeating it in a
loud tone of voice. (Reverse this process when the wife
is the active politician.) Pick out the card from the file,
kept near the phone, and read it as you answer the
phone. The delay can be held down to seconds. When
you speak to Mr. Brewster you won't make a fool of
yourself and lose a vote, or votes. Remember — he
expects to be remembered.

If you are forced to answer the telephone yourself,
you can always manage a few seconds delay by asking
the caller to hold on while you answer the door, or turn
off the radio, or something.

One of the card tables at the meeting will be occupied by a deputy registrar. In most states this is possible; in some states, unfortunately, the voter must go to a definite place, some states set a date as well, in order to register. This greatly complicates the problem of picking up potential votes by getting unregistered persons to register, and may have to be met by a volunteer automobile service as complex as that for election day. But we will consider the more usual case.

From the roll of deputy registrars of voters you will have selected a member of your own party, conveniently near, and seen to it that he (or she) is at the meeting early. Provide transportation if needed. These persons are usually paid by the head; your best bet is an elderly female who needs the money. If you are on your toes she will pick up a dollar or two each meeting and you will pick up the votes.

Later on you may be able to get your club treasurer deputized, who will then contribute the fees to the club treasury. It is an honest way to help meet expenses while gaining votes.

You will have an announcement to make during the meeting. If you are shy, write it out and read it. It will go like this:

"This is the first public meeting of the Oak Center State Republodem Club — but it won't be the last. The party has needed a way to get together in this community for a long time. The boys on the other side of the fence have kinda gotten in the habit of taking things for granted around here, but we are going to show them a little action this year and this club will be right in the middle of it. We are going to get all the party candidates down here to talk to you for one thing and let you take 'em apart and see what makes them tick and ask them embarrassing questions. We'll get better candidates that way. Maybe we'll pick out one of our own people and send him to the capital so that we will get a little representation for a change. It can be done. If I had time I could show you some interesting figures about the registration and how this area that we're in can make the difference in any election for the whole district. We'll take that up another night, maybe.

"Besides looking over the candidates and getting ready for the struggle this fall, we're going to make this a public forum where we can discuss our problems and get some of the experts in to give us facts, so that we can make up our minds intelligently and not be dependent on that yellow journal—you know the one I mean—for distortions.

"But we're going to have some fun, too. There is no reason why serious public affairs have to be conducted in a funeral atmosphere. That reminds me — stick around for some coffee and cake after the meeting adjourns . . . we have Mrs. Parker to thank for that. Stand up, Mrs. Parker. Take a bow.

"We've thrown together a provisional organization, just to get things started. We've got some working committees and we want to add to them tonight, but, unless there is objection, the provisional officers will putter along and make their own mistakes for about six weeks or two months while you folks get acquainted and decide who you want for permanent officers.

"One more thing, and I'll shut up and let the chairman get on with the program. There has been a lot of discussion as to how often we should meet. Just to start the ball rolling I want to offer a formal motion that we meet two weeks from tonight, same time and place — because I happen to know that we can get the lieutenant governor to come to speak to us that night. Will somebody second my motion—or propose another night?"

Corny again, eh? It will do, it will do. Eloquence is nice, but not necessary. You can revise that speech to meet your actual needs and it will serve every purpose you need to push at the first meeting. If you are not in the habit of public speaking type it out and hold it. You are likely to find that you will not have to refer to the text, but it will give you confidence.

Your first meeting is over, a success. You have only to do the same next time, with different speakers. There will always be business to transact and issues to discuss — politics is like that; you are not working in a vacuum. But since we have reached the subject of making speeches, let's kick it around a bit. It's not as hard as it seems. Here is a sure-fire formula which can be used over and over again:

This dodge is designed to permit you to speak before a small audience of unsympathetic people — the worst possible set up. A small group is much harder to face than a large; anybody can talk to a thousand people. You won't be asked to be principle speaker at a large meeting until you have acquired a reputation and public speaking has become second nature to you. Until that time, if you are called on to say something as a secondary speaker to a large audience you can say as little as a dozen words, speaking in praise of "good roads and good weather," complimenting the principal speaker, or the chairman, or the arrangements committee, or simply announcing your intention of voting the straight ticket. You can then say "I thank you" and sit down. The audience will appreciate your terseness and your stock will go up.

(I attended the dedication of Soldier's Field in Chicago in November 1926. The Vice-President of the United States spoke for three minutes, the Governor of Illinois spoke for seven minutes, the Mayor of Chicago spoke for ten minutes, and the city park official in charge of the field spoke for more than an hour. The audience was exposed to a driving snow and below-freezing temperature. Which speech was the most popular?)

As you become known as a politician you will be called to speak as principle speaker before small groups. The toughest assignment will be to make a non-partisan speech, not in support of a candidate nor an issue, before a non-partisan, non-political group, such as a Kiwanis Club or a ladies' church group. At first glance this seems an impossible task. How can you make a political talk and not talk about politics? There is a limit to the time you can spend declaring for good government and praising honesty in public office. Besides — it ain't news!

Watch me closely and you can learn the trick. I don't have any cards up my sleeve but I do have two dozen sharpened pencils concealed on my person.

Stand up. Bow to the chairwoman. "Madam Chairman — ladies — the worst thing about invitations like this is what it does to my waist line." Glance down. "It's an imposition to ask a man to speak after such a good lunch. What I need is a siesta.

"Audience-participation programs seem to be all the rage these days; there is no reason why we shouldn't have them in politics. I got this idea last night while listening to the Guess Again program — we're going to have a little try at being Quiz Kids." Haul out the pencils.

"Just in case any of you don't happen to have a pencil with you, I've brought a few spares. Will you ladies nearest me pass them along to those who might need them? Now take a piece of paper, each of you — wait a minute. We seem to be short of paper. I wonder if your secretary can help us out?" She can and does, and some of them turn up old grocery lists in those steamer trunks women carry. Don't provide paper yourself. Paper can always be found but there are never as many pencils in a crowd as there are people. The little flurry caused by the search for paper gives you a breathing spell and a chance to size up your audience. During this period individuals will catch your eye and smile. You grin back and they get the impression that you are good to your mother and kind to small children. Remember John Henry's hog.

"Everybody fixed up? Let's start the quiz. Write your

name at the top of your paper. Go on — don't be afraid. I promise, cross my heart, that I'll keep the result confidential. Nobody, nobody . . . will see the papers but me. But I want to be able to announce the winners and I can't do that if you insist on being anonymous. I ought to warn you that there won't be any prizes other than the pleasure of winning. Somehow I've never gotten acquainted with the sort of politics that pays off in cash. Okay? First question:

"Write down the name of the President of the United States.

(Pause)

"Write the name of the governor of our state.

"Write the names of our two United States senators."

Go on down the list. Ask for the names of the local congressman, the local state senator, the local legislator, the county commissioner, supervisor, agent, or "presiding judge" — the titles vary but you want the chief elective county executive or legislative officials. Than ask for the name of the mayor of your town or city and the name of their local city councilman, alderman, or selectman. Ask only for elected officials who represent directly the people you are questioning. You can't hold them responsible for appointed officials. Limit it to people they have voted for or against and are therefore presumed to know.

You might finish it up with these two questions: "Are you registered to vote?" and "Did you vote at the last primary election?" (Voting at a general election is no more indicative of civic virtue than is standing up when the band plays "The Star Spangled Banner.")

Then gather up the papers and look them over.

The results will amaze you and, if you are not braced for it, dishearten you. If you find one paper in which the respondent has answered more than half of the questions correctly you are justified in naming her as a praiseworthy, intelligent citizen, especially if she voted in the last primary.

But it is unlikely that you will find anyone to praise. Most of them will stop after naming the President and the governor. There will be scattered answers thereafter, very scattered and about half of them wrong. Mostly you will see blank paper.

I remember one respected matron who thought that Prime Minister Chamberlain (1938) was a United States senator and I have even found people who could not name the President of the United States — although I classed such latter cases as sheer feeble-mindedness and threw them out of my calculations.

You will now extemporize for about ten minutes on the subject of civic virtue, holding them up to themselves as horrible examples. You will point out that they voted for or against, or failed to vote, for each of the persons you asked about. You will ask them how in the name of all that's holy they can expect anything but a gang of crooks in office, and thank the stars and the mercy of heaven that a number of these public officials are honest statesmen despite the fact that the ladies of the East Squamous Community Church obviously don't give a hoot what happens to the country their ancestors and sons died to protect.

You can point to the ghosts of the martyrs of women suffrage and ask if this is the equality between the sexes they fought so hard for. You can point out that more of their family income goes into taxes than goes into groceries and ask them if it would not therefore be wise to give almost as much thought to the selection of a congressman as they do to the selection of a good head of lettuce.

The results of the questionnaire will make you so tarnation mad, when you think about the weary effort you have put into trying to drag this community up out of the mud, that you will make what may be the first really good public speech of your career. You will be feeling emotional and you will know your facts; the combination automatically produces a good speech.

Don't lambaste them too hard — resist the temptation. There are brands to be snatched from the burning even here. Try to make it more in sorrow than in anger; rouse their shame rather than stir up anger against you personally.

Some forthright old gal may state that she never wanted the vote. Don't scold her; praise her as an honest women and point out, gently, that she is free to throw away her franchise, just as the voters in Germany did. She has only to refuse to register and she automatically returns to the status of a child, a slave, or a domestic animal. Point out that it is a fair comparison since women were classed as all three only a hundred years ago.

Most women don't like those classifications, no matter how lazy they may be as citizens. They like to think of themselves as free citizens and your audience honestly believed — until you held a mirror to their startled faces — that women were a force for good in politics, somewhat superior to men. When they think of a corruptionist, they visualize him as a man, not a woman.

Some serious-minded lady, honestly ashamed, may ask you what they can do to be better citizens, better informed. If no one asks, you can invite the question, or even state it as a rhetorical question. You are here to get votes, whatever the program chairman had in mind; this is your chance.

Don't invite her to join your club; you are obligated to be non-partisan before this group. Instead tell them all about the telephone book clue (see Chapter II, How to Start). But get her name, check her registration later, and follow up. It's a fifty-fifty chance you have a new worker.

Stick the papers in your pocket and take them home. At least you have a record of the persons in that group who claim to have voted in the primaries. Check to see which ones belong to your party and add those names to your card file. They are worth carrying on your mailing list and some may eventually join your club and become active precinct workers. These women aren't worthless; they are simply in a rut.

(Gather up your pencils. They cost money.)

The results of making this talk before any all-male organization will be quite a bit better and you will be able to praise several of them as being "good citizens" entitled to the vote. At any political gathering you will find many perfect scores.

This talk can be used over and over again, year after year, before any sort of a meeting; you need nothing else on your repertoire until you find other things you want to talk about — by then speaking will be easy for you. You can even use this questionnaire gag more than once to the same crowd under the pretext of finding out what progress has been made. It never fails to hold attention and it can always be used to stir out new votes.

I feel deep sympathy for persons who are terrified at being asked to speak in public. I did not attempt it until I had been in politics quite a while. My first venture was an impromptu comment offered at a luncheon meeting. I said about two dozen words then sat down, white and shaking, so nervous that I went away without my spectacles.

On my second attempt I was very full of my subject and managed to struggle through a twenty-minute talk, but my wife told me afterwards that I paced back and forth all the time I spoke like a caged tiger while shouting my words over my shoulder.

My own difficulties were greater than yours are likely to be; in addition to a very real shyness which I have to fight against, I have a speech handicap, partly controlled, which can leave me utterly speech-bound if I get rattled. I invented the questionnaire routine in order to give me time, while facing an audience, to regain control of my vocal chords without enduring one of those ghastly pauses. If it will work for me it will work for anybody.

Experience overcame my difficulties. There came a time, shortly before the war, when I was invited to be keynote speaker at a convention held in another state. (This is sheer boasting, under the guise of giving you courage.) The speech was electrically recorded; it is terrifying to think of that disc going around and around, recording inexorably your pauses, your errors in grammar, your word blunders. I prepared a written manuscript to fortify me.

I found I did not need it. I spoke for one hour and forty-five minutes, extemporaneously, and kept the crowd with me. The recording was transcribed, printed, and bound, and the speech was sold (not by me) as a pamphlet which ran through two editions. I still get occasional fan mail about it.

I like to tell that story because it represents to me a major personal triumph. I should show, as well, that the hazards of speechifying are only mental hazards. Once you get over your fear, talking to a crowd is no more difficult than conversation around the dinner table.

What to say when punching a doorbell is more difficult — which is why I gave such specific examples at the first of this discussion.

Don't try to be humorous in making a political talk unless it comes naturally to you. A collection of funny stories, told to illustrate a point, is a useful asset but not necessary. Nor is eloquence necessary; sincerity is enough and it can do without eloquence. I once heard William Jennings Bryan speak back in the days of the spellbinders. As I recall it, it was not his rolling periods that moved the crowd; it was the evident fact that he believed what he said. His honesty was so compelling that I could not help being affected by his words, even when I strongly disagreed with him.

One of the most effective speakers today is

Congressman Jerry Voorhis — even his opponents are anxious to listen to him. Yet Mr. Voorhis has no eloquence in him and has a shy, diffident manner. But he speaks with such dead seriousness that each listener is convinced that the man is saying the exact truth as he sees it.

Can anyone forget the emotional power of the simple, uneloquent words of Edward VIII's abdication speech?

• CHAPTER VI

The Practical Art of Politics (continued)

Political Influence, Its Sources, Uses, and Abuses

How to Have Votes in Your Pocket. Many times we hear
that So-and-So has such-and-such district "in his pocket." Usually it isn't true, except by default — when the
local leader has no real opposition of any sort and has
the only vote-getting organization in his district.

It is even less likely to be true when So-and-So shows up
at headquarters, claims to have the West Heights district
"eating out of his hand," and wants to know what sort of
arrangements you want to make, i.e., how much cash you
will pay him personally for his support, such as it is.

You can disregard such fellows. Such a man usually
controls his own vote, that of his wife (if she remembered to register), and, possibly, the votes of members
of his own family living at home. I have yet to meet a
man who claimed to control a district who actually did.
Tell him you're sorry, congratulate him on his party
loyalty, assume that he is so public-spirited that he is
certain to support the cause anyhow, ask his opinions
and his advice. Tell him you wish to high heaven that
times were good and the cupboard wasn't bare. But
never, never, never give him any money!

It isn't even worthwhile to give him a little money as
a sop, to keep him from working against you. True, he
will work against you, but you can get more votes for
the money you have in more direct ways. Besides, it

isn't fair to the hard-working volunteers, many of whom need money worse than he does.

There may be someone in his district who does in fact control it but you will have to scout around and dig him (more usually her) out, as he, or she, will be busy mending fences instead of trying to cadge money at headquarters. This person, when found, can be entrusted with campaign funds — they will not be wasted.

But there is a way whereby every "volunteer fireman" in politics can have, and does have, votes in his pocket, sure votes. As your acquaintances become aware that you are active in politics they will start to lean on you for political advice, as fast as they realize that you treat it as a "hobby" (from their point of view) and not as a money-making trade.

This influence even cuts across party lines, especially with respect to the so-called "minor" offices. Many of your acquaintances of the other party, because they know you, respect you, and consider you well informed, will let you vote the whole ballot for them, propositions and candidates, except for the head of the ticket. (Votes for the head of the ticket can't be influenced anyhow, enough times to matter, except by the process of seeing to it that the lazy voter registers and then hauling him to the polls.)

This slug of votes that you control will creep up on you, without your knowing it, and grow from year to year. There will even come a time when your public endorsement, for political advertising, is sought after. You will then realize, and even then it will surprise you, that you are a powerful politician.

The first election your influence will come from private conversation, on social occasions. Your advice will be taken because you quite evidently know something about the whole, confusing ballot.

You may not be aware, the first time, of the votes you

have changed. But next year your telephone will ring steadily during the week before the election. "Say, Bill, tell me about these judge candidates. You know some of them, don't you?" You oblige. He adds, "How are you voting on the propositions?" You tell him.

You may have to explain in some detail your reasons for each vote during this second campaign. Such-and-such a judge is stupid, or plays games with the traffic patrol, or takes dirty campaign funds. Proposition #9 has a trick clause which makes it mean something different from what the title says, or #12 is a clever way to divert money from the school system. Thereafter you will make fewer explanations; all they want is the verdict — they have come to trust you.

These people are serious in their intent, mean to be independent voters, and have no intention of voting for a political machine. They welcome a chance to get any honest source of information other than the newspapers. Their votes cannot be purchased, they are not in politics themselves, and their name is legion, in any community.

You may find that fifty or sixty people make it a regular habit to call you up in the last day or two before an election and ask you how to mark their sample ballots. It is a "must" to place a typed list of your choices by the telephones a couple of weeks before the election so that even your twelve-year-old son can pass out the gospel in your absence. These people simply want your choice; they pay no attention to politics, but they do vote. You are a "find" to them — and their votes are in your pocket!

Not only their votes, but the votes of many of their families and of their friends. They become secondary centers of influence for you — dope from the horse's mouth is scarce; they are rather proud of knowing you and they pass the word along. You are safe in figuring about five votes for each person who looks you up or telephones you.

Fifty times five is two hundred and fifty — you have 250 votes "in your pocket," quite aside from all your regular campaigning activities.

Many an election is won by a smaller margin than that!

How to Mark a Ballot in a Hurry: There will come a year when sickness, or an extended trip out of town, or something, causes you to be caught with your lines of communication down. This time you don't know the answers; most of the ballot is a mystery to you. But the people who have come to depend on you will still expect your advice in marking their sample ballots.

Here is an easy, fool-proof way to get a satisfactory list in a hurry. Use it — but tell your clients that you are somewhat out of touch and may make some mistakes. The mistakes will never be important but you don't want to shake their confidence in your truthfulness and good sense. To some of them you can explain the process; to others, just give them the selections.

Here is the process: Get a copy of the newspaper you despise the most. (You have it — of course you have it. Don't you want to know what the opposition is doing?) Note their selections and vote against all of them. Make that your list.

In some cases some candidates and some propositions will be so overwhelmingly popular that you will find out afterwards that you voted the wrong way — both parties, or factions, were in agreement. But it does not matter in the least, because those candidates and those propositions, you will find, will have won by overwhelming majorities. Your mistaken vote meant nothing.

You will be able to eliminate some such cases by casual inspection and correct them as you make out the list, thereby saving yourself some embarrassment — but that will be the only significance.

You may well ask why not use the newspaper you favor most and vote for its selections, rather than against the selections of that despised opposition rag. Well, I admit I am prejudiced on this point — but I have yet to see a newspaper which seemed to me entirely altruistic and public-spirited in its policies at all times. Even with the best of them, it seems to me that the Brass Check occasionally shows through. I think I have detected some terrific swindles on the trusting public in many a list of recommendations which was, on the whole, good.

I think it is more nearly fool-proof, when you are in a hurry, to make a reversed use of recommendations which, in your opinion, come from unmitigated scoundrels.

How to Dispense Patronage: This is one of the touchiest problems in politics but one that you can't duck. No matter how anxious you may be to avoid all contact with a "spoils" system the matter is bound to come up and you will have to pass on it, as long as there are any public jobs which are filled by appointment rather than by honest competitive examination. There are still lots of such appointive jobs and there is no end in sight. Even, come the millennium, when all possible spoils are abolished, there will be appointive jobs on the policy-making level and the favor of politicians will be sought in the filling thereof.

On the policy-making level the touchstone of political belief and loyalty is both moral and a practical necessity. There has been a lot of starry-eyed guff talked about this; in my opinion the people who talk it are spiritual descendants of the mice who voted to bell the cat. Of course the policy-making administrators of the executive branch of the government should be active and loyal party members of the party in power since they will be called on to bring to life the party platform of the party in power. Any other arrangement is a swindle on the people. Would you hire a surgeon to give a Christian Science lecture? Or a Rabbi to say mass?

Under special circumstances a chief executive, state or national, may draft an elder statesman of the other party to do a difficult top-policy job for which such man is peculiarly fitted. Such statesmen, of both parties, can and usually do carry out their special assignments with high patriotism and without obstructing the program of the party elected to power. When such a case comes up, don't go overboard in being a partisan. Some pipsqueak in your county committee will pop up with a resolution condemning such a coalition action. Don't handicap your governor or president by supporting such a narrow view.

But the much more usual case is the one in which partisanship is appropriate. Your party has just won an election; there are numerous policy-level appointive jobs to fill. As an active party politician your support and endorsement will be sought; in such cases you are not only justified, you are obligated, to consider the politics of the candidates as well as their several abilities. Your governor (or mayor, or president) is entitled to assistants who are loyal and of the same political beliefs. A man can best demonstrate his devotion to the party principles by getting out and hustling for the party ticket. Such party support may not in itself prove anything, but the lack of it is does prove something — it proves either that the appointment seeker does not really believe in the party program he now asks to help carry out as a public official or it proves that he is too indolent and too selfish to make a good public servant. Thumbs down!

I want to elaborate this point because there is so much nonsense talked about it. It seems to be part of the Great American Credo that it is statesmanlike to forget all about party lines as soon as the election is over and pick the "best men" for the big jobs whether they helped in the campaign or not. It's pretty but it's not true to life. The "best men" — for this purpose — are not to be found among the spectators, nor on the other team; they are to be found among the men who were in there scrapping for what they believed in!

Although policy-making appointees should be party regular and active campaigners, there is no reason why typists, surveyors, truck drivers, or food inspectors should be selected for their political beliefs and many reasons why they should not be. Despite the prevalence of civil service, good and bad, many such jobs are purely appointive and you will be called on to help people get such jobs.

Patronage is not an easy matter and I know of no perfect solution. I suggest the following pragmatic rules for making the best of a bad situation:

(a) Accept the responsibility. When it comes to pass that you have the power, through influence or direct authority, to decide or help to decide who shall hold the myriad little jobs below policy-making level, meet it head on, make the decisions — and the mistakes — and take the consequences. To pass the buck is moral cowardice, similar to that of the person who can't bear the thought of killing but eats meat and wears fur, and it will result in someone else passing out the jobs in a fashion which may not please you and which may be contrary to public interest.

(b) Don't adopt a "spoils" attitude. Discuss qualifications for the job, not whether or not the candidate is politically "deserving." Make it quite plain that you think such jobs should be filled by civil service methods and that you are acting in trust for the public, not for your party. (This advice is contrary to that of many successful politicians, I must admit. Nevertheless I think my attitude is more practical in the long run. You will have to find out for yourself. But I submit that my advice is not only moral, it is practical — and that any other course leads to a long succession of headaches and loss of votes.)

(c) Be completely honest with the applicant. If you don't intend to help him get the job, tell him so, bluntly — and take the consequences. There is no difference of opinion here on the part of any of the successful politicians, but the advice is hard to carry out. It is so much easier to promise to do "anything you can to help him," then fail to follow through. I must admit that I balked at this hurdle when I was new to the business. I did not have the courage to disappoint a man to his face. It takes guts and I did not have the requisite supply. I have learned better — I won't make that mistake again. But it still upsets me to have to say "no."

(d) Be warm-hearted. Don't adopt a holier-than-thou attitude. Help the poor devil if honesty permits it. Err on the side of charity. After all, he has to eat — at least he thinks so. Job hunting isn't easy at best, and he, or she, wouldn't be there if the wages weren't a matter of consequence. Even if you have to say no, you can be friendly and give him the dignity that every human being wants quite as much as he wants a full belly. Sit him down, offer him a cigarette, a cup of coffee. Listen to his troubles. Perhaps, if you can't give him the job he wants, you will recall one in the course of the conversation which he is qualified to hold.

There is nothing unstatesmanlike in helping another fellow human being to find a job. It is as righteous as healing lepers or causing the lame to walk. Most of your applicants will be second-raters, but don't let that worry you; most of the world's work is done by second-raters. You won't be cheating the taxpayers in recommending a person who is merely adequately qualified instead of being an ideal candidate for the job. First-raters hardly ever seek these minor public jobs, as they can make more money in private industry.

Don't try to monkey with any job covered by federal civil service! Tell the applicant that the job he wants is beyond politics and that he should go straight to the civil service commission where he will be given, not one but many, fair competitive chances to get a job if one is available. The federal civil service commission comes as near to being above reproach as any public agency you will find.

There is one apparent exception to the above rule: Many agencies under federal civil service make seasonal, temporary appointments, without examination, to cover their peak load period. For example the railway mail service and the postal service need a lot of help around Christmas time and the Internal Revenue Service has other rush seasons. It is frequently impossible to get sufficient help from the certified civil service lists. This means jobs for clerks, typists, laborers, chauffeurs, etc. Most of the jobs require only minor skills and no experience.

Don't try to use political pressure to get these jobs for people — it's wrong and you don't need to. What you can do is make it your business to know when such jobs are available. You can pass along the tip to the unhappy creature you have had to turn down and let him go get the job on his own. Most people simply don't know the ropes; they are not too familiar with the world around them. You can often lend a helping hand just by knowing more than the applicant. He may even be grateful to you; at least you have not refused him help.

Such devices are necessary if you are to compete successfully with the Machine. Never forget that the strength of the Machine lies in giving help when it is asked. You can do likewise — and not attach strings to it. Bread cast on the water comes back of itself; you don't need to harry unfortunate people by insisting that they demonstrate loyalty to your political organization.

(Incidentally, the successful machine politicians know that fact. They will help anyone, not merely the "faithful." They count on a backlog of good will rather than on cracking the whip. The whip-cracking comes later, if at all.)

Appointments to Annapolis and West Point should be purely competitive but are not. The civil service commission will serve as an impartial referee in selecting candidates for appointment as the agent of any congressman or senator who asks for the service. You will be performing a patriotic service by urging your congressmen and senators to avail themselves of this service.

You will be approached frequently by parents of young hopefuls who want to go to one of the service academies. You can encourage such laudable ambition without mixing politics into it — but which will nevertheless redound to your political advantage! In the first place these persons usually do not know how to go about any phase of the matter; the kid has simply been struck by the bug. Full information may be obtained by anyone by addressing requests to the Adjutant General of the Army, concerning West Point, Deputy Chief of Naval Operations (Personnel) for Annapolis, or the Commandant of the Coast Guard, Treasury Department, for the Coast Guard Academy. They can get this information just as quickly from any public library or recruiting station, but they don't know that, and they will love you for your helpfulness. From the same sources you may, if you wish, obtain free pamphlets which set forth the requirements for each academy, along with typical entrance examinations. You can also obtain lists of prospective appointments and the names of the officeholders who control them.

If you have these items in your possession you will seem almost omniscient to the lad and his parents. You can also pass out some good, non-political advice. All three schools are basically engineering schools. Therefore an applicant needs solid grounding in mathematics and physical science, plus one modern language. Make sure the kid knows this. All three schools have stringent physical requirements, and the applicant should find out at once whether or not he can meet them, or whether corrective measures will enable him to meet them. It is a sad thing to see a boy spend a couple of years trying for an appointment, then eat his heart out because some disqualifying disease in his past record prevents his accepting it when it comes along.

Don't use your political influence in connection with appointments to the service academies. It may not be dishonest, but it is certainly not in the public interest. Limit yourself to helpful advice and supplying information.

I have dwelt at length on these service appointments because, first, you will be faced with the problem with certainty every year, and second, because I am advising you not to give the political help asked for. Since you are to refuse to basic request (for political influence) you should know specifically what you can do to be helpful to all comers. The matter is touchier than most requests for political favor because of the emotions stirred up by the parent-child relationship. It is easier and safer to turn down the father in a request for a job for himself than it is to refuse him help for his boy.

How to Tell a Trojan Horse from a Political Party: In any city or town in which a well-entrenched machine has been in power without interruption for many years, the party of the political label opposite to the label worn by the Machine will also have a public organization, somewhat smaller, which regularly puts a ticket on the ballot, opposing the Machine, and with equal regularity gets beaten.

One will be the "Democratic" organization; the other will be the "Republican" organization. One of them will be the party in power and will be known as the "Machine." But it is almost a foregone conclusion that they are both the Machine.

It's a partnership. They get along fine together — except in public. Each year they put on a whoop-t'-do campaign, a grunt and groan match for the cash customers. They exchange insults, demand investigations, and hold rallies — but the fight is fixed, the results certain, and the take split two ways by arrangement.

In addition to these official organizations there will be unofficial organizations of each party, reform in nature, and probably unrecognized by their respective national committee. That makes four parties — or, more truthfully, three. The latter two are honestly opposed to each other and to the Machine. More confusing than amusing, isn't it? Well, take a glance at the multiple parties of some other countries; it will make you feel better.

The question is: What should the honest citizen do when faced with this situation?

It is a very real problem, for the "reform" wings of each party usually suffer from pernicious anemia. As for the official organizations, they are not the Republican and Democratic halves of the American Eagle; they are the twin wings of a turkey buzzard. For these reasons, the honest citizen in a machine-ridden community usually stays out of politics, and limits his participation to voting for the national ticket of his choice in the general elections.

But we'll never get out of the mud that way!

If you live in a machine-dominated city and if you entered politics by the direct routes suggested in Chapter II, you probably landed first off in the Machine, either main tent or sideshow. It hasn't hurt you, but you have cut your teeth and now is the time to strike out on your own. The six months or so that you spent with the Machine has taught you more than anything else could in the same length of time.

Move in on one of the two reform organizations, take it over, and, through it, capture the party of its affiliation in the primaries. Operation time: Six months to three years.

Use the party organization you have captured to turn the Machine out of power at the following city final election. Then do your darnedest to get a satisfactory governor, state attorney general and county prosecuting attorney at the next general election in order to tie down your victory.

Does it sound too hard? Remember what was said of the people who crossed the plains: "The cowards never started and the weaklings died on the way." Don't despair; you will not be alone. There will be others marching beside you. It is not too likely that you yourself will be called on to be the generalissimo of this war; you may find yourself a non-com or a junior officer.

But it can be done. I know it can be done because I have been present when it happened. Many American cities have carried off such reforms successfully; it is not too hard to do. The hard part is to make the reform stick. The ordinary reform organization falls to pieces after the first successful campaign and the ordinary reform candidate turns out to be a sorrier specimen in office than the Machine politician he displaced. The anatomy and pathology of reformers and reform organizations will be discussed in the chapter Footnotes on Democracy. Choosing a candidate will come up in the next chapter.

Many machine politicians are so sure that a reform group will hang itself that a lost election does not worry them. They take an off-year philosophically as a chance to clean out the dead wood and strengthen the organization. Much of the organization is secure through a phony civil service; the rest can live on its fat.

You, presumably, have learned already that politics is a process that continues. You will not fall into the error of thinking that you need to plan for only one election. Let us consider then how you will choose your field of operations and what you will do.

Pick your medium on principle, not expediency, or

you will never be happy. If you are a Republican in your national politics, if Republican party principles are what you believe in, then go into the Republican reform organization, even though the Democratic reform organization may seem to have the better chance of achieving your immediate purpose, defeat of a corrupt machine. Vice versa if you are a Democrat at heart.

In some cities the local offices are "non-partisan" by law. This changes the labels but not the facts; a "non-partisan" city machine will always turn out to be owned by the leading politicians of one party, assisted by tame dogs who nominally carry the other party label. A "non-partisan" set up makes it a little easier to form a coalition to defeat a machine once — and makes it much harder to preserve a reform once instituted, because a lack of organizational responsibility and lack of basic community or interests and belief among the coalitionists.

"Non-partisan" in local affairs was a bill of goods sold to the people of this country early in this century by a bunch of starry-eyed political theorists who were not semantically oriented and thereby confused symbols with facts. They saw the corrupt city machines — party machines — and figured out that they could do away with all that by outlawing political parties in local affairs. It was a cinch for the machine boys; the labels were abolished, but not the Machine! (I wonder why that didn't occur to the theorists?) It enabled the same old corruptionists to get away with murder without leaving finger prints around the corpse.

If you still have party labels in your local affairs for goodness sake, hang on to them! Otherwise, when they steal the city hall, you'll never be able to pin it on anybody.

Let us assume a concrete case so that we can be specific. You will have to shift it around for other circumstances but the principles will not vary. We will assume partisan local offices and we will assume that your party is not in power. The only difference the latter assumption makes is that in such case it takes a primary election and a final election to gain power; in the other case, when the Machine proper wears your party label, the primary election is the only real struggle and the final election may be a pushover.

First, you and your friends take over the reform organization of your party. This is about as hard to do as beating up on a butterfly; you just join up and start running things by the techniques described elsewhere in this book. You get new members for the existing clubs and form new clubs where needed. For all practical purposes you behave as if the anemic older organization never existed; you form a new political organization and start getting ready for your first primary fight.

That is your practical, factual behavior; your symbolic behavior is something quite different. The old, moribund reform organization has its officers and notables. You will find them to be, with few exceptions, a bunch of prima donnas and political masochists as well. They never really expected anything as strenuous as success — and they bleed easily.

You must avoid hurting their feelings. They may not be much use to you but they have the power to do you a great deal of harm.

Remember the old story about the new lodge member who was elected "Lord High Exalted Ruler of the Universe"? He was not the lodge master; his was the very lowest position in that lodge. There is your technique.

Flatter them. Defer to them. Ask their advice . . . in such terms that you get the advice you want! Never ignore them. Have them speak to new clubs. Put them on "dignity" committees (people who greet visiting notables, sit on platforms during programs, and have their names printed on political stationery). Never displace them from club or organization office unless they wish to retire. You can always create new offices — "executive" this and "executive" that — without disturbing them. If some old fuddy-duddy is now chairman and can't conduct a meeting properly you can always carry out basic business in a committee-of-the-whole, with your own choice as chairman of the committee-of-the-whole — or you can through an executive committee — or provide the office of parliamentarian — or even teach him some parliamentary law if you are subtle about it. You yourself will work as floor leader, in his good graces. Be sure never to surprise him with what you bring up on the floor. Tell him about it before-hand.

But don't replace him until he wants to retire, then create some equivalent of Lord High Exalted Ruler of the Universe for him — "critic," "senior adviser," "chairman of the reception committee."

I was present once when an elderly man, just the sort I have referred to, addressed a mass meeting for twenty minutes on how he had been ignored by the johnny-come-latelies in the campaign just completed. That was his whole plaint; the campaign had been successful — he could not deny that. It had turned out a bunch of vultures and had taken over an entire state organization. But he had not been consulted; he was the dean of the reformers in the party; his nose was out of joint.

His point was ridiculous, as a reformer he had been a consistent failure. But he was a powerful, persuasive orator; he managed to convince the crowd that he had been wronged. It started a crack in the organization which widened and destroyed it.

He is nationally known but I shall not name him — he is rich in years and honors and fought many a gallant fight in his youth. I cite him only as a warning.

Some few of the old-timers will turn out to be good workers; if you are considerate of all you can salvage the useful ones as well as avoiding the dangerous pique of the dead wood.

Let us now suppose that you have won your first primary (see Chapter X) and thereby control the official party machinery. You are the Party, you and your friends, in the legal sense; this obligates the state and national committees to deal with you.

You have still to cope with the persons you have displaced. This will be a headache!

Here we are assuming that these persons are not sincerely members of your party at all; they are stooges of the Machine who wear your party label for the purpose of selling out your party. These jackals lack even the limited honesty of the ordinary successful machine politician; they are professional traitors. You cannot trust them under any circumstances.

(This case is very different from the normal post-primary situation described in Chapter X where your object would be to heal the wounds between factions all loyal to your party.)

You are likely to find it very difficult to throw these crooks out of the party. You can't keep them out of public meetings; in any case some of them will have been elected to your county committee. There is probably no method of unseating them, but this is not the time to compromise. Don't let them hold any office if you can possibly prevent it. If you let one have so much as an honorary vice-chairmanship in a subcommittee, he will go out, print up stationery with his title on it, and write letters of endorsement for the Machine which will appear to be, through judicious use of large and small type, official endorsements from your organization.

Another favorite trick, and one almost impossible to stop, is for them to incorporate a dummy political "club" under an official-sounding title, such as: The 12th District Official Republican Club or The

Democratic Assembly of Gedunkus County. Sometimes you can stop this sort of thing with an injunction, but not often.

There is no sure cure here. All I can recommend is to keep them at arm's length, don't trust them, and don't give them anything. Some of this phony organization may be poor lost souls, honestly devoted to the party and happy at the change. Very well, let them prove it by a long, long, term of volunteer work at a low level. Keep them on parole until you are sure of them.

I have elaborated this point because, once you build an organization, these termites will try to dominate it, under the pretext that they are the "real" (Democrats) (Republicans), and you will be tempted to meet them half-way, particularly because pressure will almost certainly be brought to bear on you from the state capital or from Washington by senior party members who are interested in party harmony and may not understand the local situation. Don't do it. If you know, of your own knowledge, that the official party organization you replaced had unclean relationships with the Machine you are opposing, then this is one of the times not to compromise, even though the national chairman of your party gets you on long distance to plead with you!

You have built an organization; you have captured party machinery — now to win an election!

● CHAPTER VII

How to Win an Election

The By-Election at Eatanswill

"There are twenty washed men at the street for you to shake hands with and six children in arms that you are to pat on the head and inquire the ages of. Be particular about the children, my dear sir; it always has a great effect, that sort of thing."

"I'll take care," said the Honorable Samuel Slumkey.

"And perhaps, my dear sir," said the cautious little man, "perhaps if you could — I don't mean to say it's indispensable — but if you could manage to kiss one of them, it would produce a great impression on the crowd."

"Wouldn't it have as good an effect if the proposer or seconder did that?" said the Honorable Samuel Slumkey.

"Why, I am afraid it wouldn't," replied the agent. "If it were done by yourself, my dear sir, I think it would make you very popular."

"Very well," said the Honorable Samuel Slumkey with a resigned air, "then it must be done — that's all."

"Arrange the Procession!" cried the twenty committeemen.

— From *The Posthumous Papers of the Pickwick Club*, Charles Dickens, 1837

"The place to learn to wash dishes is at the sink." The stuff in this book is pre-digested; to cut your teeth you must get out there in the field and try.

You are likely to lose your first election — let's discuss that first. With the aid of a few simple rules you can be absolutely certain of losing.

How to Lose an Election: The first thing to do to lose an election is to put out of your mind the basic rule of politics that elections are won with individual votes, each held by a separate human being who must first be convinced, then persuaded to go to the polls on election day to record his conviction so that it may be counted.

If you will neglect that rule you can lose extemporaneously. However, there are some other positive steps you may take to insure a good, rousing, landslide defeat.

Put the major portion of your time, energy and money into the indirect, superficial aspects of campaigning, and slight the direct, vote-by-vote methods, such as doorbell pushing. Accept all the speaking engagements you can manage to get, even if they take you miles out of your district and are before groups who will not permit an outright campaign speech. It gets your name in the paper, doesn't it? A candidate has to have publicity, doesn't he?

Get for your publicity man some kid who had a high school course in journalism, no experience, but plenty of enthusiasm. Then stifle his one asset — enthusiasm — by back-seat driving on everything he tries to do.

Get a lot of expensive advertising literature, printed on expensive stock. Put your picture on it, using different cuts for each sort, and fill up the space with plenty of words in small type. Limit your precinct activity to having this junk distributed loose on the doorsteps. You have too few volunteers to ring all the doorbells; this gets you name all over the district, doesn't it?

Tie up a big chunk of your available funds in radio time. Hire fifteen minutes or half an hour and make a political speech, once or twice a week, or whatever you can pay for. (Radio stations like cash on the table.) Take the radio time at the non-political rate; it does not permit you to mention the election but you get twice as much time for the same price. They will let you discuss issues as long as you don't campaign directly — and after all, your object is to educate the voters, isn't it? If they know what good things you stand for they will remember you on election day, won't they?

Plan some Big Events for the latter part of the campaign, a mass meeting, a dance, or a picnic. Have your volunteer workers concentrate on making this jamboree a success by selling tickets, and arranging a fine program. Make it the climax of your campaign.

Run for some good-sized office as your first try, such as congressman, or superior court judge. After all you are too big a man for those two-bit jobs like selectman or legislator.

Make some member of your family your campaign manager. This insures loyalty, on the part of the manager, at least.

Try to win the support of every possible sort of group by hedging your statements and carrying water on both shoulders. Chamber-of-Commerce meetings and funny-money rallies don't draw the same audience, do they? You can do a lot — a lot of something at least — by a wink and a nod. You are for the welfare of all the Peepul, and that is what matters — as for your methods, well, you have to fight fire with fire — it's a dirty business, isn't it?

(You're blinking well right it's a dirty business if you play it *that* way!)

Let each hopeful aspirant for patronage think that he has the inside track for your favor, but don't promise anything you can't weasel out of. (It doesn't really matter; you aren't going to be elected in any case.)

Don't sample your district to see how you are doing. Instead, surround yourself by your loyal supporters and listen to them. Kick out the pessimists; they are just trying to discourage your workers.

By running a campaign in the fashion described above you can enjoy every minute of it and have a wonderful time, right up to the announcement of the results. Even then, after your defeat, there are ways to turn a licking into outright political suicide.

You can skip the election party — the party after the polls are closed in which the workers either celebrate or console each other. This saves you the cost of the refreshments but doesn't cost you any votes, since the party would not take place until after the election is over, if you held it. It saves you embarrassment, too, since some of them are sure to get drunk.

Make yourself inaccessible the next day, too, and for several days thereafter; otherwise your supporters will swarm over you and cry on your shoulder. Don't they realize that you are nervously exhausted and have just been subjected to a shocking disappointment?

Of course you will have to thank them for their efforts. Just limit it to a mimeographed form letter. After all, it's impossible to write everybody a personal note; they ought to realize that.

Then bolt the party. This was a primary you just lost, naturally, since your methods would never take you to the finals. Neglect to support the member of your party who defeated you. You are morally justified; he had some of the worst elements in town around him — utterly shameless politicians. Not only did they tear down your signs, but they practically bought votes. And they dug up some things in your past and put them in the worst possible light — libel, really. You can never forgive him for that and no reasonable person would expect you to.

So take a walk. Do it literally — you can always be called out of town. If anybody ever needed a vacation, you need one now; it is a natural thing to do. So take a walk; hole up with kin folks, back in the sticks, until the finals are over.

The above routine entitles you to pose the rest of your life as a man who is disillusioned through bitter experience. You can hold forth on how democracy is a nice idea but won't work in practice, and how this country will some day have to feel the firm hand of authority — either the Best People will have to assert themselves and rule with no nonsense, or some rabble-rousing demagogue will ruin the Republic. You know — you've been through the mill!

(I'm sure you have all met this guy at some time or other.)

The above horrible example may seem too perfect to be true, but every wrong move depicted above occurs in every campaign, committed by some of the candidates, every year throughout the country. Many campaigns show the majority of the above errors. I recall one copy-book example which had all of the above mistakes — except that, wonderful to see, the candidate did not become disillusioned. He was bright enough to learn. After bolting the party he eventually came back, admitted his error, took off his coat, got to work, and rehabilitated himself.

How to Win a Campaign: Let us say it again: The key to success in politics is to remember at all times that votes are what you are after and that the votes are in the precincts.

They aren't downtown in the politico-financial district. They aren't at club meetings, not many of them. Of course you pick up odd votes wherever you find them, but the club meetings are primarily to arouse and hold together your volunteers; individually there aren't enough votes in political organizations to carry an election. Rallies are for morale building primarily and secondarily for publicity, but the persons who attend them have already made up their minds how to vote and can be counted on to vote, whether the rally is held or not.

The vote you need to win lies on the other side of a closed door in a private home; you have to punch that doorbell to get it. There is no substitute.

Having lined it up, you have to be sure it reaches the polling place — and that calls for more individual action.

It isn't hard to get adherents to your cause. The vote you are looking for is either already on your side and needs simply to be located, or it is one which can be switched to your side (from a condition of "no opinion") just by stating your case and asking for support. The "hard cases" should be left alone; it's like butting your head into a stone wall.

Your real problem, then, is not selling your bill of goods, but finding your customers and getting them to the polls.

And that, compatriot, is some problem!

You are hardly ever licked by the opposition; you are licked by your own friends who did not vote. I once lost an election by less than 400 votes; in the post-mortem I was able to tabulate names of more people than that who were personal acquaintances of mine, had promised me support — but did not vote. The shortcoming was plainly one of the election day organization. Forty election-day volunteers could have swung the district.

Unfortunately the district had been conceded as hopeless by everyone but myself and a handful of stalwarts, and we could not manage to be enough places at once on election day.

Earlier in this book I have described how Charles Evans Hughes lost the presidency when a shift of less than one ten-thousandth of the vote could have elected him — if the effort had been applied in the key state. The 1944 election is much more typical — with respect to statistics, not issues.

Mr. Dewey received only 99 electoral votes out of a possible 432. Looks like a landslide—but let's analyze it.

In 1944 there were 87,000,000 American citizens over twenty-one; only 48,000,000 of them voted. That leaves 39,000,000 "sleepers" — persons who did not register, or just failed to vote. If the preferences for president ran in the same ratios among the "sleepers" as among those who voted, then Mr. Dewey lost 18,000,000 potential votes — but Mr. Roosevelt beat Mr. Dewey by considerably less than 4,000,000 in the popular vote.

It looks as if the persons who were against the Fourth Term weren't against it enough to bother to turn out to vote!

If the Republicans had carried California, Illinois, Michigan, New Jersey, New York, and Pennsylvania, Mr. Dewey would have been elected. These are key states, swing states. None of them can be counted as normally Democratic; in the last ten presidential elections the Democratic Party has lost each of these states either half, or more than half, the time. Furthermore, all six of them either had Republican governors in 1944 or elected a Republican governor in the 1944 election.

Mr. Roosevelt's majority in these six states, taken all together, was a gnat's whisker more than a million. But 7,200,000 of the Republican "sleepers" were in these six states! If the Republican organization had concentrated its efforts in these six states — everybody knew that they were uncertain states; ready to fall either way — Mr. Dewey would have won provided one in seven of the Republican "sleepers" were delivered to the polls.

Please draw no inferences about which side had my support; I am neither weeping nor cheering — this is a clinical examination.

There is only one conclusion that need be drawn: In

this election the Republican precinct organization wasn't worth a hoot; the high command muffed the strategy and the precinct captains muffed the tactics.

Now let us suppose that it is your home congressional district and that you have vowed to unseat Congressman Swivelchair — we'll assume that you have good reasons. What are your chances and what does it take?

You live in the mythical "average" district; it has therefore 320,000 human souls. 200,000 of them are over twenty-one; of these 140,000 are registered to vote. We will assume that the district is evenly divided between the two major parties, so that you have a chance to carry the district if you gain the nomination for your candidate but will not have the election handed to you on a platter.

There are, then, 70,000 members of your party. Of these about 25,000 will vote in the primary. You need 13,000 to win a clear majority in the primary — less, if there are more than two candidates and your state permits plurality nominations.

What does it take to get the 13,000 votes? Well, if your organizational activities — the clubs we talked about in preceding chapters — can show one hundred active volunteers who are not afraid to punch doorbells and will work on election day, I'll bet the rent money on the outcome.

Cost? Anything you want to make it. Volunteer campaigns should not cost much. Can you bank $1,000 before your candidate files his nominating petition? If so, you should never have to worry about unpaid bills — provided you have an absolute veto over commitments and expenditures. If the candidate's wife is permitted to order printing, you're sunk! The same goes if you have a campaign committee which can overrule you without digging down into their pockets personally to spend money in ways that you do not approve.

The campaign will cost more than $1,000 but the excess can be raised by passing the hat as you go along, and by nicking the very persons who want to make expenditures not included in your budget.

Still, a thousand dollars is a lot of potatoes to most people. Where are you going to get it? The answer lies between two extremes: A thousand men at a dollar each and one man with a thousand dollars. Of the two the first is by far the better; volunteer campaigns come to life when the workers themselves, and their friends, foot the bill.

Suppose your first tentative campaign meeting, long before the campaign, has twenty people at it. You ought to be able to clip them for an average of $10 a head (some at twenty-five, some at nothing), cash and checks, paid on the spot. Perhaps the candidate is sufficiently well-heeled that he can put in $300 (but don't let financial condition be any criterion in selecting a candidate — a rich man can lose an election for you just as fast as a poor one).

Your clubs should be able to raise a little for you. Then perhaps you know some people who will kick in once they see earnest money in the pot. But get the thousand before you make any announcements to the newspapers; you are going to have to have it and it is much easier to raise it first when you have time for such matters, than later, when time is everything.

The opposition may spend many thousands of dollars, but don't let that worry you. Elections are not won with dollars. The only reason you have to have any money is because printing and postage take cash. One thousand dollars is, of course, an arbitrary figure. More is convenient, if you can raise it; you may even get by for less if you have real talent for making good soup out of vegetable tops and left-over bones. Most of the things that cost big money in campaigning are almost useless for vote-getting purposes in the local campaign.

(And, come to think of it — what campaign is not a "local" campaign. Votes are in the precincts!)

After the primary, money — clean money — will be much easier to raise. In addition to local sources, the National Committee is always anxious to subsidize a local organization which shows unexpected signs of displacing one of the opposition, without help in the primary and with a live, volunteer organization. Each national organization has a fund to be used only on congressional districts "in the balance" — which is not to be spent on hopeless districts nor on sure districts, but on ones such as yours. There may be only a hundred such in the country, but the fund comes from all over. Present your figures.

Now let's tabulate the situation. We are assuming that the Honorable Horace Swivelchair is not of your party; you may want to displace an officeholder of your own party, but the circumstance is less usual and the task should not be attempted except for the most grave reasons. (Are you quite sure you know all about the voting record of your co-partisan whom you wish to displace? Have you tried all methods short of war? Don't get sucked into such a campaign simply because someone is ambitious to hold office. The minimum reasons should be nothing less grave than proved moral turpitude or a consistent refusal to support party measures.)

The Situation:

District population	320,000
Persons over twenty-one	200,000
Registered voters	140,000
Registered strength of your party	70,000
Number voting in your party primary....	25,000
Required to cinch party nomination	3,000

Your assets are:

Volunteer workers	100
Cash on hand	$1,000

The problem is to turn the assets into 13,000 votes.

For simplicity we will assume that there are just two candidates out for your party nomination, Jack Hopeful and your own candidate, Jonathan Upright. If there are more, you are a cinch to win, but let's do it the hard way.

Thirteen thousand votes divided among 100 people means an average of 130 ballots in the box per worker. But it is not that bad; your candidate, in a two-man race, will get 10,000 votes just for having his name on the ballot. Your workers have to locate one hundred and thirty votes apiece, but one hundred of them will get to the polls in any case under their own steam and vote for your man. The precinct worker must sort out the other thirty votes and get them to the polls — perhaps half by phone calls and the other half by providing transportation.

It begins to look easier — one man to haul fifteen voters to the polls, in order to gain control of a district containing a third of a million people, in order to seat a congressman in a Congress where the draft law was extended, just before Pearl Harbor, by a majority of one vote.

It is easy — from that stand point, and that is the reason why the volunteer amateur can take over this country, or any part of it, and run it to suit himself. Your part is very easy if you are just one of the volunteer precinct workers — a noble ambition in itself!

But if you aspire to manage a congressional contest you will find, before you are through, that it requires all of your intelligence and diplomacy. While the job can be done — many have done it — it will call into use your highest human faculties.

Choosing a Candidate: All too often your choice is very narrow. In this country people who offer themselves for public service get a shameful kicking around. The pay is so niggardly that an honest man usually leaves office poorer than when he accepted it, and the dead cats and rotten eggs far outnumber the pats on the back for work well done — to our collective shame!

The sober, able citizens whom we need in public office know these things; very few of them are willing to make the sacrifice that public service entails. We have indeed been blessed that enough able men have always been willing, thus far, to forego their own interests that the Republic might survive.

You will probably have to persuade the candidate of your choice to make the race. If he is bright enough for the job he won't be very anxious to have it.

If he is the man you need for the job he will be aware that some citizens have to give up their natural desire for privacy, peace of mind, and financial security in order to keep democracy alive. The motivation is the same which causes men to volunteer to meet their deaths in time of war; it exists in peace time, but is a little harder to stir up.

You can expect him to be reluctant but willing to be convinced — convinced that his personal sacrifice will not be in vain. You must convince by showing him that he can be elected, in terms of district statistics, local factors, availability of campaign funds, your proposed budget, and your organization — organization above all. Since he is neither a nincompoop nor politically naive he knows that organization is the controlling factor.

If you can show him a fighting chance, he will probably go.

On the other hand you will be beset by hopeful, potential candidates who are just waiting for the lightning to strike. They will come smirking around, digging one toe in the dust, and murmuring that "Barkis is willin'." These people are usually political light-weights whose only assets are consuming ambitions to hold public office and to receive a public salary.

They will look you up — of course they will look you up; you have an organization — and get in your hair.

They will be hard to handle. It is a hard thing to tell a man bluntly that you don't think he has the character, or the intelligence, as may be, to hold public office. Furthermore you might be mistaken; some unlikely people have served the public well. I suggest that you use a counter-attack.

Ask him if he is willing to refrain from running if the organization chooses some other man to back. Press this point and press it hard. Insist that he must commit himself to support and campaign for the candidate chosen by the organization before his name goes into the hat. This commitment should be in writing.

His commitment probably isn't worth anything but it may keep him from doing what he can to sabotage your efforts.

Don't promise him anything at all except that he will be allowed to present his case before the organizational caucus which chooses the candidate — provided he binds himself to the caucus. This is the essence of caucusing, that no one shall participate in it who is not bound by it; it is an entirely fair, democratic procedure.

The pipsqueak will probably jump the caucus if he loses in it. You are then morally justified in sending several of the more influential members of the caucus to see him in order to coerce him back into line. If they are his business customers, so much the better. A caucus is a contract and should be enforceable, but the law gives no means. You are entitled to improvise means, as rude as necessary, as long as you don't step outside the law. ("Look, Joe — you signed that caucus. If you break your word to us between now and election day, your name is going to be mud in this community. We'll see to it that everybody and his brother knows just what kind of a heel you are when it comes to keeping your word. You won't be able to do anything about it, because every word of it will be true — in fact, we'd love a libel suit because that would spread it around to more people. If you don't toe the line as you promised, you are finished politically — and it's not going to do your business any good either. People don't like to do business with a man who isn't honest — starting with me!")

Your own candidate must agree to the caucus, and you yourself. This may be a little hard to take, but democracy is not a one-way proposition. Require from him also a written commitment that he will endorse, support, and make at least one public appearance on behalf of the straight party ticket and in particular on behalf of his successful opponent, in the event that he is defeated. If he won't do this he is not your man, no matter how well you thought of him. Don't waste your time on prima donnas.

A word of warning — when you bind yourself to the caucus, do not bind yourself to manage the campaign of the successful candidate. It is likely that you will be willing to undertake the grief of managing only for the candidate whom you hand-picked. If another candidate is selected, it is all right for you to drop back to the status of a precinct worker, there to do honest work but considerably less of it, if, in your opinion, the candidate is not electable or not completely satisfactory to you.

But you must bind yourself to endorse and campaign for the candidate selected by the caucus, at least on the minimum level of canvassing and carrying your own precinct.

I can almost hear your doubts and misgivings about this. Isn't such a commitment likely to land you some day in the uncomfortable position of having to choose between breaking your word or supporting a candidate you know to be unworthy of public trust?

No — not if you know your procedure. In the first place, these are your friends and associates, aren't they? Can't you count on Tom and Art and Dr. Nugent and Alice and old Mrs. Krueger to back you up in keeping any real jerk from getting the nod? If not, you are probably in the wrong pew and should be more careful in picking your political associates.

But let us suppose, nevertheless, that there is a chance that a certain party will pop up as the choice of the caucus; you are among friends but, while you are convinced that this person is a moral leper, you can't prove it. However, he is a very personable chap and many of your staunch friends are still taken in by him. This can happen — it's happened to me.

You need only insist that all the potential candidates be listed before the caucus is bound and that the caucus be limited to consideration of the listed candidates. This gives you a chance to thresh it out before you are bound.

Let's run over a typical caucus — it is one of the least understood and most necessary of the democratic techniques. We'll make it the caucus to select the organizational candidate for congress for the party primary in your district. Caucuses can be used for any sort of joint action; this one will illustrate all the principles involved.

In the first place membership in a caucus is strictly by invitation. The man, or group of men, who call the caucus is the sole judge of the membership. No one has a natural right to be a member of a caucus. You are no more obligated to invite a man to caucus with you than you are obligated to invite him to be a guest in your home. It may be politically imprudent to exclude someone who wants in — he may form a rival caucus of his own — but you don't have to. A caucus has no existence until it votes to bind itself; up to that time, if you called it, you can exclude anyone merely because you don't like the way he parts his hair.

After the caucus comes into formal existence by voting to bind itself, it may add to its own membership any person who agrees to be bound by it by either of two methods, by majority vote (or greater majority vote, as may be required) provided the original terms of the caucus permitted it, or by unanimous vote of the entire membership — not just those present — if the original terms of the caucus failed to provide explicitly for increase of membership.

The original terms of the caucus constitute an inflexible contract among the members and may never be varied except by unanimous consent of all the membership. This is a striking difference between caucuses and all other parliamentary bodies. The essence of a caucus is its unanimity. That unanimity has been arrived at by each member binding himself to support the wishes of the majority under certain conditions all of which must be explicitly stated in the original agreement. This includes both membership of the caucus and the matters which the caucus may consider and how they may consider them.

A caucus which decides by less than unanimous consent to do anything at all not set forth in the original agreement is not extending its powers; it is committing suicide. At that moment it ceases to have any existence, for the contract which gave it birth is no longer binding on anyone.

From which we draw two rules: Be extremely careful what goes into the caucus agreement, and be still more careful that each member understands the exact nature of a caucus. Give a lecture on it each time — someone present is sure to be mixed up on the subject. But get it clear before action is taken.

At this point the Lone Rangers in politics will gallop away. There are many of them and they don't like to surrender "freedom of action." They will leave, noses in the air, protesting that their high ideals prevent them giving up their independence.

Good riddance! There is probably no easier way to

avoid these political spoiled brats than by inviting them
to caucus and defining to them exactly what it means.
You will thereby remain true to your own ideals of
honest dealing and democratic consent.

Candidates are not members of the caucus which
select them. This is not a law, but it is good sense. If you
called the caucus you have also notified any candidate
who has approached you earlier and to whom you
have given a commitment for a hearing in exchange
for his commitment not to run but to support the
choice of the caucus, if not selected. You may also have
invited other candidates, in order to make the base of
your faction as broad as possible. Each person who has
been invited to caucus is also free to bring along his
favorite candidate.

The candidates are gathered in another room out of
earshot. Among them are Mr. Pipsqueak, Judge
Weathervane, and a Mr. Nemo who is acting on behalf
of his law partner, Mr. Briefcase. Your own candidate,
Jonathan Upright, is not there; you will present his
case.

You would be willing to support any of these candidates, in a pinch, except Weathervane. You speak to
the group: "Look, folks, I suggest that we listen to the
candidates first, before we take any action to caucus.
That way we will have more facts. I for one think that
we should limit the caucus to a set list of candidates,
determined before we caucus, so that no one can say he
has been taken by surprise. How about it?"

Someone objects that the purpose of the meeting is
party harmony and that the thing to do is to agree to
accept the will of the group before we get into any rows
over candidates. There is sense in what he says; therefore you must expose the rest of your hand.

"Judge Weathervane is sitting out there, by my
invitation, but he is not my candidate. He called on me
a while back and asked for my support. I didn't

promise it to him. Instead I agreed to see to it that he
got a hearing before any caucus I took part in provided
he would agree to support the caucus if he wasn't
picked. I am bound by that commitment; he's got to
have his hearing or I can't caucus. On the other hand I
can't agree to support him under any circumstances. If
he is still eligible for consideration at the time we bind
ourselves I'll have to drop out and leave the meeting.
Can you help me out?"

Let us suppose that they turn you down. You have
no choice then; you must leave the caucus. Don't get
angry — wish them luck and withdraw. You can't even
go to the candidates' waiting room and then present
Upright's name before the caucus but not as a member
of it, because you can't bind yourself and your candidate to support the result of the caucus as long as
Weathervane is still in the running. But you hang
around on the slight chance that the caucus, when it
forms, will not decide to bind candidates to the outcome. Upright may still squeak through.

More probably they will agree to your point, since it
is evident that you got into your predicament from an
honest attempt to promote organizational discipline.
The group holds a preliminary caucus and agrees
(a) to a two-stage procedure to hear any candidate who
is willing to sign a commitment to support the caucus
(this is for outsiders, like Pipsqueak, Weathervane, and
Briefcase, and has no effect on the favorite candidates
of the members of the caucus), (b) after hearing them
to include a list of candidates to be considered as a condition of the final agreement to caucus.

The candidates waiting outside are presented with a
written commitment to sign (better write it yourself)
and are then invited in, one at a time, to state their cases
and be questioned. An agreement like this will be adequate: "We, the undersigned, candidates for congress
in the umpteenth district, agree to abide by the

outcome of the caucus held at (exact address) on (date) by withdrawing from the race if not selected and by endorsing and supporting the candidate chosen by the caucus. We do this in return for the opportunity to present our several cases in advance of any decision by the caucus."

The last clause is correct and is no swindle on Weathervane. You know your own mind, but the caucus has made no decision.

Weathervane looks at it, hems and haws, then signs it with a flourish. He is confident of his ability to sway any crowd. Pipsqueak looks it over, decides not to sign it, and stalks away in a medium-sized dudgeon. He has gotten cold feet while chinning with the other candidates and this gives him an easy out. You mark him down mentally as a man to call on and dose with soothing syrup.

Briefcase's law partner asks to use the telephone, then comes back and signs. The other candidates sign.

After they have each had their hearing before the group you get down to the business of caucusing. You, or one of your friends, propose that the caucus be limited to the persons now present, that adjournment be provided for if no decision is reached tonight, and that consideration be limited to candidates' names now to be nominated before the vote to caucus is taken. This last point is a repetition to avoid misunderstanding. You may add that the business of the caucus shall include setting up a campaign committee, or anything else which suits your purpose, and close by limiting the actions of the caucus to the points set forth explicitly, except by unanimous consent.

It may be modified, but you will get your agreement as long as you are careful to make everything clear. Nominations come first; when the list is complete Weathervane's name isn't on it. You are safe.

Or perhaps Weathervane's name is there. Unknown

to you, Jim Swiftly has an agreement with Weather-vane. Here is an impasse; you won't caucus with Weathervane on the list, Swiftly won't caucus unless he is on the list. A separation is the only answer. "Those who wish to caucus with me, come over and stand beside me; those who wish to caucus with Mr. Swiftly, go over and stand beside him."

If your political fences are in good enough repair to justify the enterprise you are undertaking, Swiftly will stand alone, or joined by one or two. Now he and his friends must leave. They will probably object; they will probably want to hang around as "observers" (kibitzers). They will point out that they were invited.

But you must insist. Caucuses don't have "observers"; only the bound members may be present. Tell them to take their caucus (that's what it is) elsewhere.

When they have left you can all sign the caucus — put it in writing — and get on with the selection of a candidate.

Let everybody talk all he wants to, without limit. Present the case of Mr. Upright yourself, carefully and thoroughly. When everybody is talked out you can start balloting. Secret ballot is not necessary; at this stage a man should show his colors — but don't object if it is asked for.

There may be several ballots, with candidates dropping out of the running and regrouping taking place. Someone may ask for an adjournment; if it passes you will be busy during the intervening days, gathering up support for your man. But eventually some ballot shows a majority for one candidate who is then the unanimous choice of the caucus.

It is Mr. Upright. You've started.

Weathervane bolts his agreement the next morning. Swiftly has gone straight to him after leaving the meeting; from the two of them come loud shouts of "Fraud! Frame up! Unprincipled chicanery! Never in my many years of public life, etc." Don't worry about it. Send Weathervane a photostat of the agreement he signed and suggest that he call on you before you send copies to the newspapers. He will probably come around and offer his services, after suitable shadow boxing, in exchange for patronage or a paid job on the committee. Don't give him anything. He won't run in any case.

Swiftly will probably go whole hog and work for the other party.

Of course you can always skip all this monkey business of caucusing — just gather together Upright's friends and form a campaign committee. You can lose, too. Caucusing is worth the trouble; it can either vastly enhance your candidate's chances, or it can keep you from attempting a race that should never start.

But why did you settle on Upright in the first place, before you ever persuaded a caucus to choose him? Your criteria should be suitability, availability, and electability, in that order.

Suitability: He should be a man with whom you see eye to eye on matters of public welfare. I refer to issues — states' rights, unions, foreign affairs, national defense, poll tax, atomic control, peace-time conscription, etc. His views in these matters should be generally in harmony with the established program of your party (as are yours) and, in your opinion, wiser on some important issues than your party has shown itself to be in the past, as it is your object to improve the Republic, not to embalm it.

He should be selected from the persons you know through politics in your district, as it is quite unlikely that a suitable public servant can be found in the ranks of those who never bother their heads with public matters, no matter how able or even brilliant they may be in other fields. (Unfortunately the "Congress bug" bites quite a few who have become eminent in other lines. I suggest that you eliminate at once those who wish to start in politics at the top. A suitable candidate must have a record of unpaid, devoted public service of some sort, even if not as a precinct worker. Perhaps he has made an outstanding record on the Grand Jury, in city planning, as a Boy Scout commissioner, or in the improvement of inter-racial relations. But beware of the Prominent Citizen who has stayed out of public life entirely, even if you find him in *Who's Who* and he is willing to foot the whole campaign bill.)

There should be no question in your mind as to his integrity or character in general. H.L. Mencken once remarked that, in order to judge a man, it was necessary only to know how he makes his living. I can't endorse that as a sufficient test but it is a very illuminating one. Look into how he gets his money. Does it turn your stomach? Investigate his business reputation among his competitors. He's a lawyer — what sort of cases does he take? He is a doctor — what charity work does he do and what is his practice like? He runs a restaurant — is the kitchen clean? What are his practices with respect to his waitresses' tips? Some occupations are so notoriously dishonest that his reputation will shine out like a halo if he is an honest member thereof. In any case — check up. (I made a terrible mistake once in not doing so, the details of which are so grisly that I decline to repeat them.)

In temperament he should be conciliatory and cooperative. Don't saddle yourself with a man who gets into rows, is stiff-necked, and unwilling to meet people half way. Be sure that he understands the principle of the coordinate nature of authority and responsibility and that he has sufficient confidence in your ability to delegate the management of the campaign to you and then abide by your judgment. This will come up again under "electability."

In intelligence, education, and experience he should be of congressional caliber. Of the three intelligence is the most important.

Availability: This stumbling block, a serious one, can be dealt with in only the most general terms. In particular it means that he should be able to devote full time to the campaign for three months before the primary, another three months before the final election, and then be able to close up his affairs and go to Washington. The economic difficulties here automatically eliminate at least 90% of our best prospective public servants. A family man working as an employee can hardly ever get over this hurdle. Available candidates usually are elderly retired people, housewives, young bachelors, persons of independent income, and persons in the free-lance professions — actors, writers, lawyers, lecturers, etc. Sometimes a farmer, a school teacher, or an independent businessman can arrange his affairs to take the plunge, and once in a while an employer will cooperate by holding a job open. But you may expect to hear something like this rather frequently: "Old man, I'd like to and I appreciate the compliment — but I'm tied to a treadmill!"

This is one of the reasons why lawyers are so numerous in public office. Lawyers have law partners; they can usually arrange time off whenever the bank account can stand it. Lawyers, of course, tend to be poor law-makers, but their "availability index" is high.

If you select a housewife, count on a maid for her household as a necessary campaign expense.

The remarks about availability of a candidate apply with equal strength to yourself, the manager. Since you are likely to be a woman your problem may be simpler. But I am unable to recommend trying to carry on a campaign part time, while continuing a regular occupation, to either you or your candidate, except in compelling and exceptional circumstances; it is too likely to result in fatigue-impaired judgment during the campaign and physical collapse before it is over. A campaign is pleasantly invigorating to the precinct workers and other volunteers; it is more like an endurance contest for the candidate and manager.

Electability: From a stand point of electability the ideal candidate is male, over thirty and under fifty-five, a veteran with a combat record, strong and healthy, pleasant in appearance without being outstandingly handsome, moderately tall, a good public speaker, a friendly but not an aggressive personality, married with at least one child, very well known and universally respected in his community, a church member, previous experience in public office, previous experience as a candidate (two different things — the office could have been appointive), long service in the party, and willing to let the manager run the campaign.

I have never met such a candidate.

In fact, one of the best candidates I have ever known was female, past seventy, ugly as an old horse, no children, a poor public speaker, and not very well known. What she had was integrity that surrounded her as an almost visible aura and an evident selflessness.

None of these aspects of electability is too important. St. Peter could be elected Mayor of Hell with proper precinct organization. As long as your candidate wears shoes habitually — in public, that is — and qualifies under "suitability" and "availability," it doesn't really matter if he eats with his knife. Usually the things that make a candidate truly not electable are things which have already disqualified him under suitability.

Each deviation from the synthetic "perfect candidate" increases your problems a little, but the opposition has the same sort of problems. You may reasonably hope that the opposition will worry so much about "electability" that they will neglect more fundamental attributes of a good candidate and give you a sitting duck to shoot at. That beautiful facade may conceal a hushed-up indictment for fraud.

The only item under "electability" that need keep

you awake nights is the one about previous experience as a candidate. Being a candidate for the first time is like nothing else under the sun. "Nervous bride" is a common expression, but you have seen lots of brides who were not nervous. I'll wager you have never seen a first-time candidate who was not nervous.

Candidates are subject to a nervous disorder which I choose to term "Candidatitis." (New managers sometimes catch a milder form of it, if they have not come up the doorbell-pushing route and thereby gained immunity. Be warned.)

Candidatitis is something like measles; persons almost always catch it when first exposed, one seizure usually gives lifetime immunity, and it is best experienced early in life for the mildest symptoms and the least disastrous after-effects.

The usual symptoms are these: Extreme nervousness and irritability, suspiciousness raised almost to the persecution-complex level and usually directed toward the wrong people, a tendency for the tongue to work independently of the brain especially in public where it can do the most harm, and a positively childish aversion to accepting advice and management.

Mr. Willkie (God rest his gallant soul!) was an almost perfect candidate in most respects and an able contender for the Champ. Take a look over the yardstick of the "ideal candidate" with respect to electability and see how well he measures up. In addition he had a well-financed campaign which had been organized and directed by some of the most able public-relations men in the country; his supporters had a crusading fervor and the opposing candidate labored under the very great handicap of bucking the anti-third-term tradition which more than off-set the advantage of incumbency. (Incumbency is a questionable asset for a presidential candidate in any case, no matter how important it may be in lesser offices.)

It is generally agreed by most observers that something catastrophic happened to Mr. Willkie's campaign during the man-killing swing around the country. Some of the reporters who went with him say that it appeared that the candidate hurt his own chances, unnecessarily, on almost every occasion.

Note that Mr. Willkie had never run for any office before. Note also that he steadied down right after the campaign and assumed the role of elder statesman, which fitted him well, and was a strong force for unity and cool-headed wisdom in a country at war. Does the diagnosis of "candidatitis" during the campaign seem to fit?

In any event, if you have picked a man you want to run for congress in a year or two, or for any major office, and this candidate has never run for office before, then it would be wise to run him at once for something like dog-catcher, in order to get him blooded for the fight.

Side remark — I find I have used as major examples three cases in which Republican candidates-for-president lost; this is not bias either way. The cases happened to display the illustrative features I needed.

CHAPTER VIII

How to Win an Election (continued)

The Grass-Roots Campaign: From here on a bewildering variety of possible activities will press their claims on you. All of them will appear to be of use to the campaign; each will be eagerly supported by some member of your group as being "Just the thing we need to do!" Unless you have some touchstone rule to go by you will waste your efforts and drive yourself nuts with meaningless activity.

Consider each move, no matter how small, in these terms:

(a) Will the action help to get a specific, individual vote (or votes) in your district and registered in your party?

(b) If the effect is general rather than specific, is the shotgun spread aimed at your own district? Can it be carried out at no cost? If the activity involves time or physical effort for you or the candidate, are the probable results in votes large enough to warrant it, or would it be better to use the time in sleep, going to the movies, playing cribbage, or trying to keep up with the endless study of political news and political issues?

If you start right out thinking in these terms you will soon apply the rules subconsciously and automatically. Let's consider some examples:

Effective Methods: Anything which brings your candidate, you, or your volunteer, into direct contact with a doorbell of a private home is the best possible campaigning. Nothing should be allowed to interfere with this activity — neither storm, nor sleet, nor dark of night, nor the bland insistence of Very Important Persons. I don't care how important he is; in this country he's only got one vote!

The best doorbell-pushing is done by the candidate himself. Consider a vacuum-cleaner salesman; he shows up at your door with vacuum cleaner, ready to give you a demonstration. Compare him with a mythical salesman who attempts to sell vacuum cleaners with nothing but a sales talk and some pretty pictures — no vacuum cleaner! Which salesman will sell the larger number of vacuum cleaners?

Your candidate is the product you are trying to sell; the easiest way to do this is to let the prospective buyer see the product.

In doing so you gain an enormous advantage over the usual opposition, since the Grass-Roots Campaign has gone out of style in most parts of this country. Most of our citizens actually lay eyes on their officeholders and the hopefuls thereto about as often as they see circus elephants and with the same lack of intimate contact. A man behind the footlights on a platform is a little bit unreal; he might as well be a movie.

But the people, the individual Americans, are still interested in their candidates; to have one show up at the front door is as delightful a novelty to most of them as would be a chance to ride a circus elephant. That unreality, the candidate on the platform, on the billboard, or in the newspaper, suddenly becomes warmly human and a little more than life size.

In addition to being a novelty the presence of the candidate at the door of a private home is a flattering compliment, because it acknowledges the fact that, in this country, sovereignty is vested in the individual, not the state. (The voter may not think in those terms but the idea will be kicking around in the back of his mind. "Here is a man who really seems interested in us ordinary citizens — not like those downtown politicians.")

We can assume that your candidate has at least a moderately pleasing personality; the situation is a pushover. Most laymen will even cross party lines for anyone they have met and have no reason to dislike. The only way the opposition can off-set the advantage is by a personal call by the opposition candidate himself.

Since the ordinary opposition candidate won't do any significant amount of doorbell-pushing and since the extraordinary opposition candidate can only equal the efforts of your candidate here is a way to join a battle in which you need never be defeated. In general the properly organized Grass-Roots Campaign cannot be beaten by any other sort of campaign — and it happens to be ideally suited to the volunteer organization with little or no money.

Have your candidate punch doorbells for three months on a forty-hour week basis. Ration his other campaigning to fall outside the forty-hour week of personal calls and don't let the other activities wear him out, no matter how important they may seem (they aren't!). Inspire your volunteers to the maximum of personal calls their free time and industry will permit. Everything else is incidental. You, as manager, will pick up the loose ends and attend to the unavoidable chores. You also will do some doorbell-pushing, less than the candidate, more than the average precinct worker. You must, or you lose touch with reality and your judgment goes sour.

It is frequently objected that congressional districts have become too large for the candidate to campaign from door to door. This is not true; the more physically difficult it is to cover a district the greater is the advantage to the candidate willing to make the effort of a Grass-Roots Campaign. It is true that extremely large constituencies, such as for governor or president, cannot be covered effectively by the candidate, but in districts no larger than a congressional district the candidate can and should do personal canvassing, even if the district is spread through several counties. There are ways to save his time and make him more efficient, by concentrating on populous districts and by the use of selected lists — the latter is most important; the candidate must never go blindly from door to door. More about that later.

Even in the very largest constituency, the United States as a whole, the same principle applies, at second hand. The astute national chairman tries to know personally every one of his 3,000-odd county chairmen and shakes hands with as many thousands of the precinct workers as possible. When he takes his presidential candidate on a swing around the country he has the candidate do the same thing, so far as possible, even though the newspapers emphasize the speeches and rallies. Practical politics is an unending struggle to turn mass census figures into an endless series of individual, personal contacts.

Let's see what Jonathan Upright can be expected to do against Jack Hopeful. You have him scheduled to spend 500 hours punching doorbells. He should nail down a minimum of 1,000 votes, probably much more, but if he can't average two certain new votes per hour he had better retire to private life. The average paid, professional precinct worker will not deliver more than ten to fifty new votes (votes which would otherwise have stayed at home or voted the other way) no matter how good his ward leader thinks he is. The enthusiastic volunteer is good for at least fifty, if coached and supervised, but probably not more than a hundred and fifty because of time limitations on most amateurs.

The district has a population of more than 300,000 but in the break-down given earlier it was shown that our real interest was in 3,000 selected votes. Thus your candidate will turn out by personal canvassing about one-third of the votes you are after, over and above what accrues from conventional campaigning. He is equal to about forty paid workers, or at least a dozen volunteers and he can get votes that cannot be gotten by any other method.

If this method of campaigning is used, the task of your precinct organization is only that of equalling the efforts of the rival precinct organization — quite a task in itself, but a volunteer can equal an opposing volunteer and exceed a professional. The candidate himself can tip the balance heavily and even make up for deficiencies in your field organization. He is a one-man gang, if you keep him punching doorbells. (Free bonus: Doorbells give immunity from candidatitis — and help to create statesmen!)

Ineffective Methods: In general they are shot-gun methods; take another look at the touchstone rules.

An example — one of your warm supporters calls up, full of enthusiasm. There is, he says, a mammoth Elks Club ball Friday night at the Gigantic Auditorium. There are lots of Elks in the district — he knows, he is an Elk. And this is going to be a big affair, 4,000 tickets sold already. Now here is the angle: The program chairman is a member of our party and he can be persuaded to let the candidate pin the prize on the Queen of the Ball — not strictly political but you can get his name mentioned four or five times over the loud-speaker. The rest of the time the candidate and your eager beaver friend will circulate around meeting people and getting votes. No rule saying you can't talk politics in private conversation. Furthermore (this is the clincher) the rival candidate, Jack Hopeful, will be there — we can't let him get ahead of us, now can we? Your friend will supply the tickets and drive the candidate to and fro; it won't cost a dime and it's a wonderful opportunity to pile up votes. How about it? It's a natural, isn't it?

Your only problem here is how to turn it down

without hurting the feelings of your loyal but unmathematical friend.

The meeting is worthless when compared with the effort it entails. Even if your candidate has no other scheduled date, it is better to let him go to bed early than for him to make an appearance. Here is why:

Four thousand persons present for a meeting held outside the district — Let's apply an arbitrary factor which you will vary to suit your own actual conditions; let's say that 1,000 live in your district. The ages will run from 18 on up; nevertheless the registered voters will not exceed 800 out of the thousand. Four hundred will be of your party (or apply your own registration ratio). That's ten percent of the crowd. If Mr. Upright stirs around all evening he can meet about fifty people — if he spreads himself any thinner he can't be effective. Five of them will be registered in your district and your party; two of them will vote in the primary; one of them would have voted for him in any case; the other is a new vote.

Let the poor fellow stay home and rest. His feet hurt now!

But how about the announcement over the loud speaker? Of the 400 at least half will not listen; of the remaining 200 most of them will either not catch the name or will forget it before the evening is over. The ones who will remember, associate it with a name on a ballot, and be affected thereby, can be counted on the fingers of one thumb.

Speeches made over the radio are usually ineffective except when made by very prominent persons on issues statewide or nationwide in importance. If you can get a popular local news commentator to plug your man, fine! If your organization has a regular program which has been established for some months and you have reliable figures to show that it has a sizable audience, then it is worthwhile to put your man on it.

But don't just buy a radio spot during the campaign and have him make speeches, for he will be talking to himself. Most political programs are simply turned off.

Most meetings held outside the district are useless to the campaign even if they are political rallies. If an appearance seems necessary for diplomatic reasons, send a stuffed shirt to represent your candidate.

Signs are not worth even the cost of printing unless displayed in the district. Again some enthusiastic supporter will urge the merits of display at beaches, race tracks, junctions, and other crowded spots outside the district but which do in fact draw crowds partly from your district. Agree in principle but let him operate on his own; insist that every dime and every piece of display printing is already rationed.

Border-Line Methods: Your district has hundreds of public and semi-public meetings in it during a campaign, most of them non-political. All of them are a possible source of new votes — but an attempt to cover all of them will result only in physical collapse.

Businessmen's luncheon clubs are worth the trouble if they can be fitted into the program. Your man has to eat lunch somewhere; he might as well eat it with the local Kiwanis Club, Rotary Club, or Chamber-of-Commerce group, especially if the custom permits him to be introduced as a candidate, or if he can be permitted to speak for seven or eight minutes on a "non-political" aspect of public affairs. He will pick up a vote or two and lay a foundation for the final campaign.

Women's groups are not worth the trouble during a campaign unless the candidate can make a frankly political appearance and can attend without neglecting more direct campaigning. Usually he can meet more housewives in less time by punching doorbells — and on a much more selective basis.

Some of the new veterans' groups are openly political and show an aggressive intention to do something.

The political directions of the veterans of World War II have not yet shaped up as this is written, but these groups must not be neglected. It appears likely that many of the most active political volunteer workers during the next decade will be young veterans.

I am sorry to note that there are many groups which are usually quite limited in outlook — some of the older veterans' organizations, labor groups, "tax-payers" groups, real estate groups, old-age pension groups, etc. Avoid appearing before such groups unless your candidate and you are honestly in sympathy with the particular special program of the group. I am neither endorsing nor condemning any of these groups, but it is impossible for a rational man to agree with all such groups since there is marked conflict between some of them. There is no need to waste your time going out of your way to make enemies, even if invitations are extended. Active support is only rarely forthcoming from such groups; instead your man will be asked to make flat commitments on a basis of "Whadda yuh going to do for us?"

A politician should make commitments; he should not be a mugwump, or a "know-nothing," but there is no ethical principle requiring him to drive across town for the purpose of refusing to make a commitment.

Many groups hold formal inquisitions for the purpose of examining all candidates to the end of preparing formal slates of endorsed candidates. In my opinion such a sober-minded procedure merits the respect of attendance even when you are reasonably certain of not receiving the endorsement of the group. This is quite different from being put on the spot in front of a crowd made up of a pressure group. The atmosphere of such an examination is usually judicial and urbane; your candidate has an opportunity to build respect for himself as a man even among those opposed to what he stands for, by making direct and honest answers to direct questions. If you ignore such groups as the German-American Bund (or its successors), the Communist Party, and the Ku Klux Klan, the residuum will probably merit your attention.

Many communities have non-partisan forums or study groups intended to increase popular knowledge of public affairs. They are not the source of many direct votes but are excellent places to meet and obtain the services of new volunteer workers among the serious, public-spirited persons who attend, as well as being worthy of support in principle.

Many political meetings are not worth much effort even when held in your own district. Let the candidate attend such if his budgeted time and strength permit, otherwise attend them yourself or send a representative to speak briefly and to explain that the candidate can't be two places at one time. (It is not necessary to say that he is home in bed!) But your candidate should show up at as many political meetings as can be fitted into the more important direct campaigning. His appearance can be as short as ten minutes, then to another meeting, or home and early to bed.

The use of signs, the distribution of literature, and the place of newspapers will be discussed under "Publicity." These media are distinctly border-line; there are more ways to waste money using them than there are to get votes.

The Campaign Committee: You will have two campaign committees, the public or propaganda-purpose committee and the private or working committee; the first includes the second. The public committee will be as large as possible and will include everyone you can persuade to sign a card or a list which says, "I take pride in publicly endorsing the candidacy of Jonathan Upright for Congress," or some such, but does not say "and authorize the use of my name for advertising purposes" — or people won't sign it. You then use the list for advertising purposes anyhow for the suggested phrasing gives consent. The signers won't mind — it's just that the other phraseology looks too much like a contract. Or you might say, "I take pleasure in serving on the campaign committee of — " with the explanation that the statement carries no explicit duties.

(Once in a while some person who carries water on both shoulders will sign the endorsements of two competing candidates. It eventually causes him embarrassment; he will call up and demand that you destroy, for example, your entire stock of stationery. He may threaten legal action. If you hold his signed endorsement, brush him off. "We can't do that, old man, unless you are willing to pay for printing the new lot. No, really — tell you what — we'll draw a line through your name in red ink and mark it, 'Renegged.' How would that do?" Don't help him out of his hole and don't surrender his signed statement.)

This list of endorsers, the "committee," will be spread across the top, down the side, and eventually all over the back of your campaign stationery, and you may use it in display advertising. A personal endorsement from almost anyone is likely to drag in another vote or two. You may decide to suppress some names when you know that the persons concerned have numerous enemies and very few friends. This is legitimate; you have not contracted to use the names.

If caught out, I would take refuge in a social fib. "Your name isn't on the list? It must have been skipped when the list was copied for the printer. It's too late to add it, I'm afraid — that printing bill was $26. But I certainly will tell Mr. Upright that you wanted your name on his committee."

Follow your own conscience. My own will stand a few polite evasions when another person's feelings can be saved without damage to anyone.

The public committee will be headed by officers

whose duties are nominal unless they serve in the same
capacity on the working committee. These *de facto*
honorary officers should be selected to be as broadly
representative as possible and for maximum prestige.
The following set-up would be ideal for the typical
American community:

The Citizen's Committee for the Honorable Jonathan
Upright, Candidate for Congress, Umpteenth District
> Dr. Colin MacDonald, Chairman
> Francis X. O'Toole, Secretary
> Isadore Weinstein, Treasurer
> Muriel T. Busybody, Field Director
>   telephone Grant 0361

Mrs. Busybody (yourself) is the only working member of this list, although the others are all loyal
supporters. The names have been selected by you as
being conspicuously Protestant, Catholic, and Jewish.
For maximum effect each gentleman should be very
prominent, and highly respected in the community by
all groups. If Dr. MacDonald is a prominent Pres-
byterian and Mason and a stylish physician noted for
his charities, Mr. O'Toole a distinguished lawyer and an
active Knight of Columbus, and Mr. Weinstein both a
Scout commissioner and well known in B'nai B'rith,
then your cup runneth over.

Special offices can be devised to permit other prestige names to stand out — chairman women's division,
vice-chairman, director speakers' bureau, public relations, liaison, chairman finance committee, chairmen
for various small communities in the district, director of
research, chairman study groups, etc., without end.

It is advisable to list the rest of the committee in strict
alphabetical order to avoid hurt feelings.

There is no reason why any of these prestige officers
should not be active campaign executives. It is some-

times possible to get a busy, able person actively into the campaign by getting him first to agree to letting his name appear at the top of the letterhead, then calling him into war councils.

The working committee consists of the following — by any titles: Candidate, manager, money raiser, publicity person, office girl, field supervisors, and precinct workers. Some of these people will double in brass and all of them should do some precinct work, in order to keep their roots down. The office girl and publicity person may be paid professionals — they certainly must be professionally skilled and experienced whether they are paid or not. There is no need for anyone else in the campaign to be paid anything.

The best place for members of the candidate's family on the committee is the chairman of South America and the Eastern Hemisphere. The candidate may need and want a member of his family as a confidential secretary and this may be tolerated, but relatives of candidates are subject to an even more virulent form of candidatitis than are candidates — it is very discouraging to have to drop real campaigning in order to go around patching up gaps in your fences left by unpolitic relatives of your white hope.

Headquarters: It does not matter in the least whether you have swank offices or good equipment; the voting public will neither know nor care. A telephone call from a private phone in a modest home sounds just the same as one coming through a switchboard in a suite of fancy offices. You need a typewriter, file boxes for 3 x 5 cards (shoeboxes will do), a cheap letter file, a two-bit scrap book, the use (not the ownership) of a duplicating machine, a telephone which is not in reach of the casual dropper-in — and nothing else — nothing! Use furniture at hand, or improvise it out of scrap wood. Place the headquarters in any heated, rent-free space, your own spare bedroom, somebody's rumpus room, or a donated second-rate office over a store building.

Campaigns customarily have public offices fronting on commercial streets. The usefulness of such so-called headquarters is questionable; the vote-getting power is not better than border line. If you can get an empty store building, or space in an occupied store belonging to a supporter, and in either case absolutely rent-free and if you can get someone to remain in such donated space to answer questions and hand out literature on an unpaid but faithful basis and if such person is unable or totally unwilling to do precinct work instead, it is then worthwhile to invest in signs and printing to advertise the campaign by advertising the space as a "headquarters." Otherwise it is better to wait until the final campaign when such space is more readily available for the entire ticket.

There are distinct advantages in not having public offices and in avoiding a swank, expensive appearance. Your campaign can be well advanced, almost unbeatable, before the opposition realizes that you are a serious threat. A Grass-Roots Campaign can be as silently insidious as cancer, as long as it doesn't look like much in the early stages. And if your offices are not expensive and comfortable you will be less bothered by the chap with his hand out and by the Headquarters Hound. The latter is a practically harmless but ubiquitous lower life form which clutters up political offices, occupying chairs, taking up working time, sounding off, and absorbing anything that is free, from ice water to signs. He is related to Sunday morning quarterbacks and arm-chair generals.

If your headquarters is not in a private home, make sure that the only available telephone is a pay phone, or, if that cannot be obtained, put a lock on the telephone and take extreme precautions with the key, as well as establishing the practice of logging all outgoing calls and obtaining the charges, if a toll call, from the operator. (This will be regarded as outright tyranny by the Headquarters Hound, but it is utterly necessary if you are to avoid incredibly large deficits.)

The telephone bills that can be incurred by an open telephone in a political office must be experienced to be believed. They are not necessary; the legitimate outgoing calls which cannot be made over private, unlimited phones are very few. The best arrangement is the pay phone and a petty cash account, locked up with the stamps, and for which the office girl is responsible.

After taking such precautions, you may then, and should, make free use of the telephone. *Your* business will not bankrupt the committee.

An extension wired only for incoming calls may be added to a pay phone and placed on the desk of the office girl.

The campaign funds should be kept in a bank account as the funds of an unincorporated, non-profit society. A respected group of three, none of whom have control over the funds, should be appointed to keep a running audit. The checks should require two signatures, that of the manager and either one of two others, let us say the campaign chairman and the chairman of the finance committee. The candidate should not sign checks, though he may reasonably insist on a veto as a condition of running — but let us hope not.

The following categories of expense cannot be avoided:

- Filing fee
- Printing
- Postage
- Telephone tolls
- Refreshments for the election night
  party for the workers

The following categories of expense are not indispensable but a strong campaign will include some and possibly all of them:

- Signboard rental
- Newspaper display advertising
- Professional distribution of literature
- Publicity person's salary
- Office girl's salary
- Lunch money and gasoline or
  carfare money for volunteers
- Radio spot plugs
- Candidate's extra *political* expenses
- Manager's extra *political* expenses

Some of the expenses in the second list can be avoided by astute management, not by eliminating the type of campaigning indicated, but by getting what is needed free. An able, professional publicity person on at least a part-time basis is a *sine qua non*; if a volunteer supporter in this professional category cannot be found then one must be hired. If a volunteer typist, completely reliable and reasonably efficient, cannot be found, then she must be hired — but a volunteer is better.

The other conditional expenses depend on local conditions. Form the habit of being extremely tight-fisted about expenses in both lists of categories, necessary and conditional.

There are many other types of political expenditure; you are sure to have many well-meaning advisers who will assure you from experience that this or that must be done, which does not fall under one of the above headings. I believe that you will find in every case that the recommendation comes from experience with some other type of campaigning than the volunteer, Grass-Roots Campaign. There *are* other types of campaigning — I have expended more than thirty thousand dollars (not my own money!) on a single campaign issue in less than thirty days — but no type of campaigning is as effective as the type here described and this type is almost without expense. The expenses are all *incidental to the campaigning* and are not properly part of the campaigning at all *in this type of campaign*.

This is literally a case of "The Best Things in Life Are Free." It is easy to run a campaign with lots of money, but an expensive campaign can always be beaten by a properly organized campaign which can barely pay for printing and postage.

In addition to a headquarters or intelligence center of some sort both the candidate and the manager need some sort of hideaway — two hideaways if the manager and candidate are of different sexes, to keep tongues from wagging. A spare room in the home of a friend is ideal, particularly if it is served by a phone through which messages can be left without waking the person who is resting. There will come times when an afternoon nap, or at least complete freedom from pressure, is necessary to preserve your balance, your judgment, or even your sanity.

A remote back room in the building which houses the office will do. Don't try to use your own home for this.

Precinct Organization — Training and Management: We assumed that the precinct organization had been built up through earlier club organization; that includes the assumption for a congressional campaign that the volunteer field organization is too numerous to be managed directly by the manager. Ten is about the highest number which can be managed directly; you want and need a hundred. Therefore you will have area managers.

Talent is where you find it. The neat divisions you draw up on a precinct map can never be realized in practice for you will never have enough competent leaders to whom you can delegate authority. Many of your area leaders will be no more than messenger boys between you and the precinct worker.

To make your contact with the precinct worker as direct as possible hold weekly get-togethers with all the organizations at a fixed time and a centrally located place. Serve coffee and doughnuts. See to it that the candidate has this as an all-evening "must" date; your purpose is not only to instruct and inform your workers — and to gain information from them — but to renew their enthusiasm by direct social contact with the man they are backing. Make it as informal as possible — no lined up chairs, no standing to speak — a family party.

Another fixed weekly date which can precede or follow this one, or be held on another night, is the meeting of the working committee, for strategy, tactics, and business. It is a must for you, but not necessarily for the candidate.

The volunteer precinct workers are by far the most valuable asset of your campaign and the one most difficult to get and keep. They are not merely the rosters of your clubs nor are they a list of people who have pledged themselves to "work one precinct." No such wooden approach creates a precinct organization.

You will have winnowed out, from hundreds of political contacts made during two to four years of apprenticeship, a list of people who will back their convictions by *work* rather than by talk alone. Each time you find one you will treasure him (or her) and train him and encourage him, with loving care.

Don't expect to find the majority of them *after* you decide to manage a campaign. Some candidates and some managers seem to think that precinct workers grow on trees! If you have not already built up a following of people who believe in you, look to you for political leadership, and will *work*, then you are not yet ready to tackle anything as difficult as the management of a congressional-sized campaign. You are still in the junior-officer stage of your political career.

Even if you never have the time or the circumstances

which will permit you to undertake the management of a major campaign this chapter is still for you. The principles discussed apply to the minor leader in a campaign quite as much as to the manager, and, as a minor leader, you can help to keep the manager on the right track by your counsel. In so doing you can be the factor which turns defeat into victory, as many a manager is energetic and intelligent but inexperienced.

The volunteer precinct organization is never as perfect — on paper — as the paid organization of a political machine. But you can reasonably hope to have one good enough to swing an election.

"The moral is to the physical in war as three is to one." — Napoleon.

Napoleon was a piker. The principal advantage of the volunteer over the paid machine professional is his sincere enthusiasm. In politics the ratio expressed by Napoleon is nearer ten to one. The volunteer is campaigning twenty-four hours a day, not by intent, but because he can't help it. It gets in his blood. He is the guerilla warrior of politics, acting on his own initiative, harrying and demoralizing a force much larger, and arousing a despairing citizenry to new hope. Like the guerilla, he fights with the materials at hand and improvises what he lacks.

It is your object to inspire and direct this enthusiasm.

Leadership is not an esoteric matter. You don't need the whoop-t'do "enthusiasm" of a night club master-of-ceremonies, a revivalist, or a radio announcer. You need two qualities only, sincerity and a willingness to work. The rest you will learn, in a fashion suited to your temperament. (A sort of leadership by default can come to those who lack sincerity but are energetic, since a group will accept any leadership in preference to none.)

As a leader of political volunteers there is just one paramount rule to keep in mind:

Men do not live by bread along.

The personal pat on the back, the public praise for work well done, a button to wear on the lapel, the testimonial dinner, the letter of thanks, the election night party, a personal word with the candidate — these things are worth much more than cash or patronage. Unless he is actually starving, a man — any man and all men — is motivated primarily by "face," by intangibles of some sort which have to do with behaving in that fashion which he feels does credit to his own conception of what he is, or what he would like to be.

You may not like the term "face" — if so, don't use it — but I think you will find that *all* human motivation other than the simplest animal aspects of belly hunger, sexual rut, and physical fear can be found in a need for intangibles which will satisfy the individual's ideal conception of himself — and even hunger, rut, and fear are feeble in comparison, else soldiers would not fight, rape would be as common as shaking hands, and dinner guests would fall on their food and rend it. Even the dollar is pursued more usually for this higher reason than for the simple reason of filling the belly — to do one's duty to the wife and kids, to provide for the education of children, to live in a finer house, or simply to feel successful because one's labors command a high price. These goals are all intangibles, no matter how concrete is the symbol for the goal.

In politics this strongest of all human forces is tapped most easily by the pat on the back, in its various forms. Most people in this country like to think of themselves as "good citizens"' they have been brought up to consider it one of the important intangibles. You can convert this yearning into doorbell-punching by public and private acknowledgement that precinct work is the highest expression of good citizenship. (It probably is!)

Let everyone know at all times that no other political work carries as much honor and prestige. Be emphatic that the precinct workers are the royalty of organization, the other types of workers — office workers, speakers, and such — only the nobility, and campaign contributors merely the gentry. *Never* let a mere contributor of money have a vote in policy; don't even pay as much attention to his advice as you do to that of the least of the precinct workers — the precinct worker knows what he is talking about, in his neighborhood; the cash contributor is merely theorizing.

You might organize your field workers into a Doorbell Club and call the weekly get-togethers its meetings. Make precinct work a mandatory qualification for membership. (You have a wheel-chair cripple who should be a member; very well — let him work a precinct by telephone, but make him qualify.) Get off a few remarks at each meeting along this line: "This is a closed corporation and the only way in is by pushing doorbells. John D. Rockefeller himself can't come in that door, not with a ten thousand dollar contribution in hand, unless he can prove that he has worked in his precinct."

Your exclusion-act may antagonize some persons who are useful otherwise but who can't or won't do canvassing, but it is better to let them fall by the wayside in order to protect the morale and enhance the prestige of the field workers.

If you build up such a special club, you will not only win for Mr. Upright, you will make yourself the unquestioned boss of the district. The canny politicians will quickly recognize that you possess the *only* political power in the district; they will come to you for the yea-and-nay. You will not neglect the public clubs you have helped found or been active in, however; they then will become the feeder organizations for your campaign shock troops.

Mr. Upright is a member of the club, since you have him punching doorbells. Don't let him miss attendance at a meeting, or even part of a meeting, not even though the governor or the national chairman wants to see him that night, or your vote-getting will take a sudden slump. On the other hand, if he is home sick in bed you can use it to inspire more work.

The methods of precinct work have been indicated by examples in an earlier chapter. You will have to train them in it, since most people get stage fright at the idea. There are many right ways to do it and you will learn your own as well as the types I have given — but keep it simple!

The hardest hurdle is the opening remark when the occupant answers the door. The next hardest is the second remark in answer to the householder's reply, a reply which will follow one of about a dozen stock forms. if your worker can get past this point the rest is easy for any of us chattering simians. It is therefore worthwhile to type out and mimeo some stock phrases:

Opening Remarks

"How do you do — Mrs. Crotchet? I'm a neighbor of yours, Thomas (or Mabel) Friendly, and I'm calling on you to ask you to support Jonathan Upright in the primary next month."

"Good morning. I'm Tom Friendly, Mrs. Crotchet. We're supporting Mr. Upright for the party nomination and I'd like to tell you something about him and try to get your support, too."

"How do you do? Am I speaking to Mrs. Crotchet? Mrs. Crotchet, I am one of your neighbors, Mrs. Thomas Friendly. If you can spare me a moment I would like to tell you about a citizen's committee we have formed to try to improve the representation in Congress for this district."

Replies and Answers

("I'm for Jack Hopeful.") "So? Well, I understand he is a fine man. We're in the same party, at least — if your candidate wins the nomination, Mr. Upright is pledged to support him and campaign for him . . . and so will I." This is followed by a quick retreat, or an invitation to attend local club party meetings, depending on the response.

("Those people have moved and we belong to the other party.") "Oh, I'm sorry to have bothered you! Well, be sure to vote in any case. Mr. Upright says that if we all turn out and vote our convictions it won't matter whether Upright is elected, or Upright is defeated — the country will be in safe hands." (Note the triple mention of Upright's name in a statement which urges her to vote the other way.)

("How much do you people get paid for this sort of thing?") "Oh, we don't get paid anything! This is entirely a spontaneous effort of some of the voters. We organized it and, instead of getting paid, we pay for our own printing and hall rent and so forth by passing the hat among ourselves. We think that's the only way we can have honest government."

("I'm too busy to talk to you.") "Oh, I am sorry that I bothered you! May I leave this with you and then come back at a more convenient time? We know you folks take the trouble to vote in the primaries so we would like a chance for you to get to know Mr. Upright — your opinion is worth something."

("Oh, I never vote except in the *main* election.") (Frankly, this idiot is hopeless — however) "Oh, if you wait till fall you don't get any *real* chance to make a choice. The primary is *very* important this year — if we sent a car around to pick you up, would you make an exception? We need you."

("I intend to vote for Mr. Upright.") "Fine. It cheers me up to hear a person say that. Here is some literature about him — maybe some of your friends would like to see it. By the way, Mr. Upright is speaking at our local club next Friday night. Could I drop by and take you with me?"

*   *   *

The field workers will teach each other, through shop talk; from that shop talk you will get better examples than I can give, examples tailored to your campaign and your community.

One of the easiest ways to train a precinct worker is to send him out with an experienced one for a single afternoon or evening. You can teach a group at a time by acting out the type cases, using two experienced workers in an amplified version of the type cases given herein. Do it two ways — the right way and the wrong way — and you have the basis for an amusing club program. The wrong ways can be made very funny by persons of moderate dramatic talent — Joe Roughly arrives smoking a cigarette, knocks and rings alternately until he wakes the householder or drags her out of her bath, sticks a foot in the door, gets into an argument, and so forth without end.

I venture to predict that, with the recent enormous strides in visual-aid training, both major parties will soon have 16-mm. sound pictures available for the use of local clubs covering the above. If such pictures are supervised by persons intimately acquainted with the problems of the closed door, then they should be very useful; otherwise — hmmm! Better taste before you serve.

Get them in the habit of using the 3 x 5 card. Have a supply at the meetings with a notice that invites them to place a dime in the saucer for each pack or to take them free if they wish. Show them your own files. Emphasize that the usefulness of their work depends almost entirely on whether or not they have records on election day of where the vote is.

Your area managers may show so much talent that they will crowd you and inspire you into better work yourself; however some of them will simply be message points, persons you can telephone and who in turn will telephone their several workers or whom you can call on to pick up campaign material from the head-quarters for redistribution to the individual workers. In either case the area supervisor must be a person who works in at least one precinct. Otherwise he does not know the field problems and will botch things for you.

But there is another reason why everyone from the candidate up through the whole organization to the single precinct worker should do canvassing: The U.S. Army, shortly before World War II, added some 30% to its fire power by arming with rifles or carbines all of the non-coms and officers up to major. The same result is obtainable in a campaign organization — I have seen more than one campaign in which there were so many supervisory jobs, special jobs, and headquarters jobs that there were no doorbell pushers; then they wondered why they lost!

This is a complete reversal of opinion on my part, brought on by experience. In my first campaign I used to quote Poor Richard: "The overseer's eyes are worth more than his hands." In politics it should be rephrased, "The overseer's example is worth more than his precept — and it opens his eyes wider and gets votes in the bargain!"

Your publicity man should ring some doorbells in the district to sample the flavor — but he probably won't, whether he is paid or unpaid. Still . . . he can't shoot you for suggesting it.

If your office girl pushes a few doorbells in the evening she will understand the campaign better, but you will be happy enough if she has a civil tongue, a tight lip, and an ability to not lose track of the details.

How to Get a Selected List from which to Punch Doorbells: Your district has 320,000 residents lodged behind some 100,000 private doorways. It is most unlikely that you will have enough people to punch every doorbell. However there are only 70,000 members of our party in the district and only 25,000 of these may be expected to vote in the primary. They live in some 15,000 separate homes (this is based on statistical examination and is not a casual speculation). The problem is beginning to be cut down to your size; if you know which 15,000 doorbells in your district, 100 precinct workers plus one tireless candidate plus one manager could ring every doorbell.

Fortunately there are ways to determine with reasonable exactness which doorbells are worth ringing.

The adults in the United States fall into three groups, those who vote in primaries, those who vote in general elections, and those who don't vote at all. (The membership of the groups and the ratios between them vary slightly if city elections are considered rather than elections for state and national offices; this need not concern us at the moment as the principle is unchanged.)

The key to the matter is that these groups, though fuzzy around the edges, remain very largely the same from year to year, i.e., the citizens who vote in any one primary are almost certain to vote in every primary, circumstances permitting.

In many or most states it is customary to post outside the polls a roster of the registered voters with a check mark to show whether or not each person voted and to leave this record published for about a week after each primary or election. It is then possible to obtain the basic list you need by copying data from these lists. This is tedious and piecemeal; there is usually a better way. All states (I believe) require a voter to "sign the book." These books are returned to the registrar of voters, the city clerk, or other official charged with the custody of election records. There they remain for a period of time, depending on local law or custom, as they may be required as evidence.

You are probably entitled by your state laws to

examine these records. Whether you are or not, the way to get the use of them is to find out where they are, who has the power to let you see them, and apply to that person, a smile on your face and friendliness in your voice, for permission to see them. Ask it as a favor, not a right.

Two persons, one reading the signatures and the other making check marks on precinct lines, can get the basic list of the primary voters in a political party by this method for an entire congressional district in two to four days. The results are then transferred to alphabetical files, precinct files, and elsewhere as needed. This work needs to be done before the campaign opens and is one of the many reasons why campaigns are won between elections, not during the public campaign season.

You will need precinct lists of course. You need three or four sets of precinct lists for your entire district; such sets may be rather expensive. It is often possible to obtain free sets from the same official who let you see the election books. Otherwise you must purchase them from the contract printer.

Usually the simplest way to get anything is to find out who has it, then go directly to that person and ask him, in a pleasant tone of voice, to give it to you — free. This applies in all fields with all things, from a match to a million-dollar endowment, but it is unusually important in politics. If you use this rule you may miss on free precinct lists but you will make it up on free hall rent, free newspaper advertising, free printing, or free signboards.

When you have your basic list of persons who vote in your primary, the candidate and each precinct worker will work from it. The candidate will use no other; the precinct workers will call first on the persons listed — about thirty evenings of work for each under our assumptions — and will call on others only if they have time for it.

The precinct worker is constantly revising his card file as he works, throwing away cards of persons who have moved and adding the newcomers, as he discovers them. In addition to newcomers discovered through his calls he should make an effort to find it out when persons move into the neighborhood. The postman could give him this information quite accurately but the postal regulations are a little stuffy about employees giving out data about people. Instead he can cultivate the neighborhood cop, the milkman, and the boys who deliver newspapers and groceries. Real estate offices and moving and storage concerns can be made sources of these vital statistics. A precinct worker who is on the job can, without very much effort at any one time, know quite accurately what vote is to be expected in his primary, how it may be expected to go, what individuals by name may be counted on to vote for your man, which ones of these will get to the polls under their own power, and what ones must be carried.

The handful of cards you hand him to start with, made up from the election books, make him the equal of almost any professional ward heeler, right from scratch. You have cut it down to the size a part-time volunteer can handle.

A volunteer organization is bound to be spotty; some precincts will have no volunteers. Don't try to transfer workers from other precincts, except on election day. Let the candidate work the precincts that have no workers, concentrating on the more densely populated. He will get more votes than a precinct worker could out of the same number of calls and he stands the best chance of turning up new workers. On election day regroup and bring in the votes he has cinched, even if it means spreading your forces very thin.

• CHAPTER IX

How to Win an Election (continued)

Landmarks and Booby Traps

Don't expect a volunteer organization to make blanket distribution of political literature as the time used can be turned to better account making calls. If you decide that you can afford the shot-gun method of blanket coverage, use paid professionals. Sometimes a tie-in can be made with some other distribution such as a community newspaper or an advertising throw-away at a very low cost.

You will have many marginal volunteer workers who won't or can't do precinct work. Put 'em to work! There is an endless amount of routine clerical work in a campaign, licking stamps, addressing envelopes, copying files, preparing telephone lists for election day, etc. Be a slave driver. If you blandly assume that they want to work and keep loading it on them, they will get to work, or get out and leave you alone.

Many people will telephone and ask that the candidate, or you if the candidate is not available, come to see them. No matter how sweet they talk most of them have their hands out for jobs or money. Be most pleasant but do not call on them and do not let the candidate call on them. Insist firmly that pressure of time does not permit and suggest instead that they come to see you. Most of them won't come; you gain thereby in, I believe, every case.

The Big Operator will show up. He is a Very Good Friend of Judge So-and-So and he knows Governor Whosis personally — practically elected him. The candidate has every confidence in him, he wants you to understand, and he is going to pitch in and Make Things Hum.

He wants a desk, he wants a secretary, he wants a telephone. He will be patronizing about your methods and your budget is Simply Out of the Question — if you are careless enough to let him see it.

Oh well — put him to work. Let him lick stamps, or something equally dull. He will leave presently and complain to the candidate. You may have your only real row with the candidate over this; the Big Operator may in fact be an old friend and one in whom the candidate has much confidence. But make it plain to the candidate that this guy must raise his own funds, hire his own offices, and locate his own workers if he is to be part of the campaign — otherwise you quit. You committed yourself to serve as manager, with full authority, and in no other capacity; the candidate agreed to that. If he does not have confidence in your judgment, your resignation is available.

You won't be fired. Later you will hear that this bargain-counter Boss Tweed is letting it be known all over town that poor old Upright is heading for a sad fall since he has chosen to trust his career to the amateurish hands of That Fool Woman. This is good; it lulls the opposition without interfering with your work.

There will be the crackpot, the confirmed trouble maker, and the tired liberal. The first two need no description — give them the bum's rush in any way you can. The last, like Mrs. Much-Married, has been there so often the thrill is gone. He knows the frailty of human nature — and that's all he knows. He would like to see you win — but you won't, you know. Anyhow does it make any real difference? Upright is a fine man and he is glad to do what he can for him, welcoming people at headquarters, and lending the benefit of his advice and experience — just to help out Old Pal Upright.

Use the stamp-licking routine on him. After a bit he will go back to his ivory tower and let the grown-ups get on with the work.

You are going to get sick of it. Not only will your patience be worn thin by the volunteer who will do anything except work, you will be driven to distraction by the arrogance of pressure groups, made heartsick by the outright sell-out, and astonished and hurt by dirty tricks ranging from torn-down signs to the complete lie, the planted scandal, and the falsified document.

But keep your temper and stay cheerful. The troubles will be more than off-set by the priceless privilege of close association with the loyal and untiring. Even if you lose, this alone will make it all worthwhile.

Publicity: You must have professional help if it can possibly be obtained. Publicity is an involved profession; even if I understood all about it, which I don't, this whole book could be devoted to it without considering all the angles.

If you are forced to work without a publicity man, a few rules of thumb may save you from some of the more gross errors.

Use just one picture of your candidate and make it a trademark. Don't let Mr. Upright nor his wife do the picking; get a group consensus on effectiveness, not beauty nor accuracy of likeness. Make one cut serve as far as possible. A 50-line screen is about top for newsprint paper; slick paper can stand as high as 90 lines.

Small newspapers can use pulp mats from the cut. They are cheap.

All other things being equal, use the union bug on all

your printing including your stationery and your candidate's cards. If non-union printing can be obtained as a donation, consider the probable effect in your district as well as the political beliefs of your candidate. If you believe in unionism the matter is settled automatically, of course.

The large, or 24-sheet, signboards are associated in the public mind with heavy campaign contributions and slush funds. In fact they are not very expensive but the overtone of graft is against them. Outdoor advertising companies also rent small boards, 6-sheet and 3-sheet, which are less expensive and more effective. Even the most pinch-penny campaign can usually afford a good coverage of these smaller boards for the last month of the campaign. You don't need them earlier.

There is an optical illusion, which I do not understand, but which calls for using a much smaller proportional amount of blank area on a signboard than one uses on a printed page or ad. The lay-out which looks perfect when you prepare it in miniature looks strangely anemic on a signboard. Use larger letters and fill up more of the blank. Better yet, get it done professionally.

Don't try to say much on a sign. Make it brief, then make it briefer.

Never mention your opponent's name on signboards, in ads, nor in literature. Train your workers never to mention him by name — call him the opposition candidate if forced to refer to him at all. Don't let Mr. Upright speak his name, even when referring to him.

If your district is large and has a low-powered radio station with a good local following you may want to hire spot plugs, to be scattered through the day's programs. Make them short — five to ten seconds — and have several different wordings, all simple. Careful phrasing will permit you to use Mr. Upright's name three times in a ten-second plug. Here is a rather inane example:

"Attention, please — a message from Jonathan Upright. Mr. Upright urges you to vote in the primary next Tuesday — the Jonathan Upright for Congress Citizen's Committee."

Don't make them so frequent as to annoy.

The primary purpose of all political publicity is not to persuade but to fix the name and the office in the subconscious by repetition and, secondly, to let your friends know that they are not alone — to encourage them. The use of signboards and radio plugs does very little in direct vote-getting, but it does let your friends know that there is a campaign going on. They see the signs, they hear the plugs, and it warms their hearts. They say to themselves, whether they be workers or simply voters who are willing to support your man, "Well — *this* looks like action: Maybe we got a chance."

It isn't action, save for a few who will climb on anything that looks like a bandwagon, but enough display advertising to put on a brave front is necessary in the latter part of any campaign — to warm cold feet.

The purchase of display advertising has a marked effect on what publicity stories a newspaper will run for your candidate, even with most of the large metropolitan dailies. With the small, local papers which publish once or twice a week the customary rule is an inch for an inch, advertising *versus* publicity story. A friendly editor of such a small paper may give you the ad free, provided you will keep it to yourself so as not to jeopardize his revenue from other candidates.

Editors and staff men will help you with lay-outs and with the wording of your publicity stories, even if they don't back your man, if you will ask for help and show that you don't think you know it all. "Frankly, it stinks," should be music to your ears; you are about to receive some practical professional advice, free.

People like and respect persons they have helped; it's more common than gratitude.

Large display ads in small newspapers may be a cheaper way of getting full coverage than the blanket distribution of literature. By "large" I mean up to two columns, half a page high. If you have more money, repeat the dose rather than increasing the size.

Try to split your advertising budget among all your district editors unless a paper is actively against you. Even then it may be wise to use it if it offers the only means of reaching some area.

Newspaper ads can eat you out of house and home. The political effect of newspapers is problematical and is much less than the newspapermen think. Remember that Mr. Roosevelt won four times with about 90% of the press against him. Remember that, even if you are a Republican, and don't be stampeded into building your campaign around newspapers. A strong newspaper campaign can make you think you are winning when you are actually taking a severe licking. (See *Sampling a District* below.) You can win with every paper in your district against you.

The automobile sticker is good because it constitutes a personal endorsement and is cheap. Even better, and still in the economy class, is the bumper strip sign for automobiles. They can be homemade — there is a silk-screen stencil process which you can learn from any sign maker. The printed ones are cheap, however, and come with tin strips to fasten them to the bumpers. Home-made ones may be attached with large rubber bands or with string. They make a brave display and are read by everyone who sees them — which is not true of stationary signs. Your precinct workers, at least, should carry such signs, fore and aft, on their automobiles.

One-sheets, half-cards, and quarter-cards can be tacked up all over the district by your precinct workers without slowing up their doorbell-pushing. There are frequently local post-no-bills ordinances but they are rarely enforced.

But get a publicity man if you can, even on a part-time basis, or a cash-for-results basis.

Liaison and Party Harmony: In the primary campaign your opposition is Jack Hopeful, a member of your own party. Never forget that you will need the support of *all* your party after the primary *and never let your supporters forget it*!

This is a very touchy, difficult matter, particularly in a volunteer organization. You are certain to have loyal supporters who are simple souls, unable to think in terms other than black and white. To them Jack Hopeful is the ENEMY — they will commit excesses through misguided zeal. So also will some of Mr. Hopeful's supporters. Bad blood breeds more bad blood; in short order you can have a situation which is completely out of hand, which splits the party wide open, and which will render it impossible for your man to win in the finals.

Since the nomination is valueless in itself, being merely a necessary means to an end, you must prevent this at all costs.

You can start out with the best of intentions, determined to run your own race, to keep it clean, and to ignore the Hopeful campaign. Then comes the day when some signs are torn down, or there is some bad-mannered heckling at a meeting, and your more hot-headed supporters will go galloping off the reservation, bent on triple revenge. They can ruin all your good work in twenty-four hours, in the sincere misapprehension that they are thereby campaigning for Mr. Upright.

Even if Jack Hopeful is a bit of a heel, even if he is personally responsible for the dirty tricks (which is most unlikely!), you must try to prevent retaliation in kind. As a matter of fact the signs may have been torn down by the opposition party, rather than Hopeful's crew. It is even possible that the opposition party has paid *agents provocateurs* in both your group and

Hopeful's, with instructions to create party dissension by any means.

I know of two effective and sufficient methods — you will find others. Let Mr. Upright and yourself tell your supporters repeatedly that you intend to support Mr. Hopeful and the whole party ticket, if Mr. Hopeful is nominated. Base it on the idea that the whole democratic process consists in struggles for domination in which the majority decision is accepted amicably, the ranks are closed, and the new and larger groups move onto larger struggles. Therefore your opponents of today are your allies of tomorrow, against a common enemy. Mention that if Mr. Upright goes to Congress, he will have to work with congressmen of both parties for the welfare of the country as a whole.

Nothing is more destructive of democratic institutions than implacable hatred between factions.

The English have a good term; they speak of "His Majesty's Loyal Opposition," recognizing thereby that opposition has a constructive function and need not be ill tempered.

A more positive step can be taken under the safe rule that it is very hard to dislike any man you know well, unless he is that rare thing, an unmitigated scoundrel. The primary campaign period is a good time for party-wide social events.

Dances are good; breakfasts, luncheons, and dinners are even better and less trouble to arrange. In your district there will be restaurants with banquet halls of all sizes. The usual proprietor will be willing to serve groups meals without selling tickets ahead of time and with the understanding that he will collect from each just as he does with the run of customers, provided you can give him some idea of how many may be expected. Local knowledge should enable you to do this.

(Don't forget to see to it that a saucer is passed around for tips; otherwise the waitresses will be forgotten. To forget them is bad politics as well as bad morals.)

In a district in which I was once active we used to meet for breakfast Sunday morning at ten o'clock, monthly year in and year out, more frequently as elections approached. The county committeemen used to make the arrangements, though the custom was started by lay members who saw the need of party-wide liaison. (Party harmony makes a fine hobby for anyone. "Blessed is the peacemaker — " for he shall see his party triumph in November!)

We picked Sunday morning because that was the only date satisfactory to practically everyone — you will find it so. The Catholics went to mass before the breakfast; the Jews held their services on Friday evening in any case; the regular church-goers among the Protestants missed one morning service per month which they could make up that evening if so minded. Nobody seemed to feel that the Sabbath was being broken; there is excellent precedent in any case. See *Luke VI-9*.

During primary campaign periods a clever chairman of such a gathering will see to it that those present do not gather in cliques. "The purpose of this meeting is to get acquainted, not to huddle up with your same old crowd. I seem to see the Shannon crowd all together down at the end and up here the whole Weiss campaign committee seems to be staked out. Break it up, boys and girls! Let's find out how the other half lives. Hey — you, Joe — swap places with Mrs. Ross. Take your plates and glasses with you. Bert — gimme a hand. Tag about every other one of your boys down there and make 'em move."

They'll move and they'll like it. It is very hard to stay mad at a man when you have eaten with him and swapped anecdotes.

My wife was once a necessary factor in electing a governor; her weapons were a cookie gun — one of those aluminum gadgets which make fancy, patterned tea cakes, an eighth of a pound of tea per week, and a supply of pseudo-engraved invitations to Sunday afternoon tea. The refreshments were just props; the guests averaged a little over a cup of tea apiece and two or three tiny cookies.

The effect on the gubernatorial election was an accidental dividend; our original purpose had been only to preserve harmony in our own rather small district. But the key personnel of the major rival gubernatorial candidates for the party nomination met socially in our living room several times — and found out that the other fellow wasn't so bad, after all.

It happened that the campaign we were directly interested in failed — but there was a serious breach statewide in the party over the fight for governor. The breach was patched up, because the key leaders on both sides had come to know and trust each other.

I don't mean to say we elected a governor with tea and cookies; we didn't. But we did furnish one indispensable condition, a finger in the dike at the right time and place. You can do likewise with Jack Hopeful and his friends, varying the details but not the principles.

Alcohol is not necessary as a political lubricant. Quite aside from the moral issues it is fantastically expensive for the average volunteer. I remember a Democratic politician telling me about a time when his local county chairman had dined with Jim Farley, then left early and gone to bed, whereas another major local politico had made a night of it. "Which one," he said to me, "made the best impression on the national chairman, the pantywaist who went home or the guy who sat up drinking and smoking with him and swapping yarns?"

His own opinion was obvious but I am not sure I agree with it. Mr. Farley has a well-founded reputation, I am told, for being a teetotaler, a non-smoker, and a man who prefers a good night's sleep.

The vote that can be gotten over a cocktail but not

over a cup of coffee is too scarce to merit your attention. I am not espousing prohibition; I am simply being practical. Too many politicians do too much drinking in the belief that it is necessary instead of admitting to themselves that the drinking is really for their own pleasure — to relieve their taut nerves, usually. I have seen many a promising career wrecked through the bad judgment which comes at about the third drink. Drink if you like — but don't kid yourself; it loses more votes than it gains, unless handled with real skill — a skill I can't teach you.

Scouting and Heckling: It is legitimate and useful to scout the public meetings of the opposition, if you can spare the personnel. Heckling should be used with caution as it has a habit of back-firing. You may want to heckle if the opposition is using the outright lie. Scouting is simple, it requires only a person with good hearing and a good memory; successful heckling is an art.

Always use women for heckling and pick them for quick wit, the ability to speak, and sound judgment under stress — there are probably several such in your organization. She should either be young and pretty, or should look like somebody's mother and a DAR to boot. By preference she should be as small as possible, but you may not have a choice.

Let her dress in her very best and smartest clothes, then seat herself about half way down the hall. (Front rows and back rows are associated with heckling; she should try to look like a spontaneous case.) She will keep quiet until and unless the lie she plans to nail is used from the platform. Then she will stand:

"Point of order, Mr. Chairman!"

"Yes? What is it, Madam? State your point."

"The statement the speaker has just made is incorrect. I am shocked to hear it associated with Mr. Hopeful's campaign. I am sure that it is without his knowledge." (If Mr. Hopeful himself is the speaker, make it, "I know that Mr. Hopeful would not sponsor any such misstatement if he knew the facts; I am sure someone must be deliberately taking advantage of him.")

Throughout the encounter your woman maintains the attitude that both the chairman and the candidate are pure and innocent and tries to avoid being asked whom she is supporting; she is just the Public-Spirited Citizen, in love with the Truth.

It is to be hoped that the opposition chairman will get rattled and refuse her a hearing — in which case she rises and sweeps grandly out, and gets away from there fast: her purpose is accomplished; any votes that are on the fence are by now convinced that Hopeful's crowd is up to something shady or they would have given the little lady a chance to speak. Even some of Hopeful's committee will have misgivings which will slow them down. Most people don't like lies and other dirty tricks.

Unfortunately, Hopeful's man may give her a chance to speak. She must be all sweetness and light, reserving her indignation for the lie itself and the unnamed person who planted this foul thing on poor Mr. Hopeful. She should know, as nearly as possible of her own knowledge, the true facts and state them briefly while asserting her claim to authority in some fashion which leaves the opposition only the two gruesome alternatives of accepting her version, or of calling a sweet and gentle representative of the fair sex a liar, net. "I know because I was present when it happened," or "I have seen the court records," or "I was interested in this matter and looked up the vote in the Congressional Record, down in the Public Library."

From here on she is on her own, but she can't lose if she is bright enough to justify assigning her to heckling.

You must be prepared to deal with hecklers yourself. Most of them, unlike your own trained hatchet women, will be moderately stupid, bad tempered and arrogant — and probably self-appointed. Try this routine: "Just a moment please — will you kindly state your name and address so that the audience will know who you are?" Then interrupt before he can get unwound with, "We can't hear you very plainly. Will you kindly come forward to the platform and address the audience? We want free speech here — if you have anything new to add we certainly want everyone to hear it."

There is a good chance for the heckler to destroy himself with the crowd at this point; in any case it gives your speaker a good chance to organize his rebuttal, or — if the situation calls for it — retraction with a noble gesture, but conditioned on the tentative assumption that the heckler knows what he is talking about.

In any case your speaker makes no reply until the heckler has talked himself out and left the platform. Thank him courteously, insist that he reassure you that he is *quite* through (this is so you can get the crowd to back you in suppressing him half a minute later), then swing your own forces into action.

The key to the whole matter is to let him talk, always let him talk, and pray that he will be long-winded, boring, and displeasing to the crowd. Even if he turns out to be clever and persuasive you have cut your losses as best you can.

Hecklers from the opposition, or, more likely, representatives of pressure groups, particularly Communists, can create another type of crisis, not by the direct challenge of a statement, but by getting up and demanding an answer to a question of the Have-you-left-off-beating-your-wife? variety, such as "Do you or do you not condone the railroading of six innocent men to prison in the Midriff case?" Or "Do you think that the Veterans' Administration should be permitted to turn the attempt to house veterans into a farce by sponsoring the unreasonable practices of the building group?"

Frequently the question has nothing to do with the issues of the campaign — I have seen abstruse matters of foreign affairs thus injected into city elections, state matters forced into national elections, and *vice versa*, and judges queried about purely administrative or legislative questions. If the speaker is not the candidate and the candidate is not present, the best answer to an embarrassing and impertinent question is, "I have never discussed the matter with Mr. Upright and therefore cannot answer for him. If you will do me the courtesy of writing out your query, with your name and address, I will make it my personal business to bring it to his attention and will see to it that a full answer is made."

If appropriate, you should then add, "The question is not appropriate to the campaign, since the office Mr. Upright has consented to let us run him for is one which cannot possibly deal with the matter you have raised. However, Mr. Upright believes that the voters should be permitted to know all about him, even the brand of his tooth paste, if you are interested. Therefore I am sure that he will take time out, busy as he is, to look into the matter you are interested in and express an opinion."

If Mr. Upright is the speaker, he must answer, in some fashion. If it is pertinent to his candidacy, he should not straddle. Even if it's as hot as a baked potato, he *should* answer and a forthright answer will gain respect and lose no more votes than a straddle. If it is not pertinent it is quite likely that he does not know all the details; he may ask the speaker to meet with him, making a set date from the platform, for the purpose of digging into the matter. At the private meeting he may still insist on time for research and study, since he is not bound to accept the heckler's assertions as Gospel.

I want to make a subtle but, I believe, proper distinction between dishonest fence-straddling and reasonable prudence in avoiding unnecessary and irrelevant controversy.

There are so many different ways in which men may hold honest differences of opinion that it is possible to find reasons for like-minded, close friends to quarrel if an effort is made to determine the issues on which they differ. This truth is the basis of much shoddy politics — the injection of the extraneous and unnecessary issue.

Do you think it is decent or indecent for the women of Bali to run around naked to the waist? Whatever your opinion, will it affect the fashion in which you perform the duties of county tax collector? Is it just to ask yourself to commit yourself in public on this issue?

On the other hand the matter may be very pertinent if you are seeking an appointment to the state board of motion picture censors.

There are many issues on which people are strongly divided in opinion, not necessarily along party lines, such things as prohibition, admittance of refugees, birth control, vivisection, capital punishment, public ownership, the UN, conscription, compulsory arbitration, legalized gambling, and so forth literally without end. It makes a lot of difference in these matters whether you are running for legislator, county clerk, congress, justice of the peace, supervisor of education, sheriff, or tax assessor, whether these matters are legitimate criteria of your qualifications.

Since a majority of one — yourself — holds all of your views, I think you may legitimately avoid any issue which is quite irrelevant to the duties you will be called on to perform. But don't kid yourself nor let any candidate of yours kid himself; the duties of any lawmaker, judge, or chief executive are extremely broad; the duties of some other offices are quite narrow.

How to Sample a District: Mr. Upright's campaign for the nomination has reached the last month. You have worked hard but how well, in fact, are you doing? Should you put on more steam, or fold up and quit the race?

You can't afford the services of the Gallup poll or other professionals; your volunteers can't spare the time from direct campaigning. To be sure, they are giving you a poll of sorts, at each meeting of the Door-bell Club, but what you want now is a check on their reports. You know from experience that the reports of the field workers are usually too rosy.

There is a technique which must be learned by experience but which you may start learning as soon as you enter politics; by the time you reach a place where it matters you can be quite skilled. It consists of making predictions for all candidates and issues on the ballot for each election, both before and after some direct sampling of your own, and keeping a record of the results, which you will then compare with the election returns.

From this you will learn whether you are too optimistic or too pessimistic; subconsciously you will improve your judgment until you reach a point where you can go out into a district and almost smell a victory or a defeat weeks ahead of the event. When you can do this you are in a position to turn a potential defeat into a victory.

Make your predictions at regular intervals, from filing date to the night before the election. File them away, then get them out during the post-mortem. The whole procedure is much more entertaining than cross-word puzzles; addicts prefer it to trying to pick the horses, or to reading detective stories.

Statistical Sampling: Even if you could afford professional poll-taking, supervised by mathematical statisticians, the money is better spent on campaigning.

Does this mean you have to go it blind, perhaps to work your head off for a lost cause, or lose by a narrow margin when a small additional effort would have won — had you known it was necessary?

No, there is a fairly easy and inexpensive way to conduct a poll on a district of any size, even the largest, which will give you reliable data on which to judge how well your campaign is going and then to plan accordingly.

The secret of correct prophecy by statistical sampling of a large number of units lies first in the correctness of the methods by which you sample and second in *not trying to get out of the figures more than there is in them.*

The mathematical theories of probability, chance, and probable error are complicated and abstruse. Instead of trying to give a course in this subject I shall content myself with stating a thumb rule, giving some instructions on how to use the rule, and offering a few general comments on the mathematical methods whereby the rule was derived. Only the thumb rule need be remembered to apply the method successfully; the mathematical comments are for the mathematically-minded reader who may wish to check the derivation of the rule and, possibly, enter into a little stimulating controversy with the writer as to theory, or as to the possibility of formulating a better thumb rule for the purpose.

Rule: Poll your district at "random" (identified below) until you have fifty responsive answers — answers either for you or against you, disregarding those who refuse to answer or haven't made up their minds. Take the number of answers *for* your candidate and double it. Subtract eight. Mark your answer as a percentage. The chances are about four-to-one that your candidate would not receive less than this percentage of the vote cast if the election were held at once

. . . and there is a practical certainty that he would not fall very far under this figure. Use it *as if* it were a certainty. It is, in fact, a carefully calculated conservative estimate on the "better-be-safe-than-sorry" principle.

Example: You have taken a poll of 93 voters of your party, selected at random, before you attain 50 responses — 14 declined to answer, 29 had made no choice. Of the 50, 28 were for Upright; 22 were for Hopeful. Doubling 28 gives you 56; subtracting 8 leaves 48: Upright may expect to get not less than 48% of the vote cast if the election were held at once. It is equally true that he might get as high as 56 plus eight or 64% of the vote, but you are not interested in the optimistic side of the picture; you want to know what you have to achieve to cinch the election — therefore you use 48% as your figure.

Forty-eight percent is not enough; if he loses by 2% he *loses* — it's an emergency.

Two percent of the expected vote of 25,000 is 500 votes; you must speed up the campaign to get at least 500 more votes than your present activity insures — so you shoot for about three times that number. You call an emergency meeting of the Doorbell Club and show them only the 48% figure and tell them that means that each one will have to dig out about six more *new* votes than he had counted on, by punching additional doorbells not on the selected list until he finds six more who can be wheedled into voting in the primary. You put Upright on a 60-hour week for the balance of the campaign and you decide to spend four afternoons a week at doorbell-pushing yourself, instead of two, even though it means doing your paperwork on midnight oil.

The spurt lasts three weeks but it wins for you — when you might have lost by a heart-breakingly small margin. Perhaps you win by a fat margin and perhaps the spurt was not really necessary — you will never know but it does not matter; you've won.

Suppose your poll shows a conservative estimate of more than 50%; you are then justified in continuing your present campaign plans, without an emergency spurt but without slackening off.

Suppose the poll had been the other way around, 22 for Upright; 28 for Hopeful — your conservative estimate is then 36%. Does this mean you should quit? No, for Hopeful's conservative estimate is still less than 50%. It means a tough fight with a possibility, but not much probability, of winning. Stick with it.

Suppose Hopeful got 30 votes in the poll, indicating that he will probably beat your man by at least 52% of the vote and that he might take as high as 68% of the total. Should you throw in the sponge?

Not on your own initiative — I recommend that you talk it over with your candidate, then call a closed meeting of all workers and all money contributors, tell them the sad news and ask them to express their wishes. From a cold-blooded standpoint you might as well cut your losses and quit . . . but I predict that they will vote to stick to the finish and turn the meeting into a rally. They may even win for you. Politics isn't dice, nor statistical physics; the Spirit of the Alamo may outweigh all measurable factors.

If they decide to stick, bow to their will and pitch in. It will be a treasured emotional experience at least — and many a "lost" campaign has planted the seed for an eventual political upheaval.

The Meaning of "Random": A "random" sample is one which is as truly representative of the district as you can make it. This is most easily done by trying to keep out the personal element in the selections. For example — you want 100 names from 200 precincts: Take the bottom name, of your party, from the second column of each-even numbered precinct list. Or make up any other rule which makes the selection mechanical, with no choice on the part of the operator, and which spreads the sample evenly through the district, according to population, not area.

Never take the sample all from one precinct or one area.

If you are polling by telephone you will find that some of your choices do not have telephones. *Do not* substitute the next name having a telephone listing; the voters without telephones must be polled at their homes — otherwise you will introduce an economic factor which will falsify your answer.

Polling by telephone is best done in the evenings, in order to find both men and women at home. Do not accept the response of a spouse in place of the voter named by the random choice; it will change your results . . . there is a definite tendency for women to vote more conservatively, and in other ways differently, than do men.

Do not let the polling question suggest the answer desired. For example, here is a suitable phraseology for a telephone poll: "Good evening, is this Mrs. Mabel Smith? Mrs. Smith, this is the civic affairs research bureau speaking. Have you formed an opinion about the congressional candidates who will appear on your primary ballot a week from next Tuesday?"

It should be possible for one worker to prepare a list for a telephone poll in one evening and get fifty responsive answers in not more than three evenings. A reply-postal card poll should take about the same length of time to prepare and is about as accurate, but it takes longer to get the results and 250 should be the minimum sent out. It may be cheaper than telephoning in districts involving long-distance tolls. (These reply-type postal cards, at two cents apiece, are invaluable in penny-pinching political work.)

Don't attempt to make a straw-vote canvas door-to-door. Don't try it on the street. The names *must* be pre-selected by some non-personal method.

Mathematical Basis for the Rule-of-Eight: (Skip this, if

you like.) In any statistical sampling the larger the sample, the smaller the errors in the result, except for systematic errors — errors which are inherent in the thing being sampled. In the opinion of this writer, the systematic errors in any poll of political opinion conducted without expert actuarial help are so large that it is not worth while to use a sample larger than 100. On the other hand the "probable errors" — errors which depend on the laws of chance — are so large for samples less than 50 that trends will be masked by the inescapable "probable errors." For efficient use of time and money the smallest sample which will spot a trend is desired. For that reason, and because percentages may be obtained from a 50-sample simply by doubling (percentage problems are troublesome to some), a sample of 50 has been recommended.

Bessel's formula for probable error has been used in computing the rule-of-eight, assuming independent events of equal probability and assuming a "universe" of very large but limited numbers. The assumption of equal probability may be attacked; the pragmatic justification lies in the fact that probable errors are largest in a 50-50 division and the political situation is most critical in such a situation — a landslide either way will show in a sample of 50 without resort to probable error.

The rule-of-eight is neither the "probable error"of the engineer, nor the three-standard-deviations-equals-standard-certainty of the professional statistician; the first was rejected as too esoteric in meaning for the layman, the second was rejected because trend-spotting with it requires samples too large for the volunteer political campaign. A selected error of 8% was chosen to produce a conservative probability of about four-to-one, which was considered accurate enough for the purpose and much more reliable than most data we plan our lives by — in choosing a wife, for example!

If greater accuracy can be afforded, use a sample of 100 and a rule-of-five. Or the mathematical reader may perform his own analysis, following Peters or Bessel or others; I can't recommend direct analysis using the binomial expansion without pre-computation, even using Pascal's triangle — the figures are incredibly astronomical!

Sampling by "Smell": In addition to poll-taking and making predictions, try this—in time you will acquire skill in it: Prowl through your district. Buy a Coke and chat with your druggist. Buy two gallons of gas—chin with the man at the pumps. Ask strangers for matches, then gossip. Get a haircut. Make a purchase in an uncrowded grocery. Ask passing strangers for information—then talk.

When you have done this you will combine it subconsciously with the doorbell punching you have done (which, for the manager, should be scattered through the district) and you will end up with a curious feeling way down inside. Drag it up and into the light, take a look at it, and see whether or not it tells you that your man is going to win.

The human mind, when trained, is capable of more rapid, more flexible, and more reliable evaluations of problems containing unlimited unknowns than any of the mechanisms as yet invented. In time you will acquire this talent; you will know it when your predictions are consistently correct, not only as to results but as to approximate majorities and size of vote cast.

The acquisition of the talent is painless and almost effortless.

While acquiring the talent don't let yourself be panicked by some phony figures. Amateurs are inclined to think that their strenuous efforts must be producing a tidal wave, then are disappointed when they go out on a "sniffing" tour and find hardly a ripple. That is normal; primary campaigns hardly ever stir the general public out of their sleep. All you need is

a ripple, of the right size, and in the right place. You
know it is in the right place for you have been using the
direct vote-getting methods; now you want to know if it
is the right size.

Your district has about 200,000 adults. You question
only adults. Mr. Upright needs 15,000 votes. If one out
of four of the people you meet casually has even heard
of your man, he is a cinch for the nomination; but if it is
late in the campaign and only one in ten seems to know
that he is alive, you had better get a hustle on and see to
it that your election day organization gets every certain
and every probable vote to the polls — or you're licked!
You can still squeeze through on the one-to-ten ratio
by hard work just before and on election day, but it
won't be easy no matter what the telephone poll said.

● Chapter X

How to Win an Election (conclusion)

The Final Sprint

Last Week Mail Coverage: Your candidate has called on more than 3,000 people, possibly as many as 5,000. (Fantastic? I once rang 8,000 doorbells under similar circumstances.) Your precinct workers and you yourself have worked on the rest of the 25,000 targets. (You did not have time, you yourself? My dear lady — or sir — you *must* have time. I suggest a firm date for Tuesday and Thursday afternoons, one to five. Accept no other engagements for those hours.)

The campaign has not been perfect, but 20,000 aimed shots have been fired, in addition to the shotgun spread of publicity and meetings. However many of these shots were fired weeks ago; you need to use last minute reminders.

I suggest the use of either penny postal cards or personal letters — nothing in between. The usual political advertising, sent third class in an unsealed envelope and addressed by stenciling, then stuffed till the envelope bulges with wordy printed matter, has a way of landing in waste baskets unread.

A post card will be read because it is short, and it stands a chance of being kept around for a few days as a reminder. A personal letter of any sort, sent first class, will be read and noticed.

Even for postal cards your postage alone will be

$200, plus printing costs and the (volunteer) effort of addressing and signing — all cards should be signed by someone, even if with an "authorized" signature, not marked as such. The signing and addressing take many hours and the work will need to be done long before the mailing date.

The final mail coverage will be the largest single expense in your campaign and may be one-third of your total campaign expenses. You may be forced to use postals, rather than letters, to save time and expense, but I suggest that you consider personal letters for the persons the candidate called on, as these are your prize prospects.

("Five thousand personal notes? It would take a crack typist four months to do such a job!" So it would —)

A man named Hooven invented a sort of player-piano typewriter which types any given copy over and over again, using a standard typewriter. The pseudo-player-piano roll can have signals cut in it which stops the typing and permits a human typist to insert a name, a date, a phrase, or any other variation in the copy, without disturbing the set-up. There is no way to tell a Hooven-typed letter from one typed entirely by hand.

Hooven-typing service is available in most large cities; you can do business by mail if your community does not have it. It is much more expensive than printing and much cheaper than equivalent service by a typist. (Some day, he said dreamily, I hope to *own* one of these marvelous gadgets for the use of my own district organization.)

I suggest some such copy as this — make it short, both for economy and effectiveness:

(Letterhead)
(date)
Dear Mrs. Boggles,
I hope you will recall my visit to your home last April

3rd and our discussion of the primary election. The election is next Tuesday. Naturally, I would like to have you vote for me for the Demican nomination for Congress. I enclose a short memorandum of my qualifications and the issues I am committed to support.

Whether you support me or not, I urge that you and your family turn out and vote next Tuesday. The privilege and the duty of voting are more important to the safety of our country than an individual's candidacy.

Faithfully yours,
Jonathan Upright
JU:htc

The name and the date of the visit are the only items which require the Hooven robot to stop for an insert. If you use printed post cards you fall back on "Dear Fellow Demican" and "recent." Full coverage by post card of the persons called on is better than partial coverage by personal letter, but do not be tempted to cover the whole list of registered voters by mail — it won't pay its freight.

It is worth while for Mr. Upright to thumb through his cards and dictate as many post-scripts as possible, which are to be hand-written by the person who signs his name. "P.S. My regards to the chow puppy — JU" or "I'll be after Bobby's vote in 1960!" or "Will you write to me your opinions on that reclamation matter?" or "I hope your husband is completely well by now."

Some of your precinct workers may be able to afford Hooven service for their own precincts, or they may be industrious enough to tackle the job of writing or typing personal notes — a big job but manageable for single precincts. Otherwise you will supply them with printed postals with the "trademark" picture of Mr. Upright occupying a third of the space, and a short "Dear-Neighbor" note on the rest, following the general idea of Mr. Upright's note. Leave space for the precinct worker to sign, and use the type face which simulates typewriter type style.

You may be forced to ask those who can afford it to pay the postage. It comes to a couple of dollars per worker; it amounts to a couple of hundred dollars at least to the campaign fund. One of the inspiring things about volunteers is the way they will give till it hurts right before an election, whereas a paid worker expects everything furnished to him as well as his fee.

Special attention must be given to the unregistered potential voters turned up during the campaign by Mr. Upright and the precinct workers. You have been obtaining regular reports on these people, daily from Upright and weekly from your area supervisors, and you have been turning the names over to deputy registrars with whom you have friendly liaison. These votes are free for the asking and they may amount to a couple of thousand, enough to turn a bad defeat into a narrow victory. (These are the votes Mr. Dewey needed but didn't get in 1944 — the "sleepers.") Special attention by mail and special attention on election day is indicated. You can vary your printing or your Hooven set up.

Your mail coverage should be delivered to the post office, tied in bundles by districts, on Friday afternoon before the election.

Election Day: The campaign is over, all but the final sprint. That sprint needs careful preparation.

An ideal election day organization has block workers on every street, a precinct captain and lieutenants, a squad of automobiles directed from each precinct headquarters, a trained telephone organization, workers at the polls, a flying squad to take care of physical opposition, and another squad of legal eagles to take care of more esoteric matters. The whole thing is organized like a war ship going into battle.

You won't have any such organization; you won't find it anywhere save in some large cities east of the Mississippi, and it won't be complete even in those cities.

Your ideal organization — which you won't achieve; 80% is a fine score — will consist of three workers in every precinct, one at the polls, one at the telephone, and one with an automobile, plus roving area leaders with a telephone contact for each, a telephone and a couple of helpers for you, and two lawyers on tap who will drive to any trouble spot in a hurry. You dispense with muscles in your flying squad and depend on the fact that no one, not even a bad cop, will break the peace in the presence of a lawyer who announces himself as such.

Mr. Upright spends the day circulating around among the workers, giving them that "appreciated" feeling.

To achieve such an organization you need several times as many workers as there are in your Doorbell Club. It is not really hard to manage — for one day — if your area supervisors are active and alert. Some of them won't be. Since your efforts must be incomplete work according to the following priorities:

(a) Cover every contact in the precincts canvassed by Mr. Upright even if it means persuading your best workers to leave their own precincts completely vacant.

(b) Try to cover every precinct which has been worked by anyone.

(c) Do not put workers in any precinct which has not previously been canvassed unless you are blessed with more workers than you know what to do with, in which case completely untrained workers may hand out literature at the polls in those precincts. Tell them about any local regulation which limits how close to the polls they may work and caution them not to argue with anyone.

(d) If a precinct has but one worker he or she may accomplish almost as much as three people by working in this routine: Telephone as many as possible the night before and between eight and ten the next morning. Make dates to take people to the polls, where needed, between ten and noon — a full car-load at a time. After lunch go to the polls and remove from the files all who have voted, then get to work on the telephone with the remainder, making more transportation dates for four to six o'clock. At six o'clock weed out the files further and make frenzied attempts to get a few more to the polls during the evening, giving quite as much attention to the inactive list as to the live contacts. As soon as the polls have closed, grab a hasty supper and return to the polls for the count. Remain there, watching the count (inform the senior polling official of the intention). When the count for congress has been completed, telephone the result to headquarters, and then leave for the election night party.

It is a long day's work but it is a perfect picnic for any healthy, intelligent person.

(e) If two persons are available, the same work is split up, except that the polls are not left unguarded even for a moment from the time they are closed until the count is completed.

(f) If three persons are available one of them may try to glean a few votes just outside the polls at the required distance for campaigning. He is permitted, under most state laws, to double as a poll watcher, thus keeping a running record of who has voted for the automobile workers, provided he does no electioneering while inside the balk line. He sets up a "headquarters" — a parked car, a card table, or a packing case — and covers it with signs for your candidate, and then attempts to hand some small, simple printed reminder that Jonathan Upright is running to each person who approaches the polls. If the local administration is unfriendly and unscrupulous he may have trouble with cops. If this is anticipated, have your best lawyer have a talk with the chief of police ahead of time, explaining your intentions, going over the law, and reaching a full understanding as to just what will be allowed. If your police chief is recalcitrant, let him know that you intend to fall back on the federal authorities — there are pertinent Supreme Court rulings which can scare the boots off a local official if he knows that you know your rights.

A second poll worker is desirable, as there are usually two approaches in view of the no-electioneering balk line. Anyone who is old enough to walk can be an assistant, the younger the better.

(g) Telephone workers may be found among supporters or wives of workers who are tied down by small children or ill health but can use a telephone. They must be provided with lists, by the precinct worker, and mimeographed instructions, from you. Here is an adequate formula: "How do you do? Mrs. Duplex? Mrs. Duplex, this is the Jonathan Upright-for-Congress Citizen's Committee. Have you voted yet today? Would you like to have one of us call to take you to the polls by automobile? Oh, that's quite all right — you can take the baby with you; we will take care of him during the few minutes it takes you to vote. Is there any other member of your family who needs transportation? Very well then, suppose we pick you up sometime between ten a.m. and noon? No?

"How about between four and six? Three o'clock is better? Very well, then, we will make a special trip for you at three o'clock; I'll make a note of it. Not at all, we're glad to do it."

No direct attempt to campaign would be made in these phone calls; limit them to offering service and reminding the voter of the election, while mentioning the name of the candidate as often as possible by referring to the committee by its full name. The person who makes the pick-up limits his campaigning to signs on the car and to handing to each passenger as he gets in a copy of the same small printed item used at the polls.

Election day work is simply to turn your potential votes into real votes by seeing to it that all your supporters get to the polls. Many times your interest lies in a minor candidate or in a proposition on the ballot. Votes for these can frequently be obtained by the courtesy of supplying a ride to the polls. Many people vote only for candidates for president, governor, and senator. The votes of these people can be sewed up for Mr. Upright if one of Mr. Upright's friends supplies the transportation.

Watching the Count: These votes gained on election day can be lost on election night, in the count. One of the commonest pieces of chicanery in the counting is to take advantage of the fact that many people neglect to vote for any but the head of the ticket. If the ballot is of the style in which the candidates are grouped by offices it is very easy to mark incomplete ballots after the polls are closed. Thus with 300 ballots cast for governor of which only 250 have been marked for a congressional choice, split 110 for Doubletalk and 140 for Trueblue, five minutes work behind closed doors can change the result to 160 for Doubletalk and 140 for Trueblue without leaving any provable evidence of fraud.

Ballots arranged by tickets rather than by offices are more usually faked by throwing out as improperly marked any split ticket ballot which does not suit the dishonest polling judge and by accepting such ballots when the split does suit him, no matter how many technical mistakes the voter may have made.

Actual stuffing of the ballot box is very rare and the cash-in-hand purchase of votes is still more rare, whereas the election which is actually changed in outcome by these methods is so seldom found that it may be regarded as a museum piece.

These crude methods of blatant dishonesty are not used by the more successful city machines, even when the Machine is corrupt to the core, because they are not as efficient nor as reliable as machine methods which are technically honest. If a Machine resorts to use them it is a symptom that it is on the skids. (Cf. Kansas City vote fraud trials.)

Your watcher will not be able to do much actually to check the count, because there is so much going on. But the presence of the watcher, announced as such to the official in charge, will be an almost airtight deterrent against fraud. In addition to purportedly watching the count the watcher keeps careful track of how many ballots are discarded as spoiled and for what reasons; this can strongly affect the outcome of a contested election.

Voting machines make the above routine unnecessary. It may be possible to inject fraud into an election conducted with a voting machine other than by the crude methods of coercion or bribery, since anything that one mechanical engineer can design another can modify to produce a different result, but there is nothing for you to do *at this point*. The detection of skullduggery with the innards of a voting machine would call for a type of investigation, probably by the FBI, beyond the scope of practical field politics.

The watcher telephones the outcome to headquarters, where you and Upright are keeping your own tally while chewing your nails down to the elbows. Then she, or he, goes to the election party.

The Election Night Party: When the polls closed you moved from the office headquarters to the space in which the Doorbell Club meets. You expect three times the membership of the Club but that's all right — let 'em crowd in; it makes them happier.

You did not stop for dinner; your stomach isn't behaving quite as it should. A sandwich picked up "to go" is all you want. Upright shows up from the field about the time you get there and the two of you, alone for once, or with the office girl and one or two others, get ready for the party. You place someone at the telephone and arm her with a tally sheet. You turn on the radio to the best station for returns — the snap tallies on the major offices are already beginning to come in — and set up the big black board to post returns on the whole ballot. You place an excited, high school-age adherent in charge of this, and turn your attention to the refreshments.

Three times the membership of your organization gives a figure of 300 — three hundred quarts of beer. That's a lot of beer; you have purchased it in kegs, if you could not get it donated, and made an arrangement to return untapped kegs for credit, so you display only one keg at a time and keep the rest under lock and key. You have five hundred paper cups, *not* of the largest size.

Coffee and soft drinks are available for those who do not drink. A very small amount of food, doughnuts, cheese and crackers, has been obtained, but you hide it away and will not display it until about one o'clock in the morning.

Don't try to serve hard liquor; it will bankrupt you. Some will bring their own and some will get tipsy. It's a free country.

A few people are beginning to show up and it breaks up the depression that you and Upright have been suffering from since the polls closed. They crowd around him, shaking his hand and slapping him on the back, and urging him to have a drink "right out of the bottle." Some of them also speak to you.

After that they pour in a steady stream; the place gets crowded and stays crowded. Most of them are your friends; some of them are the perennials who go to all the election parties every election night. You wedge yourself in back of a table to get away from the press and bend one ear to the telephone while trying to watch the telephone tally and eat your sandwich and drink some coffee.

Judge Yardwide, according to the radio, has a safe

lead over the field for the gubernatorial nomination. You nod knowingly and with pleasure — with Yardwide at the head of the ticket the final election should be easier to win.

The first telephone reports come in; they are simply *awful*! Your sandwich shows a tendency to want to come up again. Upright squeezes his way through the crowd, nodding and smiling and speaking to people, then bends over and glances at the figures.

His face is suddenly grave, but he pats your arm. "Never mind," he says. "It's all been worth it, even if we lose. If I ever run again I want you to manage me."

You feel like bursting into tears, but there are too many people present.

After a while it begins to swing. Upright is creeping up on Hopeful. . . . Upright — 982; Hopeful — 1,005.

Upright — 2,107; Hopeful — 2,043. You're ahead!

Upright — 5,480; Hopeful — 5,106. You begin to breathe more easily.

Upright — 9,817; Hopeful — 8,166

Upright — 12,042; Hopeful — Wait a minute — you hear your district number mentioned on the radio, and the telephone is ringing at the same time. "Quiet! Keep quiet — please!"

You get some modicum of surcease, at least around the radio: " — minor contest seems to be settled," the announcer is saying cheerfully. "Jack Hopeful, through his manager, has just conceded the nomination in the Umpteenth District to the Honorable Jonathan Upright. The statement urges all voters to support the Demican ticket this fall. Mr. Hopeful could not be reached for a personal interview but it is understood that — "

You don't hear the rest. You've won.

The rest of the evening is pretty light-hearted. You break away from the radio and circulate around a bit even though your feet are killing you. You try a glass of beer but you let it go flat while you duck back to the radio. The attorney general fight has taken a very interesting twist; it's likely to cause some complications.

About three a.m. you and the nominee and two other faithfuls squeeze into a booth in an all night restaurant and you eat the biggest meal you have eaten in over two weeks. You've got the first edition with the preliminary returns and you eat while one of you reads the figures aloud.

At four a.m. you fall into bed and die.

Post-Mortem

Upright — 16,107

Hopeful — 11,373

Figures from earlier contests, corrected for population and registration changes, show that a candidate in a two-man race will receive 10,000 votes in your district if he files and makes a superficial campaign. Comparison with other districts and previous years on a percentage basis shows that your district had 2,000 votes more than normal.

Therefore your campaign methods stirred out about 6,000 votes, of which some 2,000 were *new* votes not normally to be expected in a primary. This is the final proof of the correctness of your technique, since winning could have resulted from the deficiencies of Hopeful's campaign rather than the excellence of yours.

Detailed examination of the results by individual precincts shows that the candidate stirred out between a third and a quarter of the majority and that the precinct workers did the rest. The decision to have Upright go directly to the homes of the voters has been justified.

The cupboard is bare but the bills are paid — all but the beer; you pledged your own credit on that. You must remember to return the two kegs left over — that will help, and perhaps you can get one or two others to divvy up while they are still feeling good over the victory. Upright intends to reimburse you but you don't want to stick him for it — his personal expenses have been a little heavier than he had anticipated.

We Was Robbed! Or perhaps you did not win. Maybe there was a bad break at the last moment, or a schism in the Club, or something. Suppose the outcome was: Hopeful — 12,785; Upright — 12,009.

It is easy to cry fraud, easy to charge it up to a machine, to dirty campaigning, to stuffed ballot boxes. But you won't be right, not one time in a thousand. No, citizen, depend on it — if you lose it is almost certain that it was because not enough people wanted your man to win and most especially that not enough supporters worked hard enough or intelligently enough.

At the very least in every election there is a high percentage who just don't vote — in a primary more than 50%. You cannot blame those lost votes on chicanery. Perhaps you did the best you could and the outcome was indeed affected by some dirty tricks, at the polls or elsewhere, but the result still represents the will of the American people, at least by passive consent. Accept it.

Closing Ranks: You won't get anything out of your workers and you won't try to — you will wait till the next regular meeting of the Doorbell Club. In the meantime you are very busy.

There is the matter of gathering up records of the primary in order not to have to depend on the county clerk's records next time. Some of the precinct area supervisors may be disciplined enough to help you do this, but the let-down may continue until the posted voting record and results have been taken down. A 35-mm. camera furnishes a convenient way to get these records without stopping to copy the data, but it's too big a job to cover the entire district single-handed even with a camera to help you. Do the best you can and pick up the rest from the official records next winter.

Your memo pad has a score of such jobs, loose ends to

be picked up. You want to get them out of the way promptly so that both you and the nominee can get at least a week's rest, out of town, after the state convention and before starting the final campaign. A shorter holiday is needed before then, too, if you can manage it. But you have got to consolidate your victory by getting the party factions inside the district together before you dare leave town or make any campaign plans.

The entire slate of county committee candidates from the Doorbell Club have been elected, yourself among them — you now control the district delegation. The nominee is an *ex-officio* member of the state committee and is a delegate to the state convention. On your advice he has appointed state committeemen, yourself among them. You must plan to attend the state committee meeting at the capital but you may not have time to stay over to observe the convention — there is so much to be done.

(Your own state may provide for party organization somewhat different from that implied here, although this is typical. You must be familiar with it, whatever it is. Don't be caught with less representation on either the county committee or the state committee than your pro-rate necessary to control your district.)

But your *first* job is to see Jack Hopeful.

We have assumed that Mr. Hopeful is a regular member of your party and not a stooge of the other party. You want and need his support in the final election. Get hold of him or his manager and invite them both to your house for dinner. Mr. Upright will be there also. After dinner you will talk over the coming campaign.

Don't offer him anything. Don't assume that he wants anything. Treat it as a matter of course that he and his manager will support the straight party ticket, including Mr. Upright. Mr. Upright will ask him to serve as chairman of the district campaign committee for the ticket, while explaining to him that the work need not be any more strenuous than he wants to make it. The office will in fact be titular, since you will dominate the executive committee and the committee as a whole. You will remain personal manager for Mr. Upright, and, as chairman of your district's delegation of committeemen, you will be in authority on any official party matters.

You don't speak of these aspects to Hopeful; you offer him the top stuffed-shirt position in exchange for his nominal support. His manager is offered a vice-chairmanship and a place on the executive committee.

They may accept, pitch in, and be most valuable. Or they may hem and haw and leave, after asking for time to "think it over." Or they come right out and ask for money or appointments or both. They may have campaign debts to meet, or they may demand outrageous salaries to campaign. Hopeful may want help in landing a major piece of patronage for himself, or he may expect you to pay off his obligation to his manager by letting him have one of the congressional secretaryships if Upright wins. For some curious reason many unsuccessful candidates seem to feel that their successful rivals owe it to the defeated to pay off their campaign debts and commitments.

It's a form of blackmail; don't give in to it.

Upright should explain that he can't promise appointments to anyone since he has consistently refused to promise them inside his own committee. Appointments will be settled if and when — after the final election. As for money — there isn't any.

They may give in with bad grace, if they have no place to go and wish to stay in good standing in the party, or they may leave. If they do, they will be self-righteous as can be about the whole matter. For some reason your refusal to pay the bills they ran up trying to defeat you will seem like a clear case of moral turpitude to them.

Bring up your heavy artillery. Get some Big Names, preferably from the camp of the party's nominee for governor, to call on Hopeful and explain to him, sweetly but firmly, that if he ever intends to get anywhere inside the party he had better stay regular, lend his name, invite in his supporters, and, as a minimum, preside at one or two public meetings for Upright and the ticket.

The chances are you will get him. But don't buy his "support"; it isn't worth it.

In the mean time you will have seen to it that personal notes of thanks are prepared (Hooven-typed, perhaps) for every worker, endorser, and contributor in Upright's campaign. Make the ones to precinct workers different from and more emphatic than the others and let all of them be a call to arms for the final ticket in the final campaign. In addition, make the first meeting of the Doorbell Club a jubilation in which each worker is thanked individually and his majority is announced.

You will want to get everyone possible out to the first meeting of the party-wide breakfast group; here is where your spade work for party harmony will pay off. In addition to gathering in Hopeful there are at least twenty party factions in the district, one for each candidate for each office on the ballot. You will need all of them and will make personal appeals by telephone to the leaders in the campaigns that lost, in addition to the usual postal card notice. You have many different fights to straighten out here, dozens of sets of feathers to smooth, but your job is easier than it was with Hopeful, as you appear in the capacity of broker for everybody's interests.

Out of it all you try to whip together a campaign committee for the whole ticket, as that is the best way to elect your own man. You turn your thoughts to "face," everybody's face and you help to preserve it by offering them all a chance to do the noble thing in public by declaring for the whole ticket. Titular offices in the campaign are passed out to anybody who seems to want one, with great fanfare (the possibilities of the words "vice-chairman," "director," "secretary," "coordinator," and "committee" have never been exhausted).

From these other groups you get new members of the Doorbell Club, at least on a temporary basis. You may retitle it, if expedient, for the duration. You now need a membership about four times the best you could do in the primary.

There is money to be considered, all over again. It is easier to raise now, but you need more of it. Better put money raising in the hands of the gubernatorial nominee's local manager, for the campaign as a whole, and handle your own resources as a separate account for the congressional campaign. Don't forget to insist that the national committee kick in for the congressional district and be darn sure some bright boy down town doesn't beat you to it and get his hands on it through a more direct pipeline to the national committee.

Some county and state committees seem to be under the delusion that the way to raise money is to assess the candidates. This is all wrong; the committee should raise money and support the candidates. If assessed, don't pay it; their help isn't worth much if that is how they work.

From a proper state or county committee you may expect some money, a lot of active help, and much free or partly free printing. Your printing bills should be small in the second campaign as the stuff you will use will be for the whole ticket.

You may want a few items in which Upright's name is emphasized over that of the rest of the ticket, by lay out and type face.

We won't run through the final campaign in any detail. In general it is just like the primary campaign, except that everything is more complicated, the numbers are larger, the emotions are stronger, the amounts of money are larger, and you have the disadvantage, as it is usually figured, of running against an incumbent. The Honorable Mr. Swivelchair has more friends and more acquaintances, but he has also accumulated a back log of enemies and mistakes. Still, incumbency is usually figured as an asset and that is the safe way for you to figure. If Swivelchair is the stooge of a tight and well-established machine, you will not only have to work harder but will have to count on some trouble of the dirty sort. The election night count in particular will have to be closer. Figure your trouble spots and make your watchers there your smallest women; they will be safe. Men might have their arms broken.

There will be more Big Operators in your hair, more blokes with votes-in-their-pockets, more people with their hands out, more hopeful patronage hounds, more of everything which makes politics complicated without adding to the vote.

There is just one thing to be remembered in the midst of all this hurly-burly and confusion:

Keep your eye on the ball!

The votes are still in the precincts. Punching doorbells still remains the only way to get out the vote you need, despite anything you may hear from the Important Politicians from down town.

Maintain your own practice of spending two afternoons each week punching doorbells.

Schedule Mr. Upright for another 500 hours of canvassing and see to it that he keeps to his schedule.

Keep your campaign centered around the Doorbell Club and don't use them for anything but canvassing until election day.

Ignore the opposition as before.

The only real differences are these:

(a) You all campaign for the whole ticket and

emphasize Mr. Upright only by getting in his name more frequently, principally through quoting him by name in support of the platform and the ticket.

(b) You canvass from a selected list as before, but this time you ignore, in your canvassing, all the members of your party who voted in the primary. With the exceptions of the ones who had to be carried to the polls (and will have to be again) these people can all be depended on to get to the polls and to vote the straight party ticket. Instead you canvass all members of your party who *failed* to vote in the primary . . . and all members of minor parties and all unaffiliated voters. The known members of the other party you ignore. You have nearly 40,000 people to reach; you haven't time enough nor people enough to do more. Your effort will be to turn out the largest possible vote *of your own party* . . . especially the vote of the "sleepers."

(c) Therefore you will put more effort than ever into organizing your election day forces. If additional help for election day can be obtained from the county or state committee you will want it, since it does not require local information, other than a prepared list, to do election day work, and it does not even take that to be a poll worker or a count watcher.

And that's all.

Along toward the last of the campaign very heavy pressures will be brought against you to change the campaign, but one will come from an unexpected source. A senior member of the party, resident in your district, a nominal member from the beginning of the Upright committee and a fairly heavy contributor to it, is likely to call on you. He won't put it quite bluntly but the idea is that you should lie down and let Swivelchair win.

He will say you have made a good fight but that Upright does not have a chance. Upright isn't quite ready yet; maybe in two years, or four years, but not this year. On the other hand he happens to know that

Swivelchair plans to go for Senator next time; on that occasion he could throw a lot of support to Upright if Upright did not cause Swivelchair too much expense this time. Why not be practical, take a long view, and get along?

You wouldn't even have to drop the rest of the ticket, naturally; just persuade Upright that there was no sense in throwing good money after bad — and get sick for a while.

As for you — well, what appointment would you like? Maybe it could be arranged.

There is no particular reason why you should not indulge in the rare luxury of losing your temper, although it won't help any. Send him about his business. Don't make it an issue — now. But don't let him sit in on any party conclave during the campaign, nor ever again, if you can keep him out. He's a Trojan horse.

Don't let it shake your faith in human nature. Instead, it should build up your faith. They would not try to buy you off if they were not frightened! It is a shining justification of your faith in the nature of the average citizen. Your methods and your beliefs are being vindicated in the most practical way possible — and the opposition knows it.

Some time later you will again find yourself seated behind a table with an election night party going on all around you. The radio will be blasting, the phone will be ringing, you will be trying to eat a sandwich and listen to the radio while thinking with half your mind about how to scrape up the postage for the eight or nine hundred-odd letters of thanks that Upright will have to send out in the next two weeks.

The early returns aren't going too badly; Upright is even running a little ahead of the ticket in some spots — but it's still touch-and-go. Swivelchair's organization is experienced and well trained; it can't be discounted.

You decide to put off worrying about the postage,

and so forth, until about Thursday. You'll find the money; you always have.

There haven't been any returns on congressional districts for about an hour. You are getting jittery. The announcer is introducing candidates and notables — why don't those stuffed shirts get off the air?

Here come some figures — 9th district, 10th district, 11th district, 12th district — the announcer stops. What's got into him?

"Just a minute, folks, some new figures just in . . . any moment now. Here's one item of news anyway. The new figures clearly show that in the Umpteenth District, in a surprise upset, Jonathan Upright has unseated old-timer Congressman Swivelchair. The incomplete returns show a lead of — "

You have elected a congressman.

You can't leave on that vacation the next day. In fact you can't leave for a couple of weeks. Besides the thank-you notes there are the post-election meetings of the Doorbell Club, the breakfast club, and the state and county committees. Upright wants to discuss appointments with you, too, of his secretaries. You don't want to go to Washington with him; you don't even want to be on the payroll as his field secretary and stay in the district, as you don't want to be his employee — your position depends on your being your own boss. This attitude gives you at least a veto in the appointments he does make — and on his later appointments.

Your own plans have more to do with tying in the Doorbell Club to Washington through a weekly newsletter from Upright and a regular procedure whereby the Club will be kept informed as to what is going on, what it means, and votes their approval or disapproval for the information of Upright and the two senators.

It is nearly a year and a half later that you are sitting in your living room, thumbing through the current Congressional Record — the only tangible thing you

got out of either campaign — when you notice a roll
call vote on a measure you have been following. It's a
good measure in your opinion, and important to the
whole country. This is the last vote, the one that sends it
to the President for signature. You note with approval
that Upright voted for it — as you knew he would; you
have corresponded about it.

It just squeaked through, by one vote. You suddenly
realize the significance. One vote — Upright's vote, for
Swivelchair had a definite record against this sort of
measure.

One vote. *Your vote!*

Your own efforts have put a constructive measure
into effect for the whole 140,000,000 Americans — *you*
did it, with your bare hands and the unpaid help of
people who believed you.

It's a good feeling!

● CHAPTER XI

Footnotes on Democracy

> *"The target is who and what?*
> *"The people, yes —*
> *"sold and sold again*
> *"for losses and regrets*
> *"for gains, for slow advances,*
> *"for a dignity of deepening roots."*
> — Carl Sandburg

"When you assemble a number of men to have the advantage of their joint wisdom, you inevitably assemble with those men all their prejudices, their passions, their errors of opinion, their local interests, and their selfish views. From such an assembly can perfection be expected? It therefore astonishes me to find this system approaching so near to perfection as it does. . . ."

> — *Benjamin Franklin to the*
> *Constitutional Convention*

The art of politics is as confused and unorganized as a plate of hash and as endless as a string of ciphers. Despite the numerous digressions many things pertinent to the art, as distinguished from the issues, have necessarily been ignored. Some of them are much too involved for available space and quite unnecessary to a basic book, as you will learn about them as you come across them, with little loss to you, if your grounding is firm.

We must pass by such matters as the workings of state and national conventions, the work of state legislatures — "cinch" bills, "must" bills, the effect the Speaker can have on producing a "do pass" committee vote, the rules committee, stopping the clock — and the inner workings of congress — seniority, cloture, the functions of floor leaders and whips, senatorial courtesy. Lobbying and lobbyists, proper and improper sources of campaign funds, blocs, the preferential ballot, the publication of political newspapers, the Hatch Act, the organization of national committees and national campaigns, the political inter-relations of city, state, and county — all of these matters will face you with fresh political problems, but your answers will depend much more on how you look at issues; the techniques will turn out to be familiar to you. Only the names will be changed.

Nevertheless, whenever a large family makes a journey, no matter how many neat pieces of luggage they may own, there are always left-over items for which there is no assigned space but which must not be left behind. These are wrapped in brown paper and carried under the arm. This chapter is such a bundle.

The Personal Expenses of Volunteer Politics: Let's be specific. You can be quite active without spending a dime, but there are expenses which make your work much easier and more enjoyable. Here is minimum budget for comfort and freedom from embarrassment:

One extra meal out per week	$1.00
Pass-the-hat collections and dues, per wk	.50
Transportation, per week	.40
Additional postage, political, per week	.25
Weekly total	$2.15

This budget permits much higher expenses during the most active weeks of campaigns because there will be many off-season weeks when the additional expense of being a politician is limited to a few postal cards and a phone call.

The budget ignores the fact that you aren't spending money on movies, bridge at a tenth, nor on other recreations or hobbies when busy with politics. Politics on the above budget is cheaper than most recreations, i.e., entering politics can save you money instead of costing you money, even though you pay your own way.

Political contributions and trips to conventions can run to any figure you care to spend. So also can any hobby. You will need the moral courage to say firmly, "I'm sorry but I don't have the money," when you can't afford it. You will be respected for it and it will cost you no political influence in the long run.

Coping with Communists: Communists are not very numerous but they get around; you will run into them everywhere. There is a popular belief that Communist infiltration is found only in the left wing of the Democratic Party; I have not found it so. A Communist cell can pop up wherever more than four people assemble. I have spotted them in organizations so reactionary that their presence, if known, would have caused deaths from apoplexy.

Communists are most easily understood if you think of them as a fanatical, evangelical religious sect. I speak here of American Communists; I have no knowledge of Russian Communists, having never met one to my knowledge and having never been to Russia.

From the standpoint of religion the peculiarities of communists form a recognizable pattern. They have an outrageously unscientific "bible" which they point to as being the last word in science. It appears in "authorized" and "forbidden" translations. They have a god — the idea of the "proletariat" — a major prophet, a minor prophet, and an apostate saint. They are absolutist in viewpoint and brook no argument. Anything is moral to them which serves to propagate the faith, no matter how offensive to the unbeliever. Theirs is a "higher" morality; what we have is a "decadent, bourgeois" morality. They are indefatigably zealous. They are usually sincerely and altruistically devoted to their cause. You will find other such characteristics.

Their favorite technique is to bore from within. The operators are usually clandestine Communists, hiding behind some other party label — this is not offensive to their own strict moral code. They will make use of democratic parliamentary procedure and the democratic concept of free speech to ends destructive of both. Their notion of free speech is one in which you hire the hall and they do all the talking, on a subject of their choice. It is strictly a one-way proposition — try it in *their* hall sometime!

A common technique is to operate in a cell of three — one to make a motion, one to second it, and the third to harangue. They generally spread around the hall to do this and may not even appear to be acquainted.

A chairman confronted with this triple play can find himself in a pickle. The subject picked by the cell is always one which can be made popular with the particular crowd and which is not overtly connected with Communism. A group of three can often stampede a crowd into some action disastrous to the objectives of the crowd but suited in some devious fashion to Communist purposes.

An able chairman can prevent this by means described earlier in this book if he spots the Communist cell.

Fortunately this can often be done in plenty of time. American Communists are hardly ever very intelligent although many display some aspects of brilliance. They tend to behave in regular patterns which they have been taught and by which they can be spotted, but they can most easily be spotted by their addiction to catch words and phrases.

These shibboleths change from season to season, but, if you are in politics, you will hear them, come to recognize them, and listen for them.

A few years back the word "activize" was such a touchstone. "People's" this and "People's" that has enjoyed a long popularity, as has "United Front." There is no way to tell you what these words will be at some time in the future. Listen for them and check the *Daily Worker* now and then to see what they are up to.

Some of them reveal themselves by calling themselves "Communist-sympathizers." This sort of person explains that he is not a Communist himself, but sympathetic to their social ideals. Consider, citizen — have you ever heard of a Democrat-sympathizer, or a Republican-sympathizer? There ain't no such animal.

Communists are merely irritating nuisances rather than dangerous. Only the timid and the mendacious profess to fear a communist revolution in this country. Anyone acquainted with the *mores* and the culture of this country can see that ninety-nine Americans out of a hundred, at the very least, don't want any part of Communism. It does not fit in with our individual ambitions.

Of what use, then, are the American Communists?

They serve one function extremely useful to you and to the country, so useful that, if there were no Communists, we would almost be forced to create some. They are a reliable litmus paper for detecting real sources of danger to the Republic.

Communism is so repugnant to almost all Americans, when they are getting along even tolerably well, that one may predict with certainty that any social field or group in which the Communists make real strides in gaining members or acceptance of their doctrines, any such spot is in such bad shape from real and not imaginary social ills that the rest of us should take emergency, drastic action to investigate and correct the trouble.

Unfortunately we are more prone to ignore the sick spot thus disclosed and content ourselves with calling out more cops.

Lawyers in Politics: Lawyers constitute around half of all our state legislators and congressmen. They hold other political offices way out of proportion to their numbers in the population. Many people take this as a matter of course and it is in fact a logical consequence of certain features of our social structure.

We have already mentioned the fact that a lawyer can run for office easier than most other people and that, in many offices, he can take a bribe in an undetectable manner. However these are not real objections to lawyers in public life; lawyers are certainly as patriotic and as honest as the average run of men and I believe that they average more intelligent than the general run.

Nevertheless it seems very unfortunate that lawyers should make laws. It may even be argued that lawyers should not be judges. The latter idea is certainly radical, but the profession of judging is by no means the same as the profession of the solicitor or the barrister. It could be a separate profession; the origin of the identification of the two professions seems to go back to Biblical times, when priest, teachers, judges, and lawyers were all one profession. Two of the professions separated out; the other two could be separated just as, in England, the two professions of solicitor and barrister are separate. There is now no legal requirement that the justices of our Supreme Court be lawyers.

But lawyers do their greatest damage in lawmaking. In the first place lawyers speak a language not known to the rest of us; they write laws in that language and then we must hire one of their guild to tell us what the law means. They assert that their special language is necessary, as ordinary speech is not sufficiently exact. One may doubt this; many semanticians have disputed the claim. A layman is surely entitled to doubt it, even without the special analytical skills of the semantician and without knowing the other language, since lawyers are forever disputing as to what a law means after they have written it.

I wonder what the result would be if one could attack the constitutionality of a law on the grounds that it could not be understood by the ordinary literate adult? The ordinary adult is required to *obey* the laws — which carries with it the implication that there must be *some* way of telling him what it is that he must do. How would it be to require that laws be expressed in such terms in the first place?

Even a lawyer cannot require me to *rimpf* unless he has some way to tell me, in English, what it is I have to do to *rimpf*.

A foreign language is a minor vice of the lawmaking lawyer, however. Foreign languages can be gotten around, more or less, through interpreters. The worst thing a lawyer brings to the task of lawmaking is a faulty orientation.

You have heard of the Fillyloo Bird? He flies backwards because he does not care where he is going but he likes to see where he has been. Lawyers as a group are strongly related to the Fillyloo Bird, by training, by lack of training, and by association. They look to the past.

That's a helluva way to try to draw up a new law to cover a new situation!

We are now confronted with the disheartening spectacle of lawyers attempting to draw up laws on the subject of atomic physics. They look to the past for precedents; there are no precedents — and their own esoteric professional training does not require that they be exposed in any fashion to science nor the methods of science.

The dilemma is not new, it is just more acute. In a myriad ways we permit a group of men who know rather less about the real world than do farmers, engineers, mechanics, or grocers make for us our most important decisions, in accordance with dusty precedents of dead men of their own clique.

The real trouble with lawyers in public life is that most of them don't know anything that really matters.

A Third Party? The emphasis that has been placed herein on the two major parties and the necessity for party regularity and party discipline may lead some to think that I oppose any attempt to form new political parties. If so, I wish to correct the impression.

Party regularity and party discipline are pragmatically necessary and morally correct in any political party if that party is to carry out its responsibilities. This is especially true with respect to unsuccessful candidates in a party primary; no man should offer himself as a candidate in a party primary unless he is prepared to abide by the majority will of the political group he seeks as a sponsor. Running in a primary is a voluntary action, very similar to joining a caucus; it carries with it responsibilities as well as privileges. A candidate need not enter a primary at all; he is always free to run as an independent instead.

In some states the right of a person to participate in a primary may be challenged and he may then be called on to prove his right by taking an oath to support the ticket which results from such primary. Such a procedure is morally correct; if universal it might do much to put a stop to the present eat-your-cake-and-have-it-too attitude of some irresponsible politicians.

Special circumstances arise from time to time when two groups, strongly opposed on basic issues, struggle for the privilege of wearing a party label claimed by both. In such cases there is usually no pretense that the losing faction will support the winner and there should be none. Consequently no obligation to party regularity exists. But the more usual case is much more like that of the spoiled brat who insists on having his own way in every respect or he won't play.

All of which adds up to this: if you decide to bolt, go whole hog. Leave the party. Join the other party or join a third party. Don't expect either the Republicans or the Democrats to permit you to wield influence if you insist on flirting with the other party whenever the whim seizes you.

The issues involved in forming a third party at this or any time are beyond the scope of this discussion, although it is evident that both parties are now wracked with internal stresses over basic issues which bring each wing of each party closer to the corresponding wing of the other party than are the right and left wings of either party, within the same party. An ideological realignment would appear rational; a third party may be the convenient means to such end.

The practical aspects — our proper business here — depend on whether or not the risk is justified by the objectives. Forming a third party is a highly speculative venture; it fails much more often than it succeeds. But it has been done successfully many times in our history. Mr. Lincoln was elected by third parties for both terms, first by the Republican party and next by the Union party — the latter fact seems to be little known. In 1864 the so-called "Radical" or regular Republicans nominated John C. Fremont, who had been the Republican nominee in 1856. The Union party was a coalition of both Republicans and Democrats.

The Failure of "Reformers": It is a truism in political history that the only thing worse than an officeholder under a corrupt machine is the reformer who replaces him.

Why should this be? Surely most of these reform gentlemen are honestly devoted to the cause of good government and have the best of intentions when they take office. Within my experience practically all of them were, I believe, sincere.

The downfall of some of them can be charged to sheer naivete; they were quite unprepared to cope with the liquor and lady lobbyists, the pressure groups, and the stab in the back. Some of them were cold zealots who could not maintain power because they did not understand what people wanted as well as did the bosses. And some were tragic cases who found themselves unable to live on the miserly stipends which we so frequently offer as a reward for statesmanship and succumbed to opportunities for graft and bribes.

But the most numerous variety, it seems to me, fail through conceit, from a type of swelled head arising from self-righteousness. I am a "reform" politician myself; this phenomenon is of great interest to me. It surprised and worried me to find out that so many of my ilk were such frail reeds when we got the chance to carry out our intentions.

The life and death of a reformer often runs something like this: He starts out full of enthusiasm and moral indignation. He is determined to have nothing to do with anything resembling what he calls "playing politics." He won't make any promises; he will remain a free agent at all times, devoted to the best interests of all the people.

Presently he finds that he has to make *some* promises; a man who isn't committed to anything can't get anywhere in any field, since social living depends on contractual arrangements. Being ignorant he usually makes the wrong promises; they become inconvenient to keep.

Here is where his swelled head ruins him —

He is surrounded (always) by sycophants who tell him what a great guy he is, a new Savonarola no less, and that he is much too big to be bound by bad promises because he has obligations to the whole people which over-ride commitments to individuals, particularly when he was trapped into them (which may be true).

A conscience which tells you that you can break your word for higher, more moral reasons is a very convenient thing to have around. You can get it trained so that it always gives you the answer you want that day. "Mirror, mirror, in my hand, who is the fairest in the land" — and sure enough, it's yourself!

After a succession of such incidents the Machine is back in office.

Political machines, both the fairly decent and the utterly corrupt, have accumulated a great deal of true information about politics. Reformers can't compete unless they know these facts and are prepared to offer all the Machine does and a little more. The two most important facts the reformer must learn from the Machine are these: (a) Promises must be kept, and (b) votes are in the precincts.

You can tear up the rest of the book.

Are Democracies Efficient? This used to be a favorite subject for pessimistic pondering during the 'thirties; we seem to have answered it definitively between December 7, 1941, and August 6, 1945. I used to be worried about it myself; I was devoted to the democratic way of life but honestly wondered if it were destined to be engulfed in this "Wave of the Future" which then enjoyed a certain popularity.

My doubts were settled permanently by a refugee from Nazi Germany. A gentile and a very prosperous Berlin businessman, he had preferred ducking over the border and landing in New York penniless and with no prospects to toeing the Nazi line.

I expressed my misgivings to him. He answered, "Don't ever let anyone tell you that any form of dictatorship is more efficient than freedom. Being made up of human beings, both systems make mistakes. The difference is this: In a free country when the mistake begins to show, somebody sets up a howl and presently it is fixed; under a dictator nobody dares to criticize, and the mistake is perpetuated as a permanent, inflexible rule."

To be sure the touchstone he used was free speech, but democracy and free speech are Siamese twins; one can't stay alive without the other.

But Can I Be Effective? Notwithstanding the pretty picture in the last chapter of Muriel Busybody electing Mr. Upright, unseating Mr. Swivelchair, and eventually thereby effecting in at least one instance the whole course of national life you are still entitled to reasonable doubts as to whether or not the case is typical. After all, I wrote the plot; I may have phonied it.

Remember Susie? Susie, the one-woman army? Susie and her kids? (When her oldest was about nine Susie announced the intention of taking them all to the mountains for a week's vacation. The kid was not impressed. "Look here, Mother," she said, "is this *really* going to be a vacation — or just another convention?")

The primary laws of the state in which Susie lives require that delegations to national conventions for the purpose of nominating candidates for president be elected by the people of the party and that the delegates be bound by law to support the candidate under whose name their names appear on the primary ballot, thus giving the people direct voice in the selection of presidential candidates. The law provides further that lists of such delegations may appear on the ballot only as a result of circulation of petitions among the party's voters and such petitions require a great many names to be valid.

Susie had volunteered to obtain for her candidate such a petition, but the Big Politicians downtown told her not to worry. "Joe Whoosis up north has the whole thing under control," they told her. "He's got the money to take care of it and he is going to use experienced, professional, paid petition circulators." There was a strong implication that her casual volunteer methods were too sloppy for this Big Time Stuff.

So Susie shut up but she did not put it out of her mind. She watched the newspapers for announcement of the filing of the petition, but failed to find it. With the deadline one week away she telephoned the Big Politician. "How's the petition coming along?"

"Huh? Oh, that — Whoosis is taking care of that. I told you."

"No forms have been filed as yet with the registrar."

"Oh, he'll file 'em up north. Don't worry."

On Friday, still seeing no newspaper announcement, Susie decided she would have to find out for herself; she put in a long-distance call to Joe Whoosis. She got his office but not him. Whoosis was sick. The petition? Well, there had been some mix-up about the money, but the secretary thought that it was probably being taken care of, down south.

Susie knew durn well it wasn't being taken care of down south; Susie swung into action.

She had a bunch of old petition filing forms thriftily saved from another election; she had her file of 3 x 5 cards; she had a telephone. It was Friday afternoon, beautiful weather, and about half the city had gone away for the weekend — including half her contacts. Never mind.

First she dug up several volunteer typists and put them to work filling out the headings of the petitions. . . . There were more than a thousand such headings to type. This started, she began calling her district leaders, thirty of them, volunteers all, the Muriel Busybodys of the organization.

She located about half of them, told them the house

was on fire — get busy! By midnight the last of them
had picked up her (or his) petition forms and had left
to marshall the forces. The next morning Susie spent
digging out secondary leaders in the uncovered
districts.

Saturday and Sunday was all the time there was, as
all day Monday, Monday night, and Tuesday would be
needed to check the forms against the Great Register,
cast out the unqualified names (about 40% on any petition) and arrange by precincts the remainder — then
file the petitions by four p.m.

A weekend is a poor time to try to circulate a petition
at best, but picnics and ball parks and union meetings
and crowds pouring out of churches provided places
where circulators could make their pitches and fill a
form fairly quickly. Susie needed — and got — fifteen
thousand names by Monday morning.

The petition was filed with twenty minutes to spare
and was eventually qualified as valid. The Big
Politicians never got around to submitting a single
name.

Now as to the significance of this amazing display of
the efficiency of the volunteer fireman — Susie's state is
large; it holds about fifty votes in a national convention.
It also holds its preferential primary for president
much earlier than the primaries or conventions of
most other states.

*If Susie's state had failed to support her candidate it is quite
unlikely that his name would ever have been offered at the
national convention* . . . and without Susie's intervention
— bare-handed, no money, no tools save some 3 x 5 file
cards — it would have been impossible under the law
for her candidate to receive the convention votes of her
state. The situation was critical and could have been
disastrous — in a fashion directly parallel to what happened to Mr. Willkie's chances in 1944 when the
Wisconsin primary went against him.

Since it is not desirable to tie this example to a particular party we will omit the matter of whether or not Susie's candidate was nominated and subsequently elected president — but I will say this: On one weekend Susie, middle-class housewife and mother of three, working from her living room telephone, drastically changed the course of state and national politics and left her mark on world affairs and on world history for some generations to come.

Many have done so on a much larger scale and much more prominently — I don't recall ever having seen Susie's picture in the papers. But at that point she was one of the indispensable factors in the present course of history, like the boy with his finger in the dike.

There are hundreds of utterly essential moving parts in every automobile, which are never noticed unless they fail. The volunteer in politics is most conspicuous when he is absent.

Still, you probably won't try to nominate a president. The wearying prospect of managing a candidate may be more than you will ever want to undertake. Is operating at a lower level worth the trouble?

The answer is emphatically "yes" — for many reasons; I will mention three.

Volunteers are trusted. This results in them being called on when the party needs a person of certain integrity in a pinch — which happens rather frequently. I remember one campaign organization which was almost entirely salaried; there were only half a dozen unpaid volunteers in the whole outfit. It was necessary at one point to disburse some fifteen thousand dollars for poll workers on election day; there were entirely proper tactical reasons, involving in part the known presence of spies in the organization, for keeping it quiet and for doing it at the last possible minute. The money had to be in dollar bills to permit small individual payments.

As a matter of course two female volunteers were selected to do the job — two because fifteen thousand one-dollar bills are bulky: I can see them now, two young and pretty housewives, each with handbag bulging with three thousand dollars and one with a shoe box under her arm, stuffed with nine thousand more pieces of lettuce. Off they went to disburse it, looking as if they had been shopping. And back they came the next day and returned four thousand dollars — which they could have snitched and no one the wiser.

No one worried about the possibility that they might head for Mexico — they were volunteers with established reputations — and it was much better than hiring an armored car with bonded messengers.

Volunteers are upgraded with great speed, while a mercenary stays in the ranks. There was the case of — we'll call her Helen. Helen had no personal political ambitions but she was always willing to get in and work. Two years after she started we had an appointment to the state committee to place and we were quite choosy about it; we wanted to be sure of point of view on issues of the person who got it.

Helen's name was not thought of at first because she had not been around much at the time; she was very busy having a baby. When she was thought of, she was at once selected. I called her up and asked her to serve. She was not anxious and pointed out that she was tied down and unable to be active. But she finally consented.

Two years later some of the female volunteers decided to get rid of the current national committeewoman; they wanted a new one and they did not want the usual Mrs. J. Huffington Puff clubwoman. Helen's election was assured before she was consulted — much to her surprise!

Two years later than that her congressman decided to retire; she was not even resident in the district (a congressman need not be) but the congressman and his manager tapped her to be his successor.

She became one of the best known and one of the most useful members of Congress, as statesmanlike as she was sweet and beautiful.

Yet in her whole political career she had never sought anything for herself. Her distinguishing characteristic was just a willingness to work, free, for what she believed in.

But the most important reason you can be effective has to do with the relative importance of various offices and of the several types of elections. The common belief about these matters is just the reverse of the true situation; most people seem to regard the office of president as the only one of importance and the presidential election every four years as the "main" election.

Nothing could be further from the truth.

The most important office in a democracy is the city councilman or selectman; the most important election is the local caucus — and so on up to the "major" offices and the "major" elections.

This is not news and it is no slur on the office of president. Most presidents have said the same thing repeatedly. It is axiomatic that the smaller the office the more closely it usually affects the citizen in his daily life. For example, the pavement out in front of my house was paid for by a city street bond lien laid directly against my home and the bonds were reputed to include eight cents per square foot of pavement of "honest" graft — "honest" graft is a name given to the condition that results when specifications are so drawn that one bidder on a public contract holds a favored position and need not hold down his price. It is done by describing, in the language of the lawyers, a particular patented product to the exclusion of all others.

("Why didn't I stop it if I know so durn much about politics?" Ouch! I did not move into this house until after this street received its present payment; I came in from out of town.)

However that is not sufficient to prove the point. We can stand a lot of graft in our local affairs — we always have! — and still muddle along. But can we stand another world war? Foreign affairs are directly in the hands of the President; from this point of view the office of president is surely the most important, even of overwhelming importance, with the character of the Congress almost as important.

True. But congresses don't grow on trees, nor are they brought by the stork. Nor do presidents spring full grown from the brow of Jove.

Elections are won in the precincts!

These "minor" elections are the major part of the process which produces a president each four years; the "main" election in November is only the last link in a long concatenation of events. The organization which is capable of electing a town selectman is the identical organization which joins with others like it to pick a president. The citizen who fails to participate in the contests for these "minor" offices is offered only a choice between Mr. Harding and Mr. Cox, or their successors. You can't be effective in politics if you limit yourself to presidential candidates. It is not possible.

Furthermore, these "minor" candidates have a way of becoming presidents. Fourteen of our presidents started in the state legislature, from John Adams to F.D. Roosevelt. Hayes was a city solicitor; Cleveland and Taft were assistant prosecutors; Lincoln a village postmaster, Coolidge was a city councilman, President Truman a county judge, Benjamin Harrison a court reporter, and Johnson started as a town alderman. Nor is the time from "minor" office to presidency very long; par for the course seems to be about twenty-six years — some made it in less than twenty. (These figures do not include cases like Wilson, Hoover, or Grant, where the candidate entered public life late in his career — these figures tell how long it takes to go the whole route from "minor" office to the White House.)

The President for twenty years from now may be in your district; you may urge him to run for his first public office. In any case the chances are better than two to one that any future president will make his start in one of the minor, local offices which the politically naive hold in contempt.

If you want to affect the destiny of this your country, take over your own precinct; with your friends, take over your own small district and elect the local officials.

There is no other route.

"Qui Custodiet Ipsos Custodes?" — which, freely translated, means "Who keeps an eye on the watchman?" and shows that the ancient Romans were no dummies when it came to figuring out the political facts of life.

In the Roman Republic the answer was "Nobody"; the republic folded up and the bosses started calling themselves Caesar.

"Qui custodiet — ?" There is no point in grousing about that "machine" unless you are willing to help form a machine of your own. "Machine" is simply an American word meaning an efficient political organization, one that lines up the vote and turns it out on election day — the Doorbell Club of the last chapter. The term has been used habitually with scorn, as if there were something dishonorable *per se* about efficient political activity.

A "corrupt" political machine is merely one which has been taken over by thieves while the citizens slept. Many of our city machines are not corrupt, unless you insist that patronage and a mild amount of favoritism are the same thing as bribery, racketeering, and gangsterism. Many machines, called so with contempt, are serving the public a good deal better than the public deserves.

But it is needful to guard the guardians.

Consider Philadelphia, city of William Penn, Ben Franklin, and brotherly love. The water is such that one prefers to buy bottled spring water; the Delaware is so contaminated that it eats the skin off battleships even above the water line. The subway runs occasionally; two major subway lines have been excavated but never finished for traffic, because somebody mislaid the money. Taxes? The place has a city income tax as well as all the usual taxes.

A private citizen attempted to take a picture of the Liberty Bell; he was arrested — it seems that pix of the Liberty Bell are a concession farmed out from city hall. The King of Hoboes complained that Philadelphia's skid row was the worst in the country.

A survey appeared to show a 30% incidence of active tuberculosis in crowded neighborhoods, a figure so high that I have trouble believing it — but the Philadelphia slums make the New York "Old Law" houses seem like choice residences. In Philadelphia a row house is described and pictured in the newspapers, with dead seriousness, as a "model home."

They licked the problem of mosquitoes in the jungles of Panama, and New York City is so free from flies that screens are hardly necessary. Both pests should be allowed to vote in Philadelphia; they own the place. Food of every sort is exposed on delicatessen counters, exposed not only to flies, but to the coughing and sneezing and fingering of the shoppers. Maybe the streets were once cleaned; there is no evidence of it.

One might expect the inhabitants of such a city to be aroused and indignant; anxious to throw the rascals out. Are they? I give you my word of honor, most of them are *proud* of it.

Many times I have asked a Philadelphian who complained about this or that specific symptom of his sick city what he was doing about it, to be met with a look of amazement, followed by: "Do anything? Don't be silly — you can't crack *that* machine. Why, I haven't voted in years!"

I remember seeing — not once but often — a stylish and beautiful woman, furred and smartly gowned, walk her dog in the Rittenhouse Square neighborhood. Presently she would wait, leash in hand, smug content on her face, while her doggie dirtied the sidewalk.

She looked to me like the Spirit of Philadelphia.

Let George Do It. Heinrich Hauser, in that amazing attack on the land that sheltered him, *The German Talks Back*, describes his notion of the typical American as an irresponsible, technically trained ignoramus, and predicts the downfall of this country because, he says, we lack social responsibility. He cites a case in which he claims to have been riding as a passenger in an automobile when his driver, a well-bred young American woman, passed by the injured victim of a hit-and-run driver — this, he says, is typical.

It is no defense to state that the German peasant is even less socially responsible than the American, nor is there much point in asserting that there is a difference between the callous behavior of an individual and the organized, government-directed brutalities of Nazi Germany. The indictment, if true, can destroy us anyhow. Personally, I'll bet ten-to-one on the Good Samaritan behavior of any member of the Doorbell Club, but honesty demands that we admit that there is a measure of truth in what this angry German says.

I know a man who seems to me a case in point. He is native born, well and expensively educated, possessed of a good job, married, and a father. He has both ample time and ample money with which to take an interest in politics — and he takes intense interest.

But interest is all he takes! His activity is limited to an occasional vote.

He is anti-Jew, anti-Negro, anti-immigrant. He thinks that the public schools should be segregated not only by racial groups but by economic classes, so that his children would not have to brush shoulders with the "lower classes." He is in business but he does not believe in free enterprise; he wants the rules rigged to favor his particular enterprise against free competition from other businessmen. The government to him is "They" and "They" are always doing something he does not like.

"They" have worried him so much that he has at last figured out an answer which pleases him. He believes that the trouble with government is government itself; we should abolish it. Then would come the millenium when men like himself would make their own rules and everybody would live happily ever after, free from the oppression of "They."

I would like to think that he and his kind do not exist in dangerous numbers, but I am not sure. If the people who hold to the "They" theory are too numerous and the volunteers too few then Heinrich Hauser was right. What the Axis failed to accomplish we will do to ourselves.

Rough Stuff: I would be less than honest if I did not admit that it is sometimes physically dangerous to be a volunteer in politics, even in your own neighborhood.

During my first campaign I took hasty refuge in a polling place until a lawyer from our side came to rescue me, because of a car filled with six thugs who did not like my count-watching activities. I did not feel bold and heroic about the incident; I am somewhat timid. It scared the daylights out of me.

It also surprised and shocked me. The polling place was in a prosperous, super-respectable residential neighborhood; it had never occurred to me that there could be any danger — that sort of thing happened only down near the river. And not to *me* in any case! I was a respectable citizen!

As a matter of fact it does not happen very often, but it is a hazard you must count on. Later the same day I found that another poll watcher had been less fortunate than myself — beaten about the face and head, left lying on the sidewalk. I myself have never been hurt, but I have had some bad moments, and I have seen permanent scars on more than a few of my colleagues who stood up for their rights. My own city has experienced political bombings at least twice in recent years; there is a former police officer serving time now for one of them.

Even though the danger is comparatively slight, is not this a good enough reason for a decent citizen to stay away from the dirty business?

It all depends on the way you look at it. If it was worthwhile for your son, or your husband, or you yourself, to fight in a foxhole, on the high seas, or in the air, then it is worthwhile to protect the victory by a moderate additional risk. This can be the "moral equivalent of war" the philosophers talk about.

Politicians and Political "Scientists": There is actually no reason why political scientists should not know something about politics and some of them do. I am sorry to say that most of them whom I have met did not; they made sorry fools of themselves the first time they stepped from the classroom into the vulgar hurly-burly. Some of them had basic horse sense, learned from their mistakes, buckled down and became real political scientists. Others did not.

This is not an attack on the late Brain Trust, nor on educated men getting into politics. If there was ever a crying need in any field for trained, intelligent men, imbued with the scientific spirit, that field is government.

Unfortunately many of the men who describe themselves as political scientists are neither political nor scientific.

Politics is a tag for the way we get things done, socially; many of them have only an academic knowledge of how we, the American citizens, conduct our affairs.

"Science" is a word with a definite meaning. It refers to a body of organized knowledge derived by a particular method. In brief that method consists of observing specific, individual facts, trying to find relations between them, setting up hypotheses, then checking those hypotheses by observing more pertinent facts. Under this method of investigation all scientific knowledge is founded on field work and laboratory work.

In some fields the basic facts can be observed on the campus, as in physics or chemistry. In others the scientist must regularly go to where his phenomena exist, because they can't be carried to the campus, as in geology and stratospheric research — if he is to learn anything new about his subject and not simply chew over what other men have said.

Is it not obvious that in order to study politics scientifically it is necessary to spend a lot of time where politics is going on?

I have at hand a letter from a friend of mine who is a professional political scientist, with all that years of post-graduate training in one of the most famous schools can give him. However he has had no experience in active politics. He writes:

"Do you think experience or practice in politics essential to an improvement in political interaction? I am a believer in empiricism in most things but believe that much more can be accomplished by scientific methods than by experience in government. That is, I feel that a man might be an effective partisan all his life, but end it with no greater ability to accomplish desirable political changes than in the beginning."

The above paragraph exhibits such complex confusion that I hardly know where to start. Let us begin by conceding that a man may be a very effective field worker in politics and still not do any good in the long run if his work is not enlightened by information and understanding in current affairs, history, economics, sociology, and many other things. Politics is the broadest of human subjects and we have dealt only with one narrow field of it herein.

But how can a man hope to "accomplish desirable political changes" if he is not experienced in the mechanisms by which political changes are brought about? For that matter will he know a desirable political change when he sees one, unless he has rubbed shoulders with the crowded millions off campus?

But note the orientation, note how he contrasts "empiricism" and "experience" as being the opposite of "scientific methods." The sad fact is that all of his degrees and training have not exposed him to the basic idea of the scientific method. *All* scientific knowledge comes from experience, experience as concrete as careful observation, careful measurements, and careful experimentation can make it. "Empiricism" is a word with several related meanings; in scientific methodology it is usually used to refer to an early stage in an investigation when the observer has too few facts too inaccurately observed to permit him to make more than rough generalizations as his hypothesis. Politics is largely at the empirical stage because of its extreme complexity. Empiricism is appropriate to politics; no other *scientific* approach is possible.

Unfortunately, other approaches are possible; one is the method of armchair speculation of the philosopher. It is the classic method in this field, used by Plato, Aristotle, Spencer, and Marx — and the work of each is vitiated by it. They might as well have spent their time debating how many angels can dance on the point of a needle. But the method is still popular!

Is it too much to hope that some day someone will found a school of government which will include as one of its required laboratory courses active field work in at least one campaign? And then perhaps to require something as strenuous and unacademic as serving a term in a county committee, or running for office, or managing a campaign, or undertaking to lobby a bill through a state legislature, before awarding graduate degrees which entitle a man to refer to himself as a *political* scientist?

I feel wistful about it. Honest-to-goodness trained men could do so much good in public life if only we had a few more of them.

Afterthoughts and Minutiae:

Don't put campaign literature in mailboxes other than through the mails. Postal regulations forbid it.

There is a small duplicating set available suitable for postal cards, which costs about a dollar. Sears Roebuck used to have them and probably does now. It uses mimeograph ink and a hand roller. Gelatine duplicators, hectograph-type process, and looking like a child's slate, may be had for three or four dollars in sizes which will take either postal cards or standard business stationery.

Unpredictable coincidences can play hob with a carefully planned campaign, leaving you nothing to do but laugh it off and forget it. I happened to pick the year to run for office that found the Nazi Sudetenland Fuehrer in the headlines; his name differs in spelling from mine by one letter!

In making a committee report it is diplomatic to say "your committee" instead of "the committee."

The difference between a caucus and an ordinary majority action is parallel to the difference between the Constitution and the laws which are made under it. A constitution is an agreement-to-agree-in-the-future, along certain lines and to serve certain known ends. So is a caucus. This may make it easier for you to explain it to the uninitiated.

Anti-handbill ordinances, anti-bill posting ordinances, and ordinances which forbid street-speaking and park-speaking without a permit should be opposed by all persons and parties devoted to democracy and freedom, as the avenues these ordinances close off are historically the only ones available at times to the poor and unpowerful. I am aware that it is a nuisance to have your doorstep littered with throw-away pamphlets, but it is still more of a nuisance to be thrown into a concentration camp. Democracy is worth a few nuisances.

Clubs should never have nominating committees; it is subversive of democracy. A motion to close nominations is never in order and should not be entertained. The proper procedure is to let a period of dead silence intervene, after inviting further nominations, then announce that they have closed. Be lenient in allowing laggards to slide home. Let them appeal to the floor if they wish.

Are you over thirty-five? Or under thirty-five? This is a touchy matter in volunteer politics for the old frequently work for the young, and vice versa. The power to keep things friendly lies with the leadership and the key to it rests in "face." When you are in a position of leadership to persons out of your own age group, whether younger or older, you will have no trouble if you go way out of your way to treat them with much more respect than you do persons of your own age.

Take a complete rest from people every now and then. Go away if you can. Being polite all the time is wearing.

On keeping oneself informed — of course you read a newspaper. But do you read the opposition newspaper as well? It is more informative in many ways. Both your state organization and that of the other party probably put out a little political newspaper; both are valuable to you. A free subscription to the Congressional Record may often be had for the asking; it is too long to read but it is well worth thumbing through for key votes and certain speeches. Keeping track of voting records is essential to an enlightened politico; once, to my shame, I supported the wrong man all through a primary because I had taken another man's word as to the voting record of the incumbent. There are convenient summaries of all significant votes for both congress and state legislatures from several different sources — major daily papers, taxpayers groups, labor unions, the *New Republic*. It is not necessary to agree with the opinions of the source for these compendia to be useful to you. Keep them on file rather than trying to memorize them. File every copy of a platform, or a candidate's promise on issues. It is common *credo* that election promises are never kept and that platforms are mere bait; in my limited experience this cynical belief has been false somewhat oftener than it has been true. It is well to know the facts on individual cases.

My wife and I have found a delightful way to celebrate the Fourth of July; you might enjoy it. We read aloud the Declaration of Independence and the Constitution. They are grand poetry of the Biblical style and it is well to refresh the memory.

Speaking of poetry, I wish that I had the capacity to write something like *The People, Yes* — , which I quoted from at the head of this chapter. I commend it to your attention. But there is music of the same sort in the sound of a thousand doorbells —

Ben Franklin pointed out to the benefit of all politicians that the easiest way to get a man to like you is to get him to do you a favor.

A lot of people want to get into politics but they want to operate on the "higher levels." I think of these high-minded but impractical people as "ballet" liberals because of an incident which took place in New York in 1942. A group representing all of the arts had met to see what the creative artist could do to help win the war. It developed that there was a strong bloc present which thought that the correct course of action was to demand that Congress subsidize a national ballet! I like ballet as well as the next but it seems a curious "secret weapon." If you want to enter politics don't expect to do so through organizations which are ordinarily non-political, women's clubs, church groups, fraternal organizations, professional groups, and the like. Or, at least, do not expect to be effective in bringing pressure on an officeholder by representing yourself as being influential in such groups. A man who has been elected to office is not likely to be a fool on the subject of votes. He knows the political feebleness of such organizations — that they do not vote as a bloc no matter how their leaders may bluster. Your petition will be discounted accordingly. If you represent a *precinct* organization you won't have to tell him so.

Amateur pressure groups, such as neighborhood indignation committees, all too frequently go to see councilmen and such and adopt a belligerent tone which suggests the officeholder is a crook and that he can be frightened easily. Both assumptions are likely to be mistaken.

Let us now praise bureaucrats. Bureaucrats come in for a kicking around from anybody at any time. As a matter of fact they are a pretty good lot. Try to imagine what a strike of "bureaucrats" would do to the country. No, don't — it's unthinkable, frightening.

And lastly — I would like to put this in box car letters — even if you become state or national chairman of your party, try to remain your own precinct captain, or some sort of a doorbell pusher. It will keep your roots to the ground. Even the Caliph of Baghdad made a practice of disguising himself and going out to talk intimately to his people.

● CHAPTER XII

The American Dream

"It is for us the living, rather, to be dedicated here to the unfinished work which they who fought here have thus far so nobly advanced...."

— A. Lincoln, Nov. 19, 1863

What of the issues?

We have piled up a whole book discussing the mechanical details of field politics, as if it were an automobile to be taken apart and repaired, put back together and made to run. Some of the details must have seemed very fiddling and far removed from the clean heights of statesmanship. It has been a worm's eye view of politics.

The activities described in this book would be bare bones indeed if they were ends in themselves. If we are to win elections for the competitive pleasure of winning, it would be better to play golf or bridge.

So what of the issues?

It is not necessary that I speak here of specific issues. Even if you have no clear-cut political opinions on entering politics you are bound to form evaluations about issues. Whatever evaluations you had before you entered politics are bound to change and you will wonder how you could have held them.

But if you enter politics with honesty, ordinary sense, and a hope in your heart that you can help out, I am willing to trust my own future and the future of our children to the evaluations you will form and the actions you will take. Whenever the American people take their affairs in their own hands, instead of letting them go by default, I have no fear of the outcome.

We need never be afraid of the vote of informed Americans. It is only the ignorant voter we have to fear, ignorant politically, no matter how fine his house or how expensive his schooling. Such people have never experienced democracy; they have merely enjoyed its benefits. It is hard to explain what democracy is; it is necessary to participate in it to understand it.

The former Berlin businessman I referred to earlier told me that he blamed his own group, people with the time and the money and the opportunity to know better, for what happened to Germany. "We ignored Hitler," he said. "We considered him an unimportant fellow, not quite a gentleman, not of our own class. We considered it just a little bit vulgar to bother with him, to bother with politics at all."

They thought of the government as "They." The only possible route to a clear conscience in politics is to accept political responsibility, either as an active member of the party in power or as an equally active member of the loyal opposition.

An adult is a person who no longer depends on his parents. By the same token a person who refers to or thinks of the government as "They" is not yet grown up. There are many such in America, too many, but not too many I think to prevent the adults from taking care of our joint welfare. I'm a believer and a hoper.

There is more cynicism in this country than there are things to be cynical about. The debunking exceeds the phoniness. There is more skepticism than mendacity. Dr. Alexander Graham Bell was sued for fraud because he claimed he could talk over the wires. The Wright brothers had to plead with people to please come look — we can fly! And none of the "smart people" believed that the pipsqueak "nation" of thirteen rebel colonies could ever hold together and form a living union. The spawn of the skeptics are still with us. "You can't fool me cause I'm too durn sly!" They are around us, busy belittling and sneering and grinning at every effort to make of this country what it can be. What it will be.

For you there is the joy of being in the know, of understanding the political life of your country, the greater joy of striving for the things you believe in, and the greatest joy of all, the joy of public service freely given, service to your fellow men without pay and without thought of pay. If you have not as yet experienced this joy, then there are no words with which to describe nor any way to convince you of its superiority to other joys; it is possible only to assure that it is so.

"War is an extension of politics by other means." — Von Clausewitz. And politics is an extension of war. The war did not end in August 1945; it goes on around you, around the world, in difficult guises. We are in more danger now than ever before in our history, dissension within, our ideas for which we fought subjected to many forms of attack, the peace we won whittled away, and over it all the menace of another war, a war that could strike in the night, defeat and utterly destroy America and the American Dream.

If we prevent that war it will not be by force of might, for we cannot expect time enough to bring that might into play. If we are to escape it, it must be by political action more enlightened and more nearly unanimous than any we have ever shown.

The "decadent" democracies showed on a hundred battered beach heads that free men could think, could lead themselves when their leaders fell, and could improvise with the means at hand. We face the new beach heads, we must face them with individual responsibility, improvise and fight with the means at hand.

I can hear the strange express-train roar of the jet planes passing overhead from the fields in the valley to the north. Soon it will be the blast of the great rockets. It is the end of an era.

If we can tighten up democracy to meet the challenge of the super-sonic speeds of the fast new world we may yet be spared the silent death from the sky. If not —

It's up to you, Mrs. Blodgett and Mr. Harrison and Mr. Weinstein and Mrs. Cleary. You, too, Mrs. Johnson and Mr. Berzowski and Mr. Lorenzo — Mr. Smith and Mrs. Jones and Miss Kelly — and up to me. I'll see you in the caucus and at the polls.

Good luck to you! Good luck to all of us.

The End

The End

● SUMMARY OF OPERATIONAL CHAPTERS

CHAPTER II
How to Start

Look up your party in the telephone book. Join your local organization. Stick with it for several months, doing any volunteer work that is offered. Then let your conscience be your guide — but don't accept pay!

CHAPTER III
Wheat & Chaff

A man's religion is an important political fact about him which you are entitled to consider.

Church groups are frequently a cause of corruption and confusion in politics. Don't expect any real help from them.

Women, as a group, are less politically enlightened and less politically honest than men. Test them before you trust them.

Elderly people, as a group, are politically selfish and socially irresponsible. Avoid organized groups of the old folks.

Reliable volunteer political workers are found most frequently among young people. However, the very best political volunteers are found in the three groups mentioned above.

Machine politicians are about as honest as the general run of people, and more honest about oral promises.

Machine politicians are friendly, warm-hearted, and will take pains to help people. An amateur who expects to compete must emulate these virtues.

A government should not be run like a business; a business should not be run like a government. They are very different.

Compromising is an honest process indispensable to free men governing themselves.

"Civil Service" is frequently a mask for a shameless spoils system. Patronage is a political liability to the politician who has to dispense it.

Public office is usually scandalously underpaid; this is the fault of the public and a frequent cause of corruption in public life. Nevertheless, most officials are too honest and too patriotic to succumb to the temptations placed before them. For that reason we have better government than the people deserve.

It is both virtuous and efficient to be partisan and party regular, but it requires both moral courage and clear thinking to accomplish it.

CHAPTER IV
Field and Club Organization
Four Thumb Rules:

1. Your purpose is to win elections, not arguments.
2. Elections are won with *votes* and *the votes are in the precincts*.
3. You win by persuading your own voters to register and vote.
4. Don't waste time trying to convert a man who has already made up his mind.

The above four rules are applied successfully through organized field activity based on personal calls and begun long before the election.

Doorbell-pushing: Always work from a list. Don't be aggressive. Cut the visit short. Record all information on a file case for follow-up.

Political clubs contain very few votes but they are indispensable (a) for organization and liaison of precinct workers (b) to keep up the morale of precinct workers by giving a "team" feeling. They also constitute seminars in democratic government.

How and When to Form a Club: Your party needs a club in any area that does not have one, but you should not found one unless you are prepared to do the working of leading it.

Leadership comes to him who works — the tedious, routine work of organization is the only "secret."

The easiest way to make people like you is to like them — and say so!

To associate names with faces, ask the owner, on being introduced, to pronounce and spell the name — then use it immediately.

You don't have to be perfect in parliamentary law to handle the gavel successfully. A moderate knowledge of Roberts' *Rules of Order*, common sense, and fairness will get you by with the aid of this rule: The assembly itself is the *final* judge of the rules; make your rulings promptly and inform anyone you overrule of his right to appeal to the house. If he appeals, take a vote on the appeal *without debate*.

Use your power as chairman to divert matters of personal bitterness into committee where you can arbitrate them in private.

A motion to adjourn is always in order and is not debatable — but, as chairman, you may remind the house of any pertinent fact before calling for a vote.

Your new club *must* have a chairman who can keep the business moving without antagonizing people. It is better to be floor leader than chairman, but you may have to take the gavel if you can't find such a person.

Learn to be a penny-pincher with club funds. Votes, not dollars, win elections.

Note: The word "precinct" is used throughout to indicate an area which one person can campaign successfully, say from 100 to 400 registered voters depending on population density.

CHAPTER V

Club Meetings and Speech Making

The First Meeting of a New Club:

(a) To get a crowd use personal invitations primarily, plus cheap methods of local publicity.

(b) Use a small hall and fill it with loud music, card tables, not too many chairs. Start with group singing. Have a dynamic speaker and some entertainment. Limit business to plans for next meeting and discussion of purpose of club. Serve simple refreshments afterwards and let the kids dance.

(c) Record on file cards all possible information about all persons present — then follow up. This file is your basic political weapon.

Speaking in Public:

Be brief. Don't worry about eloquence. Funny stories are not necessary.

You can get past your first appearance as a principal speaker by using an audience-participation quiz. This gag can be used over and over again until you gain confidence.

CHAPTER VI

Political Influence, Its Sources, Uses, and Abuses

Claims of "controlling a district" are usually nonsense. There are two major ways in which a politician controls votes (a) by being the active leader of a live precinct organization (b) by the gradual and unconscious acquisition of a following who depend on him for reliable political information and advice.

Be prepared to furnish advice to your acquaintances by doing your studying of candidates and propositions early. Thus you may expect to influence the votes of about 250 people.

A fool-proof method of marking a sample ballot without previous study is to mark it against the choices of the newspaper you despise most.

Patronage: Policy positions, except under extraordinary conditions, should go only to active partisans, but non-policy jobs should be filled without respect to partisanship.

When Called on to Dispense Patronage:

(a) Accept the responsibility.

(b) Refuse to countenance a "spoils" attitude.

(c) Be frank with the applicant.

(d) Be warm-hearted and helpful. Remember his human dignity.

(e) Don't try shenanigans with the federal civil service.

(f) There are many temporary non-certified federal jobs. Know the details about them so that you can advise people how to apply for them.

(g) Keep party politics out of Annapolis, West Point, and Coast Guard Academy recommendations. Instead be prepared to help applicants with accurate information and advice.

Moving in on a Party Organization: In cities where a corrupt machine is well entrenched the "official" opposition party organization is usually a clandestine part of the Machine. (Warning: Do not assume that a "machine" is necessarily a "corrupt machine.") To take over your own party machinery when it is owned by such a false-front group you must first take over the "reform" wing of your party and then win a primary for control of the official party machinery.

In taking over the reform group be extremely careful to preserve the prestige of its titular leaders. The process of taking over consists merely in joining and being more active than the titular leaders.

After winning control of party machinery in the primary make no compromises nor concessions of any sort under any circumstances at all to the group you have displaced, if you have certain knowledge that they have been in the business of selling out to the other side —but be sure of your facts!

CHAPTER VII

District Spadework, Choosing a Candidate, Caucusing

Even an excellent candidate can lose by neglecting the basic rule that elections are won with votes and votes are in the precincts. Don't attempt to elect a candidate until you have built up a precinct organization.

Selecting a Candidate:

1. Suitability — "sound" on issues from the viewpoint of you and your party; unquestionable character and integrity; record of unselfish public service; intelligence, education and experience.

2. Availability — able and willing to devote enough time and hard work to the campaign and able to afford the financial sacrifice of holding office.

3. Electability — if suitable and available a candidate is usually electable provided he has acquired immunity to "candidatitis" — a form of buck fever peculiar to inexperienced candidates, their managers, and their families — and provided he is willing to be managed in all respects save his stand on public issues. The superficial aspects of electability are usually quite unimportant.

A suitable, available, and electable man is unlikely to want the job — you must seek him out and convince him that his sacrifice could be worth while, through the reasonableness of your plans and budget, by your analysis of the district, and by the strength of your precinct organization.

Budgets should be prepared and funds raised before your candidate announces.

Caucusing: Caucusing is a democratic process whereby like-minded individuals agree to work unanimously to a common end; it is a usual method for getting political associates behind one candidate.

Unanimity is the essence of caucusing. The original

terms by which the caucus is bound cannot be changed other than by unanimous consent — these terms must be clear to everyone before the caucus is signed.

There are no circumstances under which a man may honorably break a caucus. Be sure what you are signing — then don't kid yourself later!

You are justified in using any available legal means to enforce a caucus once bound.

If you cannot get a strong caucus behind your favorite candidate then he is not yet ready to run nor you to manage. Drop back and be a precinct worker for another candidate.

CHAPTER VIII

The Grass-Roots Campaign

Two Rules for Effective Campaigning:

(a) Is the action directed at specific, individual votes?

(b) If not, is it directed at your own district? Can it be done without sacrificing anything under (a)? Can it be done with minimum effort and at no cost? If it costs anything at all is it covered by your original plans and budget?

Effective Methods: Anything which goes after an individual vote, especially:

(a) canvassing by the candidate

(b) canvassing by precinct workers

(c) canvassing by the manager

Put the candidate on a 40-hour week of doorbell-pushing for three months; the manager should canvass two afternoons per week.

Ineffective Methods: Meeting outside the district, signs outside the district, radio speeches.

Borderline Methods: Meetings inside the district, publicity by signs, newspapers, and radio spot plugs.

The Campaign Committee: Use a large "public committee" for advertising purposes, the officers of which have nominal duties and have been selected to represent the community — Catholic, Protestant, Jewish, and minority groups. The working committee is the candidate, manager, money raiser, publicity man, field supervisors, and precinct workers.

Headquarters: Public, swank headquarters are a waste of money. You need nothing but floor space, chairs and tables, a typewriter and a telephone. Take drastic measures to keep the telephone from being used for toll calls except by specific authority of the manager.

Campaign Funds: Handle by check, require two signatures out of three, provide an audit.

Unavoidable Types of Expense: Filing fee, printing, postage, telephone bills, election night party refreshments.

Conditional Types of Expense: Signboard rental, newspaper display advertising, handbill distribution, salaries of publicity director and office person, lunch money and car fare for volunteers, radio spot plugs, extra personal political expenses of candidate and manager.

No other types of expense should be tolerated in a volunteer grass-roots campaign.

Training and Management of Precinct Workers: Form a club with membership limited absolutely to doorbell-pushers; build its morale in every possible way. Be lavish in praise. Require the candidate to spend all evening at the weekly meeting of this club without fail.

Split your workers into area squads of ten or less using the best leader talent available. Train them at club meetings, in the field by sending freshmen out with old hands, and by means of photocopied instructions.

Emphasize recording and filing all doorbell data for election day follow-up.

Never canvas "blind" — use lists. A fairly accurate list of members of your party who vote in primaries may be prepared from official records of voters "signing the book." Don't tackle a primary campaign until you have prepared such a list.

CHAPTER IX
Landmarks and Booby Traps

Don't waste volunteers on the blanket distribution of political literature.

"Volunteers" who won't or can't punch doorbells should be worked hard at office work. Don't let them lounge in headquarters — especially the Big Operator.

Make people come to see you — unless it's your idea.

Insist that the candidate conform to your discipline. Lay it on the line!

Brace yourself for phonies, sell-outs, and other disappointments.

Publicity: If humanly possible, get a professional publicity man.

Never mention your opponent by name, neither in printing, signs, meetings, nor in doorbell pushing. Don't budget too much money to newspaper ads and publicity.

Short radio spot plugs during the last week may be worth the money.

Prefer 6-sheets to 24-sheets. One-sheets, half-sheets, quarter-cards, and bumper strips are cheap and useful.

The prime purpose of publicity is to strengthen the morale of your workers and supporters by creating a bandwagon atmosphere. Publicity gets very few votes but it keeps the campaign from dropping out of sight. Pinch the pennies — publicity can bankrupt you.

Party Harmony: A successful primary fight is worthless if it splits open your party. Keep it clean!

A party-wide Sunday breakfast club is a cheap and easy way to keep the party factions friendly during the primary.

Scouting and Heckling: Scout opponent's public meetings for information; heckle only to nail a lie. For heckling use well-dressed, well-mannered, small women who can keep their tempers and their wits under stress. Train them to attack the lie and not the liar.

In coping with a heckler, treat him with great politeness and insist that he talk himself out. Then refute him after he has returned to his seat.

If possible, give direct unequivocal answers to questions from the floor. If the question is irrelevant, impertinent, or loaded, counter-attack by demanding details from the questioner and publicly set a date for a (private) meeting with the questioner to permit detailed investigation.

Don't use the above device to duck a proper issue, even though embarrassing.

Sampling a District: Cultivate skill in predicting election results by making and recording all possible predictions, then examine your results in the post-mortem. Try to analyze your mistakes.

Check the progress of campaigning by a statistical poll. Make up a random list by taking, for example, the last name from the middle column of every third precinct list, then poll them by telephone or post card, using a question form which does not suggest the desired answer. When fifty responsive replies are in, double the number of favorable replies, subtract eight, and treat the answer as a percentage which indicates what per cent of the vote you could be reasonably sure of if the election were held at once.

Supplement this by prowling through your district, looking for chances to gossip about politics. In a primary, if one in four of the people you meet in your excursion know who your candidate is, his chances are excellent; if only one in ten have heard of him his chances are poor.

Don't expect the majority of the population even to notice a primary.

CHAPTER X

The Final Sprint

Final Mail Coverage: Send signed post cards or personal letters to all persons called on. Don't use third class mail.

Election Day: Regroup to cover the precincts covered by the candidate. The purpose of election day work is to get every certain and every probable vote, as determined by canvassing, to the polls. Telephoning the night before and election morning is used to separate the certain voters from those who must be coaxed or carried. Election afternoon is used to round up stragglers. Work from lists. Use any left-over time to carry any members of your party to the polls and thereby pick up a few stray votes in return for the courtesy of a ride.

Use poll workers if available — conform to local law.

Election Night: Have the count watched and the results telephoned in. Give a headquarters party with refreshments for workers and friends.

Post-Primary Troubles:

Don't forget:

• Personal notes to *all* who have helped.
• Get-together and rally meeting of Doorbell Club
• Heal-the-wounds meeting of the Breakfast Club
• County committee meeting
• State committee meeting
• State convention
• Official report of campaign expenditures.
• Vacations for you and for the candidate.

But your principal effort will be to bring candidates you have defeated into line *at once*.

Final Campaign: Organize a district campaign for the entire ticket and have your candidate beat his own drum by campaigning for the entire ticket.

Keep your candidate's campaign funds separate from the district funds.

In congressional contests attempt to get national committee funds allotted to your district.

Conduct the final campaign in the same fashion as the primary campaign, with the same emphasis on doorbell-pushing — despite any and all advice or pressure. Your list of selected targets now comprises the members of your own party who failed to vote in the primary plus members of minor parties plus unaffiliated voters. Ignore the other party.

Continue strenuous efforts to register potential voters.

Put special effort into election day organization and get workers in from outside the district if possible.

Guiding Principle: If you are licked, it means your friends stayed home. Your object is to stir out the largest possible percentage of your own "sleeper" by registering them and dragging them to the polls.

Post-Election Chores: Same as for primary, minus the convention and plus between-election plans for the organization . . . elections are won in the off-years!

CHAPTER XI

Footnotes on Democracy

Political Expenses: Volunteer work can be effective without costing you anything, but about $2.00 a week, on average, will make your work easier and pleasanter. This is usually offset by the money you don't spend for recreation as a consequence.

Coping with Communists: Communists pop up anywhere and make trouble — their objectives rarely if ever coincide with yours. You can spot them by their catch words and by occasionally checking to see what the current "party line" is. They will try to dominate your meetings under the pretense of "free speech." This is a false plea; free speech is not a license to interrupt others in their affairs; the group who pays the hall rent are entitled to set the agenda. Suppress them by parliamentary maneuver — usually by insisting on the order of the day.

Communists are nuisances rather than dangers, but they have one prime usefulness: Any real local success on their part is a sure sign that some group of Americans are in such dire straits as to need emergency help — not punitive action!

Lawyers in Politics: To a major extent lawyers control our economic and political life, partly through special advantages enjoyed by the legal profession but primarily by default of the laymen. Unfortunately they are not well fitted by training for such responsibilities; their training is too narrow and too impractical. They are especially ill fitted to make laws, because they speak a foreign language and look to the past rather than the future.

A Third Party? This is a practical matter. Granted that there are glaring strange-bedfellow conditions in our present party alignments there is still no point in starting up a new party just strong enough to lose. However, third parties have won more than once in the past; the enterprise is always speculative but it is not impossible.

The time to join a third party is *before* the primary; if you take part in the primary of a party you are honor-bound to stick with it through November.

Democracies are Efficient: As we demonstrated against the Axis dictatorships. Perhaps the controlling reason lies in the fact that the free speech of democracies results in criticism and correction, whereas in police states a mistake goes on indefinitely.

Can the Ordinary Political Volunteer Be Effective? Yes. (a) Volunteers are trusted. (b) Volunteers are promoted rapidly. (c) Most important, all our political action and all elections, including presidential elections, are based on small, local organizations and on the followings of minor candidates, i.e., the natural field of the part-time volunteer. In a republic the local leader is the indispensable man, on whom the national political figures are utterly dependent.

Who Guards the Guardians? Every corrupt machine reflects a body of citizens indifferent to, or even secretly proud of, their public scandals. The citizens are never helpless; the evils arise from inexcusable ignorance, smugness, laziness, and lack of personal feeling of public responsibility.

Personal Danger in Politics: Occasionally a volunteer suffers bodily harm because of his activity. The danger can be minimized through using your head but cannot be disregarded. The question is this: How does the danger compare with the dangers experienced by men in combat, fighting for the same ends? Or, which is better, to be slugged at the polls, fighting for your rights, or to be liquidated by a firing squad because you failed to protect your freedoms?

Political Scientists: This country needs many more men, in government and in teaching, trained in governmental matters by the scientific method. Regrettably, many "political scientists" are neither political nor scientific, having neither experience in politics nor training in the scientific method.

On Keeping Informed: The techniques expounded herein can make you an effective vote-getter; to be statesmanlike as well, you need broad information in social and economic matters. In addition to books about such matters, the following might be a minimum for current happenings — your own favorite daily paper plus its political opposite, the tabloid political papers of both parties, a national news weekly, and one of the publications which list key votes in Congress — and its local counterpart for your state legislature. It's a chore — but without such background you are merely a skilled ward heeler.

Keep Your Roots Down! Even though you rise to national party chairmanship, remain a doorbell-pushing precinct worker in some precinct somewhere.

● Notes

Jerry E. Pournelle, Ph.D.

Introduction to the Notes

One attempts to improve the work of a master with some trepidation; but the job had to be done. Mr. Heinlein wrote this book in 1946. We had just ended a great war, and confidently expected things to go back to more or less what they had been before the War and the Great Depression. Much had changed, and no one knew that better than Robert Heinlein; but not even he knew just how profound the change had been, and what changes were to come.

In 1940, Washington, D.C., was a small Southern Border town. There was no air conditioning, and Washington was uninhabitable in the summer. That didn't matter, because what went on in Washington wasn't very important to the average citizen. The political decisions that really counted were made in state capitals and city halls. Federal taxes were quite low, as were federal expenditures.

The War changed all that. The United States emerged victorious from World War II, but we found ourselves saddled with what seemed to be enormous debts, and we faced a devastated world. Money was needed. The Marshal Plan saved Europe, but it cost us. We had built a tax-gathering machine to finance the War; the needs of others kept that machine in place after the war ended. The result was a great increase in federal power, coupled with new international responsibilities. In the Far East, MacArthur rebuilt Japan from an aggressive empire to an unarmed liberal democracy. In Europe, General Lucius Clay in cooperation with democratic elements built West Germany into an armed liberal democracy. NATO became a permanent "entangling alliance."

We were not done rebuilding our former enemies when we found we were in a new war. The Cold War wasn't as bloody as World War II, but after Korea it was clear that it was bloody enough. It was also quite expensive. Instead of dismantling the enormous war machine we had created to beat the Germans and Japanese, we had to augment it. This required management, and Washington, swollen from the wartime expansion of its functions and equipped with new tax-gathering machinery, swelled again and again.

The Cold War brought about genuine divisions among the American people. While most (including Mr. Heinlein) saw armed militant Soviet Communism as a direct threat not only to world peace and stability but to the United States, many intellectuals thought the only threat was anti-Communist hysteria. Meanwhile, we had what appeared to be politics as usual, but with this difference: politics became more important than business; more important than the churches; more important than anything else we did. The growing tendency of political decisions to affect our lives inevitably attracted more professional politicians: the long era of amateur government was coming to an end.

That end came in the Johnson era. The Great Society programs were intended to make fundamental changes in the power structure of the nation; and they did. The changes wrought were probably not those intended. Then came the Watergate scandals, and a perceived need for reform.

The reforms deliberately crippled the party structure. Power was fragmented, doled out among the 435 representatives and 100 senators, divided among endless committees and sub-committees — but never returned to the people.

By 1975 the world described in this book had ceased to exist.

These notes have two purposes. First, they explain terms no longer in use, or used differently two generations ago. They also provide the opportunity to show where Heinlein was exactly right, or, more rarely, where he is known to have changed his views. Robert Heinlein began his political career as a moderate Democrat. His attempts at electoral office ended when he was defeated for the Democratic nomination to the California State Assembly by an up and coming Los Angeles Irish politician named Sam Yorty, who went on to win the Assembly seat, and later to become mayor of the City of Angels. Years later, Mr. Heinlein visited me when I was campaign manager for Yorty's successful bid for a third term as mayor. By that time, Heinlein had made many changes in his political philosophy, moving closer to the Libertarian position.

Thus the notes: the world changed a lot after this book was written, and so did the philosophical views of the author. I have attempted here to deal with both changes. Since this is a work on practical politics, I have tried to keep political philosophy to a minimum; but since the practical value of this book is as a manual of operations for a political system that doesn't exist, but which can be reclaimed, clearly we can't avoid the question. At the least we have to decide whether the system can be restored, and if so should it be.

On that question I feel comfortable: Robert Heinlein loved the America of this book, and would have loved to see it come back.

However: since we can't just turn back the clock,

there will inevitably be questions about which changes to the system are acceptable and which are not. In some cases we know, from other works, particularly *Expanded Universe*, some of what Mr. Heinlein might have said. In others I can only guess, and rather than do that, I give my own opinion. So far as I know Mr. Heinlein and I were in agreement about most basic philosophical issues — hardly surprising given his influence on my life — but not on all. As an example, we disagreed profoundly about conscription. Ironically, when Heinlein wrote this book, he supported peace-time conscription (while recognizing that there were legitimate contrary views) and had absolutely no doubts about the necessity for the wartime draft; positions which I hold now, but which he rejected in his later years.

Therefore, you must think of these notes as my commentaries. I speak as an unabashed admirer of Robert A. Heinlein; as one whose formative years were profoundly influenced by his writings, and whose later years were enriched by our friendship and his generous support of my career; but I speak for myself. I wouldn't dare try to speak for Robert.

Jerry Pournelle
Hollywood, California
July 1992

NOTES

1. *(See page 6)* Unfortunately, while some forgot the lessons of the past, others learned the wrong ones. In the rush to "reform" the political process after Watergate, changes were made that insured that the "senile congressman" would stay in office. So would all the others. By the 1980s the turnover rate in the House of Representatives was lower than that of the British House of Lords, or of the Politburo of the U.S.S.R. This was not the intended consequence of the "reforms" but it was a predictable effect.

It's important to note that the post-Watergate "reforms" took place largely because many good people became disgusted with the political process and turned away from it, leaving the reformation to be organized by zealots and incumbents. It probably should have surprised no one that given their heads, the incumbents made it nearly impossible to defeat them, but in fact most were surprised. The incumbents were shocked to discover that they could no longer be voted out of office.

Whether term limits are a good idea or not is legitimately debatable, but there's no question that term limits address what has become a very real problem.

2. *(See page 8)* Roosevelt had permitted Stalin to send Soviet forces into Iran as a safeguard against a Nazi presence there. When the war ended, Stalin didn't want to leave. President Truman insisted and went so far as to threaten war if the Soviets did not pull back behind their own borders. This prevented the Iranian oil fields from falling into Soviet hands, and had a profound effect on the future of the Middle East.

The U.S. presence in Korea was tested a few years

later, and we're still there. Britain left Egypt and, largely because of U.S. pressure, did not retain any rights to the Suez Canal. This led to the Suez crisis of 1956, which, coupled with the failed Hungarian uprising, convinced many people that the Communist system would eventually spread worldwide.

Heinlein has chosen as examples issues which turned out to be important throughout the century.

3. *(See page 8)* The Smythe Report on nuclear energy was an early study that concentrated on fission weapons, largely of the Hiroshima class. It has been replaced by *The Effects of Nuclear Weapons*, available from any Government Printing Office for about ten dollars.

One could conclude from the Smythe report that industrial civilization would be grievously harmed, but not destroyed, by a nuclear war. After fusion weapons — H-bombs — were developed, it was pretty clear that a post-war world would be a very devastated place.

Some, however, would survive. Civil defense could be important, and Heinlein built and stocked a fallout shelter at his home in Colorado Springs during the 1950s.

4. *(See page 9)* It was rather daring for Heinlein to quote Booker T. Washington in 1946, an era in which segregation was quite legal in a quarter of the nation. In those times racial prejudice was not only widely acceptable, but in many circles practically demanded. It's clear that Heinlein, who believed passionately that people weren't equal but race had nothing relevant to say about a person, quite deliberately chose to open this chapter with a quote from a black intellectual. I can only speculate on why, but my guess is that he hoped thereby to discourage the average bigot from reading any further. . . .

Today, of course, it is extremely Politically Incorrect to quote Booker T. Washington, who is seen by the Politically Correct as an "Oreo cookie" or Uncle Tom. More fools they.

5. *(See page 13)* The world was smaller then, and precinct politics a very great deal more important. As late as 1965 it was traditional in political science classes to point out that Hughes lost California by one vote per precinct.

In 1969 when I managed Sam Yorty's successful campaign for a third term, I would cheerfully have given this book to every one of my campaign workers as a practical manual for political operations. By 1973 campaign tactics had changed. Professional managers were much in vogue; and professional managers never did care much for precinct organizations. They would rather hire people. Volunteers tire; boiler room operatives are paid to stay energetic. Volunteers require persuasion; paid operatives can be given orders. Perhaps more to the point, most professional political managers own an advertising agency through which all campaign expenditures are funneled. They collect a fee, generally 15 percent, of all that money; and of course there is no percentage fee involved with the recruitment and management of political volunteers.

This is not to negate Heinlein's point that your activity matters. It matters a lot. If we are to reclaim the republic from the professional politicians, it will require more, not less, effort by the citizens. The rewards will be correspondingly greater.

6. *(See page 13)* Political clubs hardly exist today. In the early part of this century clubs like Tammany Hall were part of the governing fabric of American life. They could be again, but they will have to be rebuilt nearly from scratch.

Political clubs failed for two reasons. First, of course, movies, radio, and television provided alternate sources of entertainment: it was no longer necessary to go down to Tammany Hall or some other political clubhouse to meet people, play cards, and otherwise kill time. TV can absorb all the time one has and then some.

The second and more important reason for the

decline of political clubs has been the centralization of politics. When the decisions important to you are made at a local level, it makes sense to have a place to discuss those decisions; but when everything is decided thousands of miles away by people you will never meet, the incentive to be part of politics through a political club tends to vanish.

The reconstruction of some equivalent to the political club — possibly through electronic networks or interactive television — is a matter of some importance if we are to reclaim the republic.

7. *(See page 15)* Local party officials no longer have much for volunteers to do. The success of the Perot movement may change that. Perot's campaign was completely built by volunteers, much as Heinlein describes here. It is likely that the other parties will pay attention to that lesson.

However, it is also likely that the professional politicians will make every effort to gain control of any such movement. You have been warned.

8. *(See page 17)* An important point. There's nothing magic about political parties, and little continuity about what they stand for. Prior to World War II, the Democratic Party regularly had a platform advocating "Tariff for revenue only," i.e., decrying protectionism. The Republicans, on the other hand, wanted tariff to protect American industry. Nowadays the Republicans tend to be for free trade, and the Democrats demand an "industrial policy."

Incidentally, this issue isn't as easily decided on ideological grounds as it used to be. As an example: is it protectionism if the U.S. places a tariff on imported goods which make use of technology developed in U.S. institutions from research subsidized by U.S. tax money? Trade relations will be extremely important over the next few years, and it is not at all clear what the optimum trade policy ought to be.

The Perot phenomenon illustrates another case in point. As I write this, there is no Perot party. It is pretty clear that if the Perot supporters hope to reorganize the national political process they will need a party: either to capture one of the existing parties, or, more likely, to form their own. The United States has historically had little use for parties organized around a single person. De Gaulle disliked parties and politics, and tried to govern France by forming his "rally" rather than a party; but today it looks much like any other French political party. It is likely that the Perot supporters will discover they have no choice but to form a permanent institution which will probably look a lot like a party. Clearly those who get in on that early using the techniques described in this book will have considerable influence over what that institution looks like.

9. *(See page 20)* This would have been impossible in the 1980s; but if we are to reclaim the Republic it must be again. The Perot movement may help.

In the 1960s I went through much the same process that Robert describes, moving from precinct worker to district leader. I then moved from Seattle to San Bernardino, California, where within weeks I became county chairman of a major party, largely because of the connections I had built in Washington state. In those days the position of county chairman carried, if not precisely influence, then certainly access to the influential.

10. *(See page 21)* It used to be said in political science classes that the true governing class in the United States consisted of about 200,000 self-selected political party officials; and it was quite true. Of course in those days government was not as important as now. Alexis de Tocquiville was astonished at how much of what would in Europe be done by government was in the United States done by volunteers in association. That too remained true until the professionalization of politics.

When politics changes the rules so that it becomes the only game in town, it should not be surprising that unscrupulous people will try to get control of the game: meaning that the citizens who want to retain the republic must work even harder.

Regaining control over our lives clearly will be incomparably easier if the centralization process done in wartime and continued during the Cold War is reversed. This not only means devolving as many issues as possible from Washington to the states, and from state capitals to local government, but also divesting government of many activities which aren't properly its business in the first place.

11. *(See page 22)* Again, this is how it used to be. Alas, nowadays the paid political professionals have very great influence, and often end up as appointed officials. It is precisely those who refuse to become professionals (and thus have to earn a living) who find themselves frozen out.

When Heinlein wrote this, most state legislators were underpaid and met only for a few weeks each year. The notion of a full-time paid City Council would have been ludicrous.

Yet Heinlein is right: those with real power don't much care for the hired help. However at the moment they can't do without them. If enough people take Heinlein's advice that could change.

12. *(See page 27)* Heinlein's views on Communism, both foreign and domestic, changed considerably from the time this book was written. Today Communism is no longer armed with ICBMs and H-bombs and thrives mostly in American universities.

13. *(See page 27)* And Whitaker Chambers went precisely from Communism to Quaker. His book *Cold Friday* remains one of the most readable accounts of just why Communism had to be taken seriously right up to the moment it fell. Chambers, incidentally, died

convinced that he had abandoned the winning side for
the losing when he left the Communist Party of the
United States.

14. *(See page 28)* As a native of Tennessee I have to say
that while the restriction on teaching evolution was in
full force all during my high school years there, it had
no effect whatever on what was actually taught; we
learned modern biology including evolution.
Nowadays there may be no law against teaching evolution, but the schools are incomparably worse. Note,
however, that most of this section is as valid in 1992 as
in 1946; indeed given the proposed Voucher System
and the utter failure of public education, that debate
couldn't be more timely or important.

15. *(See page 31)* One could wish that the post-Watergate reformers had read this passage.

The fact is that most laws have unintended consequences. Milton Friedman has proposed as
explanation an "Invisible Foot" that inevitably mucks
up any great reform scheme. It's hard enough to
knock down needless social mechanisms; it's hard
enough for government to prevent harm. For it to
positively do good may be possible, but experience
shows it's not easy.

Probably the most important lesson here is that any
proposed changes ought to have a built-in mechanism
for its own destruction. Just in case.

16. *(See page 32)* Probably nothing dates this book
more than Heinlein's remarks about women.

Heinlein was personally convinced that women
were at least as smart as men, and suspected that they
were smarter. This suspicion was reinforced by his
association with his wife, Virginia, former research
chemist and officer of the U.S. Navy, and demonstrably
as good an engineer as he was.

His public views were colored by what he thought
would be the readers' expectations. In any event most

of this section is of historical interest only. The "political streetwalkers" he describes here may have been common in his day, but were rare in the 1960s, and have pretty well vanished today, doubtless due to the changed economic situation.

17. *(See page 33)* This too is hardly a modern view: but then the "daily occupations" of women are no longer what they were in 1946. See note 16 above.

18. *(See page 35)* The club woman is still very much with us. The important point here, though, is the conclusion: "Be a politician who happens to be female." Hardly a startling conclusion today, but a fairly bold thing to say when written.

19. *(See page 36)* The United States is aging. Over the next twenty years there will be a 75 percent increase in the number of people 50 and older — and only a 2 percent increase in those younger than 50. This has never happened before, in the history of the U.S. or of any other country.

It's something to worry about. We can hope that Heinlein's assessment of older people in politics is exaggerated, or plain wrong. Alas, the politics of the American Association of Retired People doesn't contradict what Heinlein says here. Note also that since this was written the United States has spent our grandchildren's inheritance and saddled them with debt; but Social Security remains "untouchable."

20. *(See page 37)* Old vultures some may be, but we had better find a way to incorporate the elderly into the political process in a way that remains acceptable to those who are actually producing goods and earning money.

When Social Security began, some eight workers paid into the fund to support each one who took money out. That number is down to about three to one today, and will actually go the other way after the turn of the century: that is, more will be drawing from the fund than paying into it. Clearly this is a matter of great concern, since if the democratic process attempts to enslave the young to the old, soon thereafter the democratic process will be set aside in favor of something more realistic.

21. *(See page 37)* Punching doorbells used to be the most common form of political activity. One rang doorbells and offered to talk politics. If the people inside liked what you said, you tried to recruit them to go work on their neighbors. You also got a small donation, on the theory that anyone who gave a dollar to a political campaign would almost certainly vote for the candidate — a principle that remains valid today. Much of this book deals with how to do that, and everything said is spot on.

However, it has been about 20 years since any political worker came around my neighborhood. The professional politicians have found what they consider better ways. I'm not so sure of that, myself, and I suspect — indeed hope — that things will change so that punching doorbells is once again a common political activity for volunteers. It's part of the process of reclaiming citizen control of the republic.

22. *(See page 39)* I have managed five political campaigns (won four) and worked in countless others, and I want enthusiastically to second what Heinlein says here. The mainstay of three of my campaigns was a group of elderly men and women.

23. *(See page 42)* Another sign of the times: today's regulatory environment has become so complex that it's impossible even to know what the laws and regulations are, much less keep each unbroken. We all break some law every day; there's no help for it, since some of the laws are contradictory. The result is to give great discretionary power to the law enforcement officials, and to undermine the whole concept of the rule of law.

The remedy for this is obvious.

24. *(See page 43)* "An honest politician is one who

stays bought," goes the old political maxim. I grew up in Memphis, Tennessee, when the city was dominated by E. H. "Boss" Crump, one of the last of the old-time political bosses. I have to say that the city was well run, we were all pretty happy about city government, and most of my friends look nostalgically on those days before politics was "reformed."

Most "reform" movements dissipate power, on the theory that this will reduce corruption; the result, alas, is to dilute responsibility until it becomes impossible to know whom to blame. That's been my observation, anyway.

25. *(See page 43)* I completely agree with both the substance and the spirit of what Heinlein is saying here. Do note, though, that we all have seen one "successful" politician make a solemn promise and break it. "Read my lips. No new taxes." Of course as I write this his continued success is very much in doubt.

26. *(See page 44)* My partner is fond of pointing out that the Beverly Hills Police Department has no doubts about whom the police work for. That's not the case in Los Angeles and many other places. The result is that the police, afraid of prosecution for excessive violence, tend to avoid the violent criminal and concentrate their efforts on enforcing the law among the middle class who don't resist arrest and don't start shooting. That in turn adds to the disaffection of the middle class. It's all part of the problem mentioned in note 24 above.

Heinlein's contempt for political "reformers" knows no bounds. In formal political science courses these people are known as "goo-goo's" (from "good government"); and many a political mess can be traced to their efforts. Heinlein's point is that the only effective reform is constant citizen participation in government. In other words, eternal vigilance is the price of liberty....

27. *(See page 45)* Note that Heinlein refers to the crisis that left France vulnerable to the Nazi invasion. This book was written before the French defeat in Viet

Nam, the Suez Crisis, and the subsequent loss of the French Empire.

28. *(See page 48)* Signs of the times. Today it's April 15th. And the tax laws are far more complex and contradictory than when Heinlein wrote this.

The federal government takes in far more money than anyone other than an out and out Socialist would have dreamed possible in 1946; yet it's still broke, and the nation is in such a sea of debt that our grandchildren will not be able to pay it all. We tax capital gains as if they were ordinary income. Anyone want to bet that tax law won't be important 20 years from now?

29. *(See page 48)* In Heinlein's day the Post Office was a courteous and efficient place, not yet the butt of national jokes. Robert was fond of telling stories about that efficiency, including a time when they delivered a package that had been nearly destroyed in a rail accident; attached to the package was a bag of candies which had spilled when the package wrapping tore. Those were the days. . . .

30. *(See page 49)* TURN THE RASCALS OUT! was long the traditional cry of voters who had had enough. Today the rascals are very thoroughly entrenched.

Heinlein's comments on civil service and patronage are as relevant today as when written, but I doubt he would today have as much faith in written (as opposed to oral) examinations. The problem is the entrenched nature of civil servants and their immunity to political responsibility: for my own part, I think I'd rather see a spoils system for the non-technical work of government.

31. *(See page 50)* How far have we come. Since that was written we have built an enormous welfare bureaucracy which has a heavy financial interest in keeping up the supply of poor people as clients. NASA has become swollen with civil servants appointed on

merit but entrenched in a system that produces little
but paper. It is needless to multiply examples.

32. *(See page 51)* It's pretty clear that Senator Byrd
was right and Heinlein wrong in this instance.

33. *(See page 51)* All that has been changed. Congresscritters get enormous perks as well as quite good
pay, and have access to other sources of income and
perks. State legislators are well paid, and often are full
time.

The original notion of a legislature was that a group
of citizens would go approve laws they then had to live
and work under. That got lost, in part due to well
meaning "reform" efforts. Heinlein argues that the
laborer is worthy of his hire: the evidence is that in
politics if you pay the legislator what he is in theory
worth he will cease to be a representative, and become
a professional politician. What happens is that when
the salary is worth competing for, people will compete
for the salary.

It's possible that what's needed is a legislature made
up of one full-time paid professional house and one
part-time amateur house.

In any event, one can hardly argue that legislators
are underpaid today: or that paying them a lot more
solved more problems than it raised.

34. *(See page 51)* The public trough used to be slim
pickings, but things are very different now. An obvious
reform is to go back to what Heinlein describes.
Government today dispenses a much larger part of the
Gross National Product than when this was written.

35. *(See page 51)* Nothing has changed here, of
course. The lawyers dominate all the legislatures:
which may or may not have a bearing on why the laws
are always so complex as to require the citizens to hire
lawyers in order to obey them.

36. *(See page 52)* Ed Crump used to distinguish
between "honest graft" and "dishonest graft."

Dishonest graft was stealing from the public; making work that didn't need to be done in order to be paid for it; overcharging for services to the public; that sort of thing.

Honest graft was patronage: channeling money that had to be spent to one's friends or associates, or where it would do the most political good, always insisting that the work or services bought be honestly delivered. Although Crump probably wouldn't have cared for Affirmative Action (Memphis was legally segregated during his era), he would almost certainly have included Affirmative Action, Hire the Handicapped, etc., as "honest graft" since those programs involve transfer of public money to people selected by political means.

37. *(See page 52)* I don't know what Heinlein's views on this would be today. My own are that the experiment was tried, and now we need term-limit laws. See above: the problem is that if you pay people a living wage to be politicians, they will make a living as politicians: which removes government from the people and hands it to a political class.

38. *(See page 52)* The disgust of the public with officeholders is stronger today than when that was written, despite our having made most legislative offices full time and highly paid. See note 37.

39. *(See page 53)* I agree: moreover, I think it was a very good thing that many of our political leaders were mostly motivated by patriotism. In fact, by professionalizing public office we made it more likely that office holding would be merely another job, not a patriotic act. Clearly I am in disagreement with what Heinlein says earlier in this book. I don't know what his views would be today. I doubt he'd have been much impressed by the current group of officeholders; I seem to recall him saying once that the California Legislature was the finest money could buy, but whether this was intended as jest or serious comment I can't say.

40. *(See page 53)* The heart of the matter. Be a party regular. That, however, presumes that the parties matter. Increasingly they don't.

The federal structure of the United States has always made life difficult for national political parties. The state parties were far more important. Members of Congress and senators were part of the state party system, generally drawn from the same pool and acting interchangeably with state legislative and executive officers. Periodically the state parties would get together to select a national standard bearer; that was usually as a result of discussion and debate and "power brokering."

Today it's far different. The parties have little role in selecting a president; that's done in a series of endurance contests called primaries. Primaries are supposed to be more democratic than a party caucus: this supposes that the ordinary voter, who generally knows no more about a candidate than has been reported in the newspapers and conveyed on TV in 30-second sound bites, will make a more intelligent selection than a party official who may know all the candidates fairly well. It's not a compelling theory, and the results could be imagined if they weren't all too clearly in front of us.

The Founding Fathers of the United States hated political parties, which they called "factions"; but they soon found they couldn't govern without them, and Madison, whose Federalist Papers essays denounce "factionalism" in ringing terms, had no choice but to participate in the building of a party system. For those familiar with the details behind *Marbury* vs. *Madison*, the case in which John Marshall asserted the right of the U.S. Supreme Court to strike down acts of Congress as unconstitutional, the irony is delicious: Madison as Secretary of State under Jefferson was acting as a party leader when he failed to deliver the judicial commission demanded by Marbury (who had been appointed by Adams in his outgoing hours).

Heinlein is saying here that parties, particularly local parties, are the most important part of citizen participation in politics; that parties are, and should be, worthy of your support and loyalty.

This is a view not much held any longer; but it is a view very much worth attention. In my judgment Heinlein has come to the heart of the matter: you cannot have citizen control of government without strong LOCAL political parties; and you cannot have strong parties without the kinds of activities he describes.

I wish every citizen concerned with reclaiming the republic would read this section carefully and reflect on it.

41. *(See page 54)* Exactly so. I've put a note here to draw attention to the text, not because I have anything to add.

42. *(See page 56)* Still true, although the Congresscritter will pretend to be impressed. The simple fact is that Congresscritters pay attention to PACs bringing money and not much else. There is a standard price for an hour of a Congresscritter's time, and every PAC leader knows it.

It used to be that Congresscritters paid a lot of attention to people who held party office; what we have to do is make that true again.

43. *(See page 57)* More of the heart of the matter. Some of Perot's support comes from people who never before took part in politics. Others are people disaffected with their parties.

If these people are to have any lasting effect on the American political scene, they must organize along regular party lines: either take over an existing party, or build their own.

The alternative is to chop away the "reforms" of the past 40 years and return the system to what it used to be: but in that case they will still have to join the regular parties to keep control.

There is nothing more temporary than the enthusiasm of a reform movement. Parties endure. Reform movements flare and vanish.

44. *(See page 58)* What Heinlein is saying here comes right out of old Boss Flynn's book *You're The Boss*, and it's spot on.

45. *(See page 59)* While most of us agree that divided government is not a good idea in theory, the Cold War produced some odd — we can hope unique — situations. The Left demanded a number of domestic political concessions, notably the Great Society, in return for allowing the Right to conduct the Cold War and continue building up defenses. The Carter presidency demonstrated that the Democrats were not optimum for handling the Cold War. By the time Reagan was elected, Congresscritters of both parties were the beneficiaries of such powerful incumbency advantages that it was impossible to bring in Republican control of the House. Whether having a Republican majority in both houses would have been a good thing is another matter, and one subject to legitimate disagreement.

However, Heinlein's principle is good. Divided government means no one is responsible.

46. *(See page 60)* Alas, most of this chapter, and the rest of this book, is obsolete. It doesn't have to remain so; but before we can return control to citizens in general, we must devolve many to most government controls back to local areas. It is far more difficult to get people involved in politics when the decisions are made thousands of miles away; if they're made close by, it's another matter.

I've always called that the horsewhip theory: if the important decisions affecting my life are made by people we can get at with a horsewhip, we're probably in good shape.

This chapter and those following are wonderful

introductions to the arts of political doorbell punching, club organizing, and general local politicking, and with luck and a lot of work these will become the most relevant chapters of the book; for the moment parts are more of academic and nostalgic interest.

On the other hand, if enough people pay enough attention to organizing political clubs, the problems of the country just might solve themselves. Meanwhile, Heinlein, like Dale Carnegie, gives timeless advice on how to win friends and influence people. His final chapter exhorting people to political action is both eloquent and important.

One could only wish that his advice had been taken before we lost control of the political process.

AFTERWORD TO THE NOTES

All the above was written at blinding speed: I only got this assignment a couple of days ago, and the book has to be typeset three days from now. This is as far as I got before the deadlines were called.

That may be just as well. I began this hoping I'd make Heinlein's book more understandable. I may have done that. What I have certainly done is convince myself that we lost a lot when we lost the world Heinlein describes, and that getting it back may be the most important thing we can do for our children.

If we do recover control of our country, we'll need new books, new manuals of operation; but I suspect this work will never quite be obsolete.

Political organizations change rapidly. People change slowly. Politics is people, and whatever his other talents, Robert A. Heinlein understood — and liked — people.

I do hope he isn't too offended at having his book footnoted by a former professor of political science. Like him I've little use for the academic political theorist; in my defense I can say I've also seen the elephant.

Now let's go get our country back.

J.E.P.
July 4, 1992